Also by Cat Sebastian

THE LAWRENCE BROWNE AFFAIR

Also by Cat Sebastian

The Soldier's Scoundrel

THE LAWRENCE BROWNE AFFAIR

CAT SEBASTIAN

AVONIMPULSE

An Imprint of HarperCollinsPublishers

An excerpt from *Talking Dirty* copyright © 2016 by Candice Wakoff.

An excerpt from *Daring to Fall* copyright © 2016 by Tina Klinesmith.

Digital Edition FEBRUARY 2017 ISBN: 978-0-06-264250-9
Print Edition ISBN: 978-0-06-264251-6

Avon Impulse and the Avon Impulse logo are registered trademarks of HarperCollins Publishers in the United States of America.

Avon and HarperCollins are registered trademarks of HarperCollins Publishers in the United States of America and other countries

AM 10 9 8 7 6

This book grew out of stories I had been telling my children about an inventor who had a giant dog and an anxiety disorder that closely mirrored my own. I probably don't need to explain that I told my kids these stories to teach them—and maybe remind myself—that love and life are possible even when every fiber of your being wants to be in a pillow fort. This book is for everyone who needs that reminder, from my pillow fort to yours.

Acknowledgments

Many thanks to my editor, Elle Keck, not only for being a delight to work with, but for possessing the uncanny ability to see what a story is, what a story ought to be, and how to bridge that gap. As always, I'm grateful for the enthusiasm of my wonderful agent, Deidre Knight.

I'd like to thank Margarethe Martin, not only for untangling the utter confusion of the first draft, but for helping out with the scientific background. Any errors, omissions, and episodes of hand waving are entirely my own. Laura Tatum did an emergency beta read in record time, zeroing in with laserlike precision on the manuscript's fatal flaw, and for that I'm very grateful.

I'm endlessly thankful for my husband and children, both for their support of my writing and as a general state of affairs.

CHAPTER ONE

Cornwall, 1816

All this fuss about a couple of small explosions. As far as Lawrence cared, the explosions were entirely beside the point. He had finished experimenting with fuses weeks ago. More importantly, this was his house to burn to the ground, if that's what he wanted to do with it. Hell, if he blew up the godforsaken place, and himself right along with it, the only person who would even be surprised was the man sitting before him.

"Five servants quit," Halliday said, tapping Lawrence's desk in emphasis. Dust puffed up in tiny clouds around the vicar's fingertips. "Five. And you were woefully understaffed even before then."

Five fewer servants? So that was why the house had been so pleasantly quiet, why his work had been so blissfully undisturbed.

"There was no danger to the servants. You know I keep them away from my work." That was something Lawrence insisted on even when he wasn't exploding things. The very idea of chattering maids underfoot was enough to discompose his mind even further. "And I conducted most of the actual explosions out of doors." Now was probably not the time to mention that he had blown the roof off the conservatory.

"All I'm suggesting is a sort of secretary." Halliday was dangerously unaware of how close he was to witnessing an explosion of the metaphorical variety. "Somebody to keep records of what you've mixed together and whether it's likely to"—he puffed his cheeks out and made a strange noise and an expansive gesture that Lawrence took to represent explosion—"ignite."

The Reverend Arthur Halliday did not know what was good for him. If he did, he would have fled the room as soon as he saw Lawrence reach for the inkwell. Lawrence's fingers closed around the object, preparing to hurl it at the wall behind the vicar's head. Sod the man for even suggesting Lawrence didn't know how to cause an explosion. He hadn't invented Browne's Improved Black Powder or even that bloody safety fuse through blind luck, for God's sake.

"Besides," Halliday went on, "you said you need an extra set of hands for this new device you're working on."

Oh, damn and blast. Lawrence knew he shouldn't have told the vicar. But he had hoped Halliday might volunteer to help with the device himself, not badger Lawrence into hiring some stranger. The vicar was convenient enough, and when he wasn't dead set on sticking his nose where it didn't belong, he wasn't entirely unpleasant company.

"I've had secretaries," Lawrence said from between gritted teeth. "It ends badly."

"Well, obviously, but that's because you go out of your way to terrify them." Halliday glanced pointedly at the inkwell Lawrence still held.

And there again was Halliday missing the point entirely. Lawrence didn't need to go out of his way to frighten anyone. All he had to do was simply exist. Everyone with any sense kept a safe distance from the Mad Earl of Radnor, as surely as they stayed away from rabid dogs and coiled asps. And explosive devices, for that matter.

Except for the vicar, who came to Penkellis Castle three times a week. He likely also called on bedridden old ladies and visited the workhouse. Maybe his other charity cases were grateful, but the notion that he was the vicar's good deed made Lawrence's fingers tighten grimly around the inkwell as he plotted its trajectory through the air.

"I'll take care of the details," Halliday was saying. "I'll write the advertisement and handle the inquiries. A good secretary might even be able to manage the household a bit," the vicar said with the air of a man warming to his topic, "get it into a fit condition for the child—"

"No." Lawrence didn't raise his voice, but he slammed his fist onto the desk, causing ink to splatter all over the blotter and the cuff of his already-inky shirt. A stack of papers slid from the desk onto the floor, leaving a single dustless patch of wood where they had been piled. Out of the corner of his eye, he saw a spider scurry out from under the papers.

"True," Halliday continued, undaunted. "A housekeeper would be more appropriate, but—"

"No." Lawrence felt the already fraying edges of his composure unraveling fast. "Simon is not coming here."

"You can't keep him off forever, you know, now that he's back in England. It's his home, and he'll own it one day."

When Lawrence was safely dead and buried, Simon was welcome to come here and do what he pleased. "I don't want him here." Penkellis was no place for a child, madmen were not fit guardians, and nobody knew those facts better than Lawrence himself, who had been raised under precisely those conditions.

Halliday sighed. "Even so, Radnor, you have to do something about this." He gestured around the room, which Lawrence thought looked much the same as ever. One hardly even noticed the scorch marks unless one knew where to look. "It can't be safe to live in such a way."

Safety was not a priority, but even Lawrence wasn't mad enough to try to explain that to the vicar.

"Villagers won't even walk past the garden wall anymore. And the stories they invent…" The vicar wrung his hands. "A secretary. Please. It would ease my mind to know you had someone up here with you."

A keeper, then. Even worse.

But Lawrence did need another set of hands to work on the communication device. If Halliday wouldn't help, then Lawrence had no other options. God knew Halliday had been right about the local people not wanting anything to do with him.

"Fine," he conceded. "You write the advertisement and tell me when to expect the man." He'd say what he needed to in order to end this tiresome conversation and send the vicar on his way.

It wasn't as if this secretary would last more than a week or two anyway. Lawrence would see to that.

These past months of soft living had rendered Georgie Turner sadly unfit for an evening of dashing through alleys and capering across rooftops. His new Hessians were better suited for a tea party than for climbing up drainpipes and shimmying through attic windows.

Still, he landed lightly on the bare wood floor and soundlessly closed the window behind him, not even daring to breathe until he heard the patter of his pursuers' footsteps on the roof overhead, then receding into the distance. He had lost them.

For now, at least. Georgie had no illusions about evading Mattie Brewster's men for long. Georgie was a traitor, an informer, and the Brewster gang would make an example of him. And rightly so.

Heavy footsteps were coming up the stairs. Familiar ones, Georgie thought, but these days he didn't trust his judgment enough to wager his life on it. The door swung open, and Georgie held his breath, wishing he had a knife, a pistol, anything.

"That had better be you, Georgie," came the rough voice of Georgie's older brother. "Of all the people for you to cross, it had to be Mattie Brewster?"

Georgie let out his breath in a rush that wasn't quite relief. "I don't think I led them here," he said, hoping it was true.

"To hell with that. You think I can't put Mattie off for a bit? He and I were pinching ladies' handkerchiefs before you were even born." Jack lifted a lantern and peered at Georgie's face. "When was the last time you slept?"

"Not since leaving the Packinghams' house." Which somehow was only yesterday. "You know everything?"

"'Course. Mattie came here last night, all friendly like. I told him to bugger off, equally friendly like. He's had a man across the way, watching the house, naturally."

Georgie winced. It wasn't right to bring his troubles to his brother's doorstep. Jack could hold his own, but what if Brewster decided to pay a visit on their sister? A chill trickled down Georgie's spine. "I needed to catch my breath, and this was…" He let his voice trail off. This was the only place on earth where he wouldn't be arrested as a housebreaker or murdered as a traitor. He had hardly anywhere else to go, hardly anyone else to turn to. He could have fallen from the rooftop and been equally lost. "I'll leave in a few minutes. As soon as I catch my breath."

"Like hell you will. Come down and have supper with us."

Georgie nearly laughed. "This isn't a social call."

"Oh, were you engaged to dine elsewhere?" Jack paused, as if expecting an answer. "No? Then eat with us, and we'll figure out what to do with you. I doubt your enemies want to murder you badly enough to poison my soup. Oliver will be glad to see you're well."

But then Georgie would need to endure the confused sympathy of Jack's high-minded lover. Which wasn't to say that Georgie objected to Oliver; he was fine enough, in a stiff-upper-lip sort of way. Georgie was in no frame of mind, however, to make conversation with a fellow who likely thought Jack's wayward brother deserved whatever punishment he had coming his way. Hell, Georgie was inclined to agree.

"If it's all the same, I'll stay where I am, thank you." He heard the edge in his own voice. Georgie wasn't used to living off anyone's kindness. He wasn't the sort of man who inspired acts of benevolence, nor the sort to accept anything he hadn't earned—or stolen. He knew he ought to be grateful to Jack, but he was only annoyed—mainly with himself.

He had earned himself a place among London's criminal classes, and he had done it with nothing more than a bit of cunning and a complete disregard for decency. He stole and he cheated, he swindled and he lied. His favorite targets were overbred nobs who were too greedy to look closely at what Georgie offered, too blinded by visions of their own prosperity to ask the right questions. They were begging to be swindled, and Georgie was happy to oblige.

And then he had thrown it all away. He didn't know whether this was what it felt like to have a conscience, but he simply couldn't take that old woman's money. He had tried to persuade Mattie to go after another mark. When Mattie refused, Georgie had taken matters into his own hands, and now Georgie was persona non grata in London, and probably everywhere else that wasn't the bottom of the Thames.

Jack grumbled and disappeared downstairs. When he returned he carried a supper tray, which, Georgie noticed, held enough to feed two people. If Georgie would not go down to dinner, then Jack would take his dinner here in the attic. Georgie tried to muster up the appropriate gratitude but found his gaze shifting to the window he had come through and the darkness of the sky beyond. He wished he hadn't come here.

"I got a letter from a vicar in Cornwall," Jack said, and Georgie gathered that they were to attempt normal conversation. "Or rather Oliver did, and now he wants me to look into why some barmy fellow won't leave his house."

Georgie poked at his meat with a fork. "Vicars and lunatics aren't in your usual line." Jack made a living solving other people's problems, but—as far as Georgie could tell—only if the problem was an aristocrat and solving it involved a fair bit of what Jack liked to think of as retributive justice.

Jack shifted in his seat, drawing Georgie's attention like a hound catching a scent. Georgie had been swindling and stealing since he could walk, and he knew what a man looked like when he had something unpleasant to say. More importantly, so did Jack. There was no such thing as Jack Turner accidentally letting someone get a peek at his cards. If he looked uncomfortable, it was because he wanted Georgie to know it.

"The vicar went to school with Oliver," Jack said, his gaze fixed on some point over Georgie's shoulder. "The fellow who won't leave his house is Lord Radnor."

Now Georgie wasn't a hound catching a familiar scent. He was a shark, and somebody had just dropped a bloody carcass into the water. For the first time in two days, he forgot about his predicament. "The Mad Earl?" Georgie had heard of him. Everybody had. "Tell the vicar the man won't leave his house because he's absolutely crackbrained." And murderous too. There had been a missing courtesan, a dead bride, and so many duels it was nearly tedious. "And then charge your usual fee."

"This fellow isn't the Mad Earl. That was his older brother, who died a few years back. I think the father was mad too, but he wasn't such a nuisance about it. Nobody knows much about the present earl, except that he's nine and twenty and as rich as Croesus. But he can't be as bloodthirsty a bastard as his brother was, or I suppose the vicar would only be relieved that he didn't leave the house."

"And instead the vicar is enlisting the help of his old school chum's *petit ami*."

Jack ignored that. Likely because he didn't speak any French and didn't care about Georgie's barbs anyway.

"Sounds like a matter for a doctor." Georgie's interest was fast slipping. He made a great show of examining his fingernails, which were in a terrible state after the day's mishaps.

"Trouble is how to get the doctor in there without the earl's permission," Jack mused.

"Are you going to take the case?" Georgie couldn't see his brother leaving his snug townhouse long enough to travel to Cornwall to appease meddlesome vicars and investigate aristocratic hermits.

"I was thinking that I might send you, actually." It wasn't every day Jack Turner looked that shifty.

Georgie put down his fork and folded his arms across his chest, almost eager to hear whatever convoluted nonsense Jack was going to say next. "And why would I do that?"

"You could pose as his secretary, just long enough to let me know whether he's right in the head."

"There are a great many things I *could* do." He could step out the front door and wait to be attacked by his old friends and left for dead, for example. Or he could march right over to Bow Street and turn himself in. Georgie's life was a positive cornucopia of bad ideas these days. "What I want to know is why you think I ought to."

"Do you have something better to do?" Jack gestured around the empty attic. "Oliver wants to help his old friend, and I want to keep Oliver happy. Sarah would like to see you far away from anyone who wants to stick a knife between your ribs or a noose around your neck. The recluse needs a secretary. So, you go to Cornwall, and we all win." A pause. "You'd have my fee, of course."

Lurking beneath the surface of Jack's offer was the unpleasant reminder that Georgie's presence in London was putting everyone he loved in danger. "Send Sarah out of London. I don't want Brewster going after her." He scrambled to come up with a reason for flight that his sister wouldn't balk at. "She can fit Oliver's sister for some new frocks."

"Is that a yes?"

He did need to get out of London until this mess died down a bit and he figured out a way to make it up with Brewster, some way to earn back the man's trust and protection, which was the only way he'd be able to keep Jack and Sarah safe.

"Fine," he said, ignoring the look of triumph in his brother's eyes. "But I'll take half the fee in advance."

CHAPTER TWO

Georgie pounded again on what he hoped was the main door. Penkellis, a disorganized assemblage of mismatched wings and asymmetrical towers, was the sort of house that had no shortage of doors, but he'd be damned if he was going to spend what was left of the day trying each of them in turn. As he let the knocker fall, chips of half-rotten wood landed at his feet, joining the crumbling stone of the steps.

What was even the point of being rich if you lived in a place like this? Georgie's old lodgings were kept in better shape than this hellhole. And it couldn't be for lack of money—for all the things people said about the Earl of Radnor, nobody ever said he was poor. It had to be sheer bloody-mindedness.

Still no answer. The cold wind smelled of the sea as it whipped across the courtyard, and the sun was low in the sky. He didn't want to have to make his way back to the coaching inn in the dark and the cold. No, he wanted to get inside this miserable house and eat something hot while warming his feet by the fire. Even mad earls had to eat and stay warm, he reasoned.

He leaned a shoulder against the door and thought he felt it budge, ever so slightly, but enough to make him try again, this time putting all his weight into it. The hinges groaned and the wood scraped against the flagstone floor. A few more shoves, and he succeeded in forcing the door open just wide enough to squeeze through.

He found himself in what must have once been the great hall. No fire burned in the huge open hearth, despite the chill of the November afternoon. The curtains that covered the high windows were tattered and moth-eaten and had faded to an indeterminate shadowy hue. Random furnishings dotted the floor—an overturned chair, an old-fashioned clock, a harp without strings.

"Is anybody here?" Georgie heard his own voice echo. Really, he ought to be ashamed of himself for the shiver that crawled down his spine, but as his eyes adjusted to the dimness, he wouldn't have been surprised to discover dead bodies or puddles of blood. Georgie had seen houses that had been closed up—holland covers on the furniture, draperies drawn, carpets rolled up, valuables locked up right and tight to foil the plans of men like Georgie himself—and this wasn't it. This looked like a house where the inhabitants had been killed in their beds or spirited away by kidnappers.

His heart pounded in his chest when, out of the corner of his eye, he saw a flicker of movement in the shadows. But then he heard a soft and proprietary scuffling, the sound of an animal going along its merry way. Georgie was the intruder; the animal was quite at home. He dearly hoped it was a cat, but cats didn't do much in the way of scurrying.

It was as cold in here as it was outside, if not somehow colder. The wind had found a way into the hall, through bad chimneys or loose windows, and it whistled disconcertingly.

There was no way out but through, he told himself, and he crossed the room, choosing a doorway at random. This led him along a series of equally derelict chambers, as abandoned as the great hall but filled with objects that Georgie instinctively inventoried. A pair of silver candlesticks, easily pawned; a painting that would fetch a few guineas at the right auction house; a pricey bit of Chinese crockery that would be just the thing for his brother's Christmas present.

It was like stepping into Aladdin's cave, only one never thought of how dusty that must have been. The place was filled with things that simply begged to be stolen, and there didn't seem to be a soul about who would be the wiser for it.

He found a set of tightly spiraling stairs and started climbing. The sooner he got started, the sooner he could get out of here, maybe a few candlesticks the richer.

Lawrence woke on the sofa in his study. Judging by the scant light making its way through the dirty windows, it was either dawn or dusk, but he couldn't remember when he had finally fallen asleep, so it hardly mattered. Barnabus was curled before the fire, snoring deeply. Lawrence stretched as well as he could on the cramped sofa and was shaking out a sleep-numbed hand when he heard the sound of footsteps.

Before he could even form a thought, he leapt from the sofa towards the noise, grabbed the intruder, and all but threw him against the wall, hard enough to bring flakes of plaster crumbling to the floor.

"Who the fuck are you?" he growled, his voice hoarse from disuse and his mouth still dry from sleep.

"I'm George Turner, my lord," the man answered, his cheek flat against the wall, his back flush with Lawrence's chest. The bones of the intruder's shoulder felt fine, almost delicate, under Lawrence's hands. "Mr. Halliday engaged me as your secretary." He sounded almost bored, but Lawrence was close enough to feel the heavy pounding of the intruder's heart. By all rights, he ought to be quaking in his boots, being attacked by a madman nearly twice his size.

"Like hell he did. Halliday's man isn't due to arrive until the twelfth." Lawrence took a deep breath, inhaling a scent that spoke of London parfumeries and time spent before a looking glass. He couldn't remember the last time he had been this close to another person.

Turner blinked, and Lawrence saw the flash of a cold obsidian eye. "Today is November twelfth, my lord."

Damn. That happened to him sometimes. Whether it was because he was in the habit of working all night and therefore lost track of days, or because he simply was not in his right mind, he didn't know and he didn't care. It all came down to the same thing.

He let his empty hands drop to his sides but didn't step back.

"And who the hell gave you permission to come in here?" Lawrence snarled, wanting to be left alone, without the reminder that he had somehow lost three days of his life.

"I wouldn't have thought a secretary needed permission to be in his employer's study, my lord. Besides," Turner went on in that same cool voice, still facing the wall, his palms resting against the chipped plaster by his head, "I knocked for a full minute before coming in, and then when I found you, I couldn't shake you awake."

"You shook me?" This man had touched him? Lawrence could almost feel the echoes of that touch on his arm. One hand drifted absently to his own shoulder, as if to call back the unremembered sensation.

"Would you have preferred a bucket of water on your head? For a moment I thought you were dead. That would have made things awkward for me. Did you take something? A sleeping draught? Laudanum?"

Lawrence was about to respond that he never touched the stuff, his brother and father having provided cautionary tales of how badly madness and intoxication mixed. But before he opened his mouth to speak, Turner began to pivot slowly away from the wall. At that same moment clouds must have blown away from the setting sun, because Lawrence for the first time got a good look at his new secretary.

He was—there was no way around it, as much as Lawrence might have wished—ridiculously beautiful, with fine features that looked carved out of ivory. Black hair and eyes that were blacker still, cool and polished and fixed on Lawrence. Lawrence wanted to stare, to admire this man the way one might admire a sketch tacked to the wall of a prison cell, an unlooked-for reprieve from the dismalness that surrounded him.

Then he remembered himself.

"To hell with you and your impertinent questions," Lawrence snarled.

They were still standing too close. Turner tipped his head against the wall and looked up at Lawrence with lazy indifference. Most unsecretarial. But Turner didn't seem afraid, and Lawrence didn't know how to feel about that. He was so accustomed to fear that the absence of it was unsettling.

"I thought you were an intruder." Lawrence took a full step backwards, bringing them to what he hoped was a normal conversational distance. "I might have hurt you."

"I'm not easily hurt. Are you expecting intruders? I should have thought any burglars would be quite satisfied to make off with the contents of the rest of your house. What do you have up here besides…?" He gestured around the room, as if indicating that there was nothing worth stealing.

Lawrence watched him survey his surroundings, one finely arched eyebrow lifting ever so slightly when he noticed the stacks of papers littering the floor, his slender frame going momentarily rigid when a mouse scurried clear across the middle of the room, nimbly darting between bits of debris as if it had made this journey often, which it likely had.

"We have another hour or so of daylight, such as it is," Turner said, and his voice was as cool and remote as the rest of him. "Shall I get to work straightaway, or would you have me wait until tomorrow?"

At the reminder that he would have to actually work with Turner, Lawrence felt the too-familiar sense of rising panic, that even in this room he was not safe from the chaos of the outside world. The man meant to stay here, to meddle and talk and distract; he planned to smell good and be handsome and obviously Lawrence should never have agreed to any of this. "I told you to leave."

When Turner still did not move, Lawrence felt his chest tighten, his lungs constrict, as if he were being buried alive. He needed to be alone, to be in control, to do whatever he needed to make these sensations stop. Blindly, he reached for the first book he laid his hands on and threw it at the wall beside Turner's head.

Turner neatly sidestepped the book, as if he were used to people throwing things at him. A man so glaringly useless, so pointedly ornamental, shouldn't know how to avoid getting hit by books thrown by madmen. Every inch of him was neat and tidy, despite having undoubtedly traveled by the common stage. He smelled clean and cool too. Lawrence found his thoughts drifting in a decidedly unclean and uncool direction before remembering that this way lay madness. Literally.

Turner flicked a bored glance at the book, now lying in a heap on the floor, and then idly examined his fingernails. It ought to be easy enough to get rid of this fellow. The last secretary had been a mousy thing who packed his bags after the first faulty fuse, and he had come with references testifying to his diligence. Turner didn't look like he had ever worked a day in his life. It really wasn't possible to imagine a man like this even existing in the same world as Penkellis, let alone standing amidst the wreckage of Lawrence's study.

Barnabus, who had slept through the arrival of an intruder and the clunk of a book hitting the wall, now stretched lazily before the hearth. He must have finally grasped that there was a stranger in his midst, because he suddenly became a furry blur headed in the direction of George Turner.

"Please have your mongrel desist," Turner said, sounding slightly shaken. Good. Perhaps Barnabus would succeed where Lawrence had failed and send this distractingly exquisite specimen away from here.

"He likes you," said Lawrence, not moving to help. Barnabus might look like a hell hound, but really he was harmless.

"He'd like to eat me, you mean," Turner replied acidly. "Ha!" he said, finally getting a grip on the dog's scruff and holding him at arm's length. Barnabus shot his master a helpless look.

"Come, Barnabus." The dog wriggled free of Turner's grasp and came, panting and confused, to Lawrence's side. "Good dog," he said, crouching to nuzzle the animal.

When he looked up, he saw that the other man was staring at him. Well, there was a lot to stare at, so it stood to reason. Lawrence and Barnabus together exceeded twenty-two stone, and it was anybody's guess which of them was hairier at this point. It had been a while since Lawrence had bothered with having his hair cut or shaving regularly.

But it wasn't fear or curiosity that Lawrence read in Turner's gaze. He was familiar with both those expressions, and this wasn't either of them. Lawrence might not have any interest in interacting with his fellow man, but he was a student of science and he liked being able to classify and categorize. This look of Turner's didn't fit into any of the looks he was accustomed to receiving. It was something darker and lighter and colder and warmer all at once.

Disconcerted, Lawrence looked away. "Get out. We'll start work in the morning."

Out of the corner of his eye he saw Turner step over the ruined book and slip noiselessly out the door.

Lawrence momentarily regretted having damaged the book, but he didn't bother picking it up. It could join the collection of flotsam on the floor. When he stood, he thought he caught a trace of an unfamiliar scent, something refined and clean that didn't belong in this musty study. Lawrence had become accustomed to the smell of dogs and explosives, with an undercurrent of dust and damp. This scent came from a bottle and had been carried in by Mr. George Turner.

He was visited by the image of his new secretary readying himself this morning at an inn, stripping before the fire and sponging off before splashing himself with that eau de cologne. Lawrence couldn't get his imaginings beyond a rough and unsatisfying sketch of slender limbs and graceful movements.

Even after he set about lighting candles to work by, that half-formed image wafted across his thoughts as surely as the man's scent had wafted into his nose. The picture would not shake loose from his mind.

CHAPTER THREE

Lawrence was trimming what had to be the hundredth wool disk when a gust of wind blew his bedchamber door open, sending each painstakingly cut-out circle scattering across the floor. Damn it. The secretary must have opened or shut a window, or tampered with the flue, or done any of the dozen other things that caused draughts to turn into gusts·in this house.

Fuming, Lawrence stormed into the study, where he found Turner sitting amidst stacks of paper. "What the bloody hell are you about in here?" he growled.

Turner flicked him a cool glance. "Sorting through your correspondence, my lord. Were those bedclothes especially unsatisfactory?"

Lawrence looked down at the quilt and scissors he still held. "Electrolyte," he muttered, not intending to deliver a lecture about voltaic piles or anything else. "You'd better not have lost or ruined anything."

"My dear fellow"—and why did such cheek sound more fitting than the correct *my lord?*—"half these papers are already ruined. I think a good number of them have been ruined for years. At least if you consider evidence of rat droppings to indicate ruin, which I do."

"It's not a rat. It's a mouse." More likely mice, plural, but Lawrence couldn't pretend to have made a thorough census.

Turner's inky eyes opened fractionally wider. "Oh, in that case I stand corrected. In any event, I didn't destroy anything, no matter how foul or revolting."

Lawrence glanced searchingly around the study, as if he could possibly have noticed the absence of an important paper. Even on the best of days, locating anything in this room involved a good deal of guesswork. Orderliness was not Lawrence's strong suit. But now there were patches of bare wood visible on his desk where yesterday it had been covered in a thick layer of unfinished correspondence and jumbled notes. He traced his fingers along the nicked and stained wood. "You can't possibly have understood half of what you read."

"Quite right." Turner's voice was brisk. "Unposted letters go into this pile." He gestured with a languor that seemed at odds with the geometric precision of the papers. "You have a dozen letters that have been franked and addressed, but never made it to the post. Most are addressed to some fellow in London."

"Standish," Lawrence supplied. "He's building a similar device." No wonder Standish never seemed to know what was going on, if Lawrence wasn't remembering to post the letters he had written to the fellow. Annoyed with himself, and with Turner, and—unaccountably—with Standish, he gathered up the unposted letters and tossed them into the hearth. Barnabus opened one eye to see what all the fuss was, then closed it again.

"I gather that this device"—he gestured at the bits of copper wire that littered the work table—"is the explosive?"

"Explosive? No, no." Lawrence could hardly look away from his desk. Each stack of paper was arranged into a neat block. Turner must have picked up each pile and tapped it on the desk to align the edges and then arranged each stack equidistant from its neighboring stacks, as regular and symmetrical as if he had used a carpenter's ell and a ruler. "That's all done. Already in use in the mines. So is the fuse. What I'm working on now is a communication device."

None of this was right. These orderly papers felt like an intrusion, like a stone at the bottom of his boot. Goddamn Halliday and his good intentions, goddamn this secretary with his clean fingernails and precise diction. This room was meant to be Lawrence's own refuge, silent and constant, safe from the unpredictability of the outside world. Having somebody rearrange his belongings quite defeated the purpose.

Lawrence toppled one stack, just for the hell of it. "What's the rest of it?"

Unperturbed, Turner pointed to the next stack. "This is anything pertaining to your estate. And this is anything in your own hand. Notes or plans, I gather." Turner went on, placing one long finger on each stack in turn. Lawrence had a hard time attending to the man's words.

Turner himself was as much an intrusion as his stacks. Lawrence's gaze drifted unwillingly to the secretary's face, taking in the sweep of dark lashes, the dimple that appeared on one cheek as he smiled—oh, damn it. Now the man was looking at him, and with a sly expression that suggested that he knew exactly what Lawrence had been up to.

Lawrence snapped his fingers to summon Barnabus and stormed gracelessly out of the room.

Well, it wasn't every day one drove a man into a towering rage simply by sorting some papers. Georgie still wasn't sure what had gone wrong, and he didn't care one jot. The earl could be as mad as a March hare and it wouldn't make the least difference. Georgie would detail the earl's behavior in a letter to Jack and then fill his own pockets on his way out the door.

He bent to retrieve the papers from the hearth. There had been no fire—Cornish giants evidently did not feel the cold to the same degree as ordinary mortals—so the papers were intact. Sitting at the earl's desk, he placed each paper into the proper pile and entered its description in the ledger he had tucked into his coat pocket. During a previous swindle, he had served as private secretary to a barrister, so he had a fair idea of what needed to be done. It was satisfying, too, to create order out of utter chaos. It was like untangling a thread or picking a lock.

Georgie had always liked things clean and tidy. Maybe it came from growing up in confusion and squalor. He tried to keep his thoughts as organized as his desk. Marks and potential marks were in one neat little pigeonhole. Friends—which was to say criminal associates—were in another. Jack and their sister, Sarah, were the only two people who existed outside those two pigeonholes. It made things simple, keeping everybody where they belonged.

The trouble was that Georgie's mind had started assigning people to the wrong pigeonholes, and he had started to look on old Mrs. Packingham as a friend, and Brewster as an enemy.

As he didn't know how to stop that disorder from occurring again, he tried to dismiss the thought and return to Radnor's disgusting papers. In the window casement he found a spool of twine that would serve to tie the correspondence into neat bundles, keeping them organized even if the earl threw another tantrum.

Through the clouded window, he could see the earl and his monstrous dog in a garden that managed to look simultaneously overgrown and quite dead. The dog, predictably, was asleep. If Radnor kept that mongrel for any purpose, Georgie had yet to discover what it was, because the dog had slept straight through the two hours Georgie had worked that morning. There were rugs with more energy.

Radnor was fiddling with a blade of some sort—an ax by the looks of things. It took Georgie a moment to fully comprehend the incongruity of the sight. The earl was preparing to chop firewood, which wasn't by any stretch a normal task for a peer of the realm. But Georgie hadn't come to Penkellis expecting anything resembling normal. Nor had he seen any evidence of the earl's madness, however. If untidiness, rudeness, and fits of mild violence constituted madness, then Mayfair was filled with madmen—just ask any lord's servants.

As he watched, the earl began swinging the ax. The thwack of the split wood echoed off stone walls. Another thwack, and another, until he settled into a rhythm. Radnor was making fast work of it, only pausing long enough between swings to set up the next log. Well, it stood to reason that a man so large had to be strong.

Georgie let his mind linger on those adjectives a trifle too long: large and strong. Good heavens, was he ogling the Mad Earl of Radnor? No, he reminded himself, he was leering at the Mad Earl's brother. That settled, Georgie folded his arms and leaned against the casement, enjoying the show.

Radnor's hair, which had earlier been messily tied back in a hopelessly unfashionable queue, now hung loose around his shoulders in waves the color of caramel. He had several weeks' worth of beard, which Georgie felt as a personal attack on order and cleanliness. Terrible. Simply awful. Really, he shouldn't be wondering what it would feel like against his skin.

And then—oh, his kingdom for a pair of field glasses. The earl dropped the ax long enough to strip down to his shirtsleeves. That couldn't be necessary, given the chill in the November air. But on another, purely aesthetic level, it was quite, quite necessary for this man to take off his clothes whenever the spirit moved him. Perhaps he ought to go the full distance and take his shirt off too. No sense in doing things by halves.

Georgie used his handkerchief to clean a bit of the window for a better view. It would have been a sin and a shame to let a sight like this go unseen. The earl filled out his dingy linen shirt quite nicely, and now the fabric was sweat-damp and clinging. Every swing of the ax caused the man's muscles to ripple and shift. Strong thighs, solid chest, arms that simply beggared belief.

The man was a beast.

Georgie licked his lips. He had felt the solid mass of those broad shoulders under his fingertips, through layers of wool and linen, when he tried to wake the earl yesterday. When Radnor had grabbed him and pushed him against the wall, Georgie had felt that strength firsthand. Georgie had let it happen, had let himself be shoved and manhandled; a man didn't keep the company Georgie kept without learning how to take care of himself in a fight. Lord, but being pressed into that wall had given him ideas, ideas that were crystallizing into something gratifyingly obscene now that he was seeing Radnor in action.

This wasn't the first time Georgie had desired a man he intended to cheat or rob. Sometimes desire even added to the thrill of the swindle, as long as one made sure to keep everybody in their proper pigeonhole. It was like having a fine dinner served on a silver charger that one intended to steal later on. The trouble was that, looking out the window, Georgie didn't know whether he was looking at the charger or the meal. His pigeonholes were in danger of getting disordered.

Besides, there was desire—simple, selfish, easily satisfied— and then there was whatever Georgie had wanted when he felt Radnor's overlarge presence behind him. There was nothing simple about that.

He turned abruptly away from the window and surveyed the contents of the room. Radnor had expected housebreakers. Perhaps that was a mania of his, but perhaps he had something worth stealing. If so, Georgie couldn't fathom what, unless there were thieves with a fondness for mouse droppings and stained papers. But who knew what might lie buried beneath the haphazard piles of books or within the half-decayed trunks. All the more reason to bring this room to some semblance of order.

Lawrence sluiced himself off with water from the well. The water was cold, but he was hot, and evidently he didn't have any servants to draw him a bath, even if he'd wanted one. He wondered which brave, misguided souls had remained. Not that he was going to visit the kitchens and find out. They'd likely flee at the sight of him, shirtless and dripping wet, like something that had washed ashore. And, truth be told, he didn't care who his servants were as long as they stayed silent and left his supper outside the study door.

"Good God, man." It was Halliday. "You'll catch your death."

Lawrence made a noncommittal noise, too physically and mentally drained to enter into a debate about the dangers of standing outside in wet clothes. Instead he proceeded to wring the water out of his hair while Barnabus greeted his friend. "Firewood," he offered after a moment. "It's too cold to swim."

"Ah." The vicar had known Lawrence long enough to be familiar with his habits. "I see."

Lawrence had learned years ago that when he felt the creeping unease that signaled what he had come to think of as an attack of madness, he could sometimes set his mind to rights by exhausting himself. It was probably only a temporary reprieve, only delaying the inevitable moment he went as fully and irretrievably mad as his father and brother. But temporary relief was better than no relief, so in the summer he swam in the sea, and in the colder weather he chopped enough wood to warm a house far grander than Penkellis. He didn't know why it worked, but he imagined his mind as a fire with too many twigs. Some of the tinder had to be burnt off before the fire was any use at all.

"Did the secretary arrive?" Halliday's voice was too casual.

"Yesterday."

"Is he settling in?"

"I mistook him for a housebreaker and nearly throttled him. Later I threw a book at his head. This morning he sorted my papers and I threw them into the fireplace."

Halliday winced. "That would be a *no*, then."

"He's a London popinjay." Lawrence pulled his shirt on over his head. "He smells like flowers."

"His references were—"

"He'll be useless." Worse than useless. Distracting.

Lawrence slid his braces up over his shoulders, then shrugged into his waistcoat and coat, all while the vicar shuffled and looked around the garden as if it held anything of interest.

"David Prouse had another sheep stolen," Halliday finally said.

Like as not it had fallen off a cliff into the sea or been stolen by a neighboring farmer. These things happened and always had. "Am I supposed to have stolen this one too?"

"The general sentiment is that you sacrificed it as part of an eldritch rite."

Lawrence snorted.

"I wish you'd take this seriously," Halliday protested. "Show your face at the village fete, buy some jam and pie at the ladies' auction. Otherwise people make up their own stories, and every little thing that goes wrong within a league of Penkellis is laid at your doorstep. It's only a matter of time before something serious happens and you're blamed for it."

Lawrence wasn't concerned about his tenants thinking the worst of him. After his father and brother, they had every reason to suspect the Earl of Radnor of any and every crime. "If the villagers are indulging in superstition, perhaps they need stronger spiritual instruction." Lawrence shot a pointed glance at the vicar.

Halliday threw his hands up in surrender. "Don't think it hasn't occurred to me. I lie awake nights wondering what I've done wrong here. Do you know, when I went to Bates Farm to read to the old lady, I found salt sprinkled on the windowsills."

"Salt?"

"To keep away the evil spirits, I gather," the vicar said, his voice weary.

If only it were that simple, Lawrence thought. If only evil could be kept away with a dusting of salt, a bowl of iron filings, an old incantation. But he knew that the madness that ran in his bloodline would one day fully claim him as surely as it had claimed his brother and father.

Georgie tried to orient himself within the rabbit warren of rooms and corridors, heading towards what he hoped was the back of the house. Because if there were any servants—and he reassured himself that there simply had to be, despite all appearances to the contrary—they'd likely be in the kitchens.

Even the most mazelike places had a certain logic to them. Georgie, born and bred on the labyrinthine streets of London's rookeries, could often intuit how a new place was laid out. When he found himself in a new town, at a new house, among a new set of people, he knew how to detect the various currents that led towards money, towards pleasure, towards power.

That was what Georgie did: he slid into places he didn't belong. Nobody realized what had happened until the damage was done, like a stiletto in the heart. It was only a matter of the right words spoken to the right people and a total indifference to the truth.

Quietly, casually, he would mention that he had invested his small inheritance in a business venture: canals, mines, shipping…it hardly mattered. Interest was piqued, greed uncovered. Georgie would offhandedly mention the name of the firm in question, the greedy gentleman invested, and Georgie disappeared into thin air, as effortlessly as he had appeared, taking half the proceeds with him.

Mattie Brewster took the other half in exchange for tolerating Georgie's doing business on Brewster's own ground. It had seemed a good deal ten years ago, when he had been too young and foolish to consider what it would be like to have a man like Brewster as his enemy. As his family's enemy. Now it was too late to renegotiate. It was too late for a lot of things.

Georgie had never felt bad about his swindles until he became foolishly fond of old Mrs. Packingham, with her perpetually tangled embroidery floss and the equally tangled tales of her youth. Before her, he had taken from people who were greedy enough to throw caution to the wind and rich enough to spare money on rank speculation. They were no better than gamblers, and nobody wrung their hands when high rollers lost their money, did they?

As he wound his way through the passageways of Penkellis, brushing aside cobwebs and stepping lightly over creaky floorboards, he checked for signs of civilization, some clue that would bring him closer to a hot meal and a working chimney: a sconce that had been dusted, a carpet that had been rolled up rather than left to molder, the telltale lemon scent of cleaning polish.

But he found none of those things. All the rooms outside of the tower that held Radnor's study were in various states of ruin. No attempt had been made to stop the progress of decay. The house had simply been given up as a lost cause. All the doors Georgie opened led to rooms as bad as the one he had slept in last night. Some weren't even furnished at all; others smelled of damp and mushrooms.

Finally, he smelled bread baking. Thank God. A few paces later he heard voices, then arrived on the threshold of the tidiest room he had seen yet in this shambles. It was a small kitchen for this size house but neat as a pin. Two women were having what looked like a comfortable coze near a blazing fire. One of them, a girl of maybe eighteen, combed out her golden hair while an older woman shelled walnuts.

Georgie cleared his throat and both women leapt to their feet.

"We're decent women!" said the walnut-sheller, walnuts and baskets skittering all over the flagstone floor.

"I've got a knife," said the hair-comber, producing a small blade from the depths of her apron.

"I'm George Turner." He held up his hands as if in surrender and tried to sound like the sort of man decent women didn't need to fear, which was no more than the truth. "I'm to be Lord Radnor's secretary." He gave a slight bow and his best smile. "I apologize for having taken you unawares."

"Flimflam." This from the walnut-sheller again, a stout woman of about five and thirty, dressed in a tidy gray cotton frock and sturdy-looking cap. "His lordship has no secretary."

"Which is why he's engaged me," Georgie offered. "Will you tell me what time supper is served?" Since arriving yesterday, he hadn't had anything to eat but some bread and cheese he had tucked into his pocket at the inn, and that had been finished hours ago.

More staring, and then the women shook their heads.

"If I were you, I'd put up at the inn," the older woman said. "This house ain't fit. Rats. And worse."

"Yes, so I've gathered." The room where Georgie had slept last night had been little better than a barn. Bone tired from days of traveling, he had managed to fall asleep despite musty-smelling bed linens and the unmistakable sound of mice in the straw mattress. A younger Georgie might have gladly bedded down for another night in far worse accommodations: mice didn't bite much, at least not compared to rats. But his time living—and thieving—among the gentry had gotten him used to beds that didn't have creatures living in them and sheets that didn't make him sneeze. "But it's cold and dark, and I'm not leaving this house tonight, or indeed until I complete my employment with his lordship."

The women exchanged a glance. "There's some bread over there," the older woman said, gesturing with her chin to a tray bearing cold meat and a few loaves of bread. Neither woman moved.

Georgie thanked the women and helped himself to a loaf of bread, temporarily giving up his hope for a hot meal as a lost cause. Then he bowed his way out of the kitchen as suavely as he would have left a duchess's drawing room a few short weeks ago.

CHAPTER FOUR

After another day of organizing dirty papers, Georgie despaired of ever enjoying a decent meal, a proper fire, or a tolerable conversation. Radnor grunted or, when pressed, emitted a grumpy monosyllable. Twice, a tray bearing cold ham, bread, and apples appeared mysteriously outside the study door, and Radnor fetched it in as if this were an utterly unremarkable event. Georgie helped himself to an apple, and Radnor stared, as if it hadn't occurred to him that his secretary required feeding.

This wasn't the only time Georgie felt Radnor's intense gaze. Perhaps it was because the earl had been alone for so long that another human's presence was a novelty worth noticing. Perhaps it was Georgie's own isolation at Penkellis that had him hoping those penetrating stares had more behind them than curiosity. But Georgie had too much practice deceiving others to be able to deceive himself. He darted a glance at where the man sat with his absurdly huge boots propped up on his desk, one muscled arm hooked behind his neck. He wanted Radnor. Badly. And, if those stares meant anything, Radnor wanted him at least a little in return.

Perhaps Penkellis had more to offer than a couple of candlesticks.

At some point in the evening—it was hard to say precisely when because none of the clocks kept proper time, but it was after they had burnt through several candles—Radnor wordlessly got up, strode into the adjacent room he used as a bedchamber, and slammed the door shut. Georgie interpreted this to mean the day's work was done.

Georgie stood and stretched, stiff and restless from so many hours sitting still. Despite the late hour, he was too fidgety to sleep. He'd take the opportunity to explore Penkellis. No, explore wasn't quite the word. Browse, more like. As a child, he used to loiter outside the butcher's shop, eyeing roasts and joints he could never afford, planning what he'd buy in the dimly imagined future where he had enough coin.

That was what he did as he twisted through the dusty corridors of Penkellis; he planned what he'd stuff his pockets with when he finally went back to London. What would he bring to Mattie Brewster to bargain for his life, for his family's safety? A rolled-up painting? A couple of silver candlesticks? None of it would be adequate to purchase his freedom, so this was just as much a game of make-believe as it had been when he was a child.

He'd have to search the study more carefully, find out whether the earl really had something he was worried thieves might take. Georgie was conscious of a nagging sense of shame when he thought of duping the earl. Before he could berate himself for the miserable state of his pigeonholes, his foot went through a rotten piece of floorboard.

"Blast!" he muttered. This house was beyond simple dilapidation. There was something decidedly *not right* about this place. He had always enjoyed solving puzzles, and Penkellis—and its master—seemed a puzzle very much in need of solving.

What a bloody waste to let a house like this rot. Radnor ought to be ashamed, but then again he took no better care of himself than he did the house. He hid in his tower, surrounded by disorder and decay, utterly alone.

Georgie could hardly stand it and was working up a righteous anger when he pushed open a set of double doors.

"Oh hell—" His words caught in his throat.

It was a library. Or, rather, it had once been. A window had blown out, and Georgie could see ivy trailing into the room, creeping onto the tall bookcases. Everything about this room was wrong. It smelled of the sea and loamy earth, not like an indoor place at all. A shaft of moonlight shone through the broken window, illuminating a toadstool growing out of the floor.

It wasn't the decay that was so troubling as much as the way the strangeness of the place warped one's expectations. A specter could float by and Georgie wouldn't be in the least surprised. He'd wave to it, wish it good evening.

Even the sounds didn't belong: an owl called from far too short a distance, and wind rustled through bare trees only yards away. And further off, the sound of something like hoofbeats and carriage wheels, but it couldn't be, since the roads all bypassed Penkellis. It wasn't as if his lordship expected visitors, Georgie reflected gloomily.

He crossed the room, blindly reached for a book, and found himself holding what was little more than a handful of pulp. Still gripping that sad corpse of a book, he turned on his heel and marched upstairs.

Lawrence had very nearly fallen asleep when he was startled to full consciousness by a pounding on his door.

"Radnor!" It was the secretary, damn him. "Radnor, open this door!"

That was quite a lot of pounding. Perhaps the house was on fire. Lawrence very nearly smiled at the thought of Penkellis lying in a heap of rubble and ashes.

The door swung open, revealing Turner poised on the threshold, lit only by the moonlight. "What's the meaning of this?" Turner asked, waving something at Lawrence.

Lawrence sat up in bed. Try as he might, he couldn't smell smoke or detect any other signs of a conflagration. "How the fuck should I know?"

"Then I'll tell you," Turner continued, undeterred by Lawrence's coarse language. "You have a library of hundreds—if not thousands—of books downstairs, and you let them rot." So it was a book Turner was waving about, brandishing like a weapon. "Do you have any idea what that does to any person of sense? It's obscene, I tell you."

"I don't give a damn about the library."

"Plainly not! But you could have given the books to a school, or…I don't know, a lending library."

It was the middle of the night. Even Lawrence thought this a strange hour to discuss lending libraries. "But I didn't, so kindly get out of my bedroom."

Turner made no move to leave. "It ought to be cleaned out, to check whether anything is salvageable. Why did the servants not see to it? I understood that you had more servants in residence until recently."

"Damned if I know. I'm not a housekeeper. Perhaps they were lazy. Perhaps they liked rotten paper. Perhaps you ought to get out of here before I lose my patience entirely." Lawrence narrowed his eyes, a terrible idea occurring to him. "Unless you plan to share my bed. Perhaps all this fuss about a couple of moldy books was only a pretense for you to gain entry to my bedchamber." Now, that ought to get rid of the man.

Turner went utterly still, and for a moment Lawrence thought he might scurry away as he ought.

But then Turner's posture relaxed into something sinewy and dangerous. His mouth curved slowly into a smile that had Lawrence cursing himself for not keeping a fire or a lamp or anything that would illuminate the man. To Lawrence's mingled horror and wonderment, Turner began to laugh, soft and low. "If that was meant to frighten me, you're wide of the mark, my lord. To be frank, you're punching above your weight."

Did that mean what Lawrence thought it meant? Or, rather, what Lawrence's prick thought it meant? Because God knew his brain wasn't capable of any thought whatsoever. Lawrence became intensely aware that he was in his bed, shirtless, in the middle of the night. And he had just told his secretary a good deal more than he meant.

Lawrence would have sworn that Turner's dark, dark eyes dipped low at that moment, to skim over Lawrence's bare torso. But no, that couldn't be. It had to be a trick of the moonlight.

Years ago, immediately after his father's burial, Lawrence had escaped Penkellis in order to join his brother in London. There, among Percy's group of broad-minded friends, he had finally met men who shared his own inclinations. But Percy's set had all been utterly crackbrained, a bunch of half-mad, thoroughly drunk, opium-eating libertines. Any practice or desire Lawrence found in common with them seemed proof of his own incipient madness. It had been a chaos of hedonism, of freedom, of all the things he had been denied. He had started to believe he was as bad as Percy, or perhaps even as deranged as his father had always insisted, and when one of Percy's friend's sisters fell pregnant by a married man, Lawrence had volunteered to marry the girl. They had fled back to Penkellis, and he had never left.

The room-spinning giddiness he felt at Turner's hungry glance echoed that mad whirl of pleasure he had experienced in London. It seemed further confirmation that his mind was unbalanced. Surely it was not normal for the room to whirl about in such a way.

Apparently recovering his composure, Turner coolly tossed the book onto Lawrence's bed and turned towards the door.

"If you must know," Lawrence said, suddenly not wanting Turner to leave quite yet, "the library was already a lost cause when I inherited. My brother had a fancy for ruins and wished to see how long it would take for Penkellis to crumble."

"A pity he's not alive to see his dreams come to fruition." Turner's mouth was a tight line.

"No." Lawrence's jaw set. "Not a pity." He picked up the book Turner had brought and examined its spine. The moon was full, but he could barely make out the faded title. *The Discourses of Epictetus*. "Are you much interested in Greek?" he asked, surprised.

"What? No, not in the least."

"The library is mostly Greek, with a bit of Latin here and there. My grandfather bought books at random to fill in the shelves." Lawrence had salvaged anything of interest to him at the first sign of Percy's neglect. "Except the pornography, which my brother sold to one of his wastrel friends." And if that wasn't Percy in a nutshell, then nothing was. "But if you're looking for something to read, you're free to borrow anything you find in the study."

Turner tilted his head a bit, as if he hadn't quite understood. "Thank you," he said, after a moment. "But I've already read most of your notes and correspondence, and I've made a dent in the scientific papers."

If Lawrence had been standing, he might have fallen over. "You have?"

"Well, yes. Of course I have. Any secretary would." Perhaps it was Lawrence's imagination, but the man didn't seem quite certain of that fact. "I would be of little use to you if I were ignorant of your work."

An idea occurred to Lawrence, something even more daring and dangerous than his foolish jest about sharing a bed. "Are you by any chance interested in natural philosophy, Mr. Turner?"

The secretary shifted on his feet, looking discomfited for the first time since arriving at Penkellis. "Perhaps."

"Because it seems to me that you'd have to be, in order to read that quantity of material in"—he wrangled with the always-slippery days and hours to calculate how long he thought Turner had been here—"two days."

"I have a good many interests." Turner sounded defensive, as if Lawrence were accusing him of prurient interests rather than scientific ambitions. In fact, when Lawrence *had* suggested that he had prurient interests, Turner had only laughed.

The prospect of conversing with an actual human being who shared his interests almost stupefied Lawrence. Imagine, being able to talk about the relative merits of brine and acid as electrolyte solutions, rather than depending on the post to communicate with Standish or one of his other correspondents. It was something he had never dared to so much as hope for.

"I could...if you wished, I could teach you." If there had been enough light in the room for Turner to see him, Lawrence might not have had the courage to speak. But since he was facing away from the window, all the moonlight fell on Turner's face, not Lawrence's own.

And Turner's face, coolly impassive as ever, revealed nothing. This was not the face of a man with a burning desire to hear about voltaic piles. It was certainly not the face of a man who was harboring carnal desires towards his employer. Of course it wasn't. Lawrence must be growing even more delusional.

"Never mind. I have neither the time nor the temperament for tutoring secretaries in natural philosophy."

There was a pause that lasted too long. "Good night, my lord." And then Turner left, closing the door soundlessly behind him.

Only later did Lawrence realize that for the first time in years, perhaps ever, he felt disappointed to be left alone. As sleep eluded him, he sought comfort in the certainty that he preferred solitude, that he hated being bothered with company, and that therefore he could not now be lonely.

CHAPTER FIVE

"Explain it again." *Slooooowly*, Georgie wanted to add. He leaned back in his chair and waited for the show.

At some point over the last few days, Radnor's coat had gone missing. Probably Georgie ought to make some effort to find it. But he wouldn't, not so long as the man kept working in shirtsleeves, rolled up to expose thick forearms that were dusted with hair.

"No," Radnor said, his voice gravelly and his tone rude. "I've already explained it twice. You don't seem like an imbecile, which means you're being deliberately obtuse."

True, Georgie already more or less grasped the concept, but as Radnor talked, he stroked his beard with those big hands. Georgie could watch him all day. It wasn't a burden to listen to him either. Radnor didn't have the slick and polished drawl of most of his peers. Instead his voice rumbled and slurred, lilted and skipped. He looked and sounded more like a blacksmith or a woodcutter than an earl.

And somehow, without either of them ever alluding to their conversation in the earl's bedchamber, Georgie had become Radnor's pupil. Instead of grunting and swearing, Radnor favored Georgie with technical explanations and disquisitions on some Italian fellow. Georgie, who fancied himself more skilled in faking an education than in actually acquiring knowledge, was surprised by how drawn he was to Radnor's world of invisible particles. He felt like he was in on a secret that few others knew.

"Now you repeat it back to me," Radnor commanded. "I'll tell you when you've got it wrong." He sat, propping his feet on the table that held the device he had finished assembling that morning. Composed of metal and wire, scraps of cloth, and fragile-looking tubes of acid, it looked like something that would be equally at home in a sorcerer's workshop or a torture chamber. It was hard to say which looked more dangerous, the equipment or its burly, scowling creator.

"All right." Georgie smoothed his trousers and crossed the newly cleared floor. It had taken the better part of a week, but Georgie had made progress with this sty of a room. The papers were properly cataloged; the rubbish was burnt in the fire he insisted the earl let him light. He had even brought a kitchen cat upstairs to frighten away the mice, despite Barnabus's vocal chagrin. He truly wished someone else were here to bear witness to all he had accomplished, because God knew Radnor didn't seem to notice or care. But Georgie felt like a magician.

For one reckless moment, he thought that maybe honest work wasn't such a bad idea after all. But no. If a man were born in the gutter, honest work couldn't take him far enough away from it. He would always be able to smell the stink of the gutter, waiting for him with one month's missed rent, one costly doctor's visit. Georgie wanted to be safer than that. *Needed* to be safer than that.

"This," Georgie said, pointing at one part of the apparatus, "is a stack of disks that will kill me if I touch them at the wrong time."

"It's called a pile, or a battery, and the disks are copper and zinc electrodes."

"And I die if I touch them. Don't forget that part."

The earl made a grumbly noise that Georgie took to mean that death was a trifling, petty scruple. "I may have exaggerated the danger. Or maybe I didn't. Either way, don't touch."

Georgie's eyebrows shot up. Was that humor he had detected in the earl's tone? Wonders never ceased. "In between each disk is a piece of your bed quilt that you cut up and soaked in seawater."

"Electrolyte," Radnor corrected. When he frowned, which was almost always, his eyebrows were dark diagonal slashes across his forehead.

"And this," Georgie said, pointing to what looked like a pair of miniature trestles connected by wires, "is what will burn the house down or eat a hole in the floor, depending on how things wind up going awry."

"Electric telegraph." If Radnor had detected the facetiousness in Georgie's tone, he did not acknowledge it.

"Right." The trestle had thirty-odd wires, each in a glass tube filled with some doubtlessly poisonous liquid. The wires coiled together for a yard, then separated where they connected to another small trestle. At each point where the wires met the trestles, a letter or number was inked on the wood in Georgie's own neat hand. "On one trestle, you apply the current to the wire for whichever letter you wish to send, and bubbles pop up on the other trestle next to the corresponding letter."

"More or less," Radnor conceded.

"Has anyone managed to make something like this work? To actually send a message, I mean?" Georgie tried not to sound as if he were really asking if the earl was deluded.

When Radnor rubbed the back of his neck with one broad hand, a strand of hair the same color as the copper disks escaped his queue. "A fellow in Munich did something similar. And Standish will try once I send him the final plans."

By now, Georgie did not need to ask who Standish was. For all he was a hermit, the earl was an enthusiastic letter writer who maintained regular correspondence with several men of science. Every post brought a stack of letters.

"With longer wires, messages could be sent over greater distances," Radnor continued.

"From the house to the village?"

"From the coast to London, more like."

Georgie arched an eyebrow. "That's a lot of wire."

"And a lot of tubing to protect it. Perhaps if it were only one wire," Radnor murmured. "But I can't see what use a single signal would be."

Georgie was about to open his mouth to agree but then remembered tapping a warning onto a closed door, the night watchman peering through the window of a warehouse Georgie's friends were burgling. Before he even knew his letters, he had learned the taps and scratches that boys used to communicate with one another during robberies. Georgie was slight and dark and very quick, the perfect lookout. Three taps on the window pane meant the watchman was coming, hold still. Six taps meant cut loose and run fast. Four scratches meant all clear. But he couldn't very well tell the earl any of that.

There were other signals too. A finger held at the hip meant take care, this cove has a knife. A tip of the cap followed by crossed arms meant let's dive into this bloke's pockets. All these little gestures—a secret language used for centuries by thieves to ply their trade and keep one another safe. And it was all lost to him, maybe forever. He was as good as exiled, transported to a land where nobody spoke his native tongue.

"Three taps could mean an unfriendly ship has been sighted. Two taps could mean a storm off the coast. That sort of thing," Georgie suggested.

Radnor was staring at him with an unreadable expression. Most of Radnor's expressions were unreadable, to be fair. There was frustration and impatience, but the rest were totally opaque. Perhaps it was the beard.

"And the message would travel faster than a horse?" Georgie asked, trying to return to a safe topic.

Suddenly Radnor smiled, such a totally unexpected sight, Georgie very nearly smiled helplessly in return. "Yes, faster than a horse."

"Faster even than a very fast horse?"

Now the smile was even broader, almost wolfish, and the earl folded his hands behind his head. "A message would travel from Penkellis to London in a matter of minutes, if only the wires could be placed."

Minutes. That sounded too good to be true. If Georgie were to gull marks into investing in this device, nobody would believe it. They'd spot him for a fraud immediately.

An idea came to him, dangerous and brilliant, like a knife in the dark. He *could* sell this device. Or, better yet, he could steal the plans and give them to Brewster. There might be enough value in the device to buy Georgie's clemency, to earn his return to the world he missed, to protect Sarah and Jack. He could get his life back.

But he couldn't very well write a letter announcing his whereabouts and hinting vaguely at a contraption that might theoretically result in almost instant communication from the coast to London but might instead be the delusion of a madman. Brewster would send someone to kill him, make no mistake.

Georgie would wait and see if Radnor's device worked. Then he would draw up plans, complete and detailed, and use them to broker a deal with Mattie Brewster.

Radnor wouldn't like it, once he found out that his former secretary had deceived him, had stolen the fruits of his labor. But that was his problem; he was wealthy and titled and could do without one poxy contraption. Georgie stamped out any stray thought that suggested otherwise.

"All right." Georgie sat at one end of the table. "Let's get this thing working. Send me a message."

Lawrence stared at the wires. If he were a proper man of science, instead of a tinkering eccentric, he'd have already thought up a suitable message, likely something in Latin, something fittingly grand for the first use of this device. He looked down the table at his secretary, as if Turner's too-handsome face would hold an answer. But Turner only looked patient, expectant. Likely bored.

Bugger Latin. He tapped out a few letters. Anxiously, he waited, watching the bubbles rise on the opposite end of the device, watching his secretary's face as he deciphered the message.

Turner's mouth quirked up in a small, surprised smile. Not bored now. "Truly? You, *you*, my lord"—he raked his gaze over Lawrence's sloppily attired person—"are commenting on *my* mode of dress?"

Lawrence's message had been short. Thirteen characters. *Thatwaistcoat.* Turner didn't look the slightest bit offended, though. Likely he took Lawrence's sartorial judgment for what it was worth—which was to say precisely naught. "I don't think there's been red embroidery within ten leagues of Penkellis in my lifetime."

"I'll be sure to parade it through the village later on, then. If your contraption hasn't killed me, that is." He smoothed one hand down his waistcoat, his long fingers as finely wrought as the embroidered flowers that swirled and twisted across the gray silk of the fabric. "And I'll have you know that my sister, who is an expert in matters of dress, assures me that the thread is scarlet, not anything so vulgar as red."

He was joking, Lawrence realized. That arch smile was meant to be playful. It was for Lawrence's own benefit. Lawrence could hardly remember a time when smiles were for him. Had Isabella smiled at any point during their marriage? Father and Percy had never smiled at anyone. Simon had smiled at him, though, toothless and absurd.

He shook his head, clearing the thought, sending it back to gather dust with the rest of the things he wasn't to think of.

It was, he understood, his turn to talk. He needed to say something that matched Turner's tone. He wasn't capable of witticism; he could no more engage in banter than he could fly. "Your sister is an expert on dress," was what he settled on, forgetting to make the words into a question.

"She's a dressmaker. A modiste," Turner amended. "In London."

Lawrence imagined Turner surrounded by bolts of brightly colored fabrics, running his hands along smooth silk and soft velvet. Perhaps the sulfurous scent of the electrolysis was affecting his thoughts, because he could almost hear the rustle of the costly fabrics as they gave way under Turner's touch. He must have let his reverie go on too long because Turner sat back in his chair and rolled his eyes.

"Yes, I know. You expected to have a gentleman as a secretary, but you're a shocking brute, so you're stuck with me."

It took Lawrence a moment to grasp what Turner meant. "Oh, that's not... Wait." He furrowed his eyebrows, reaching for the question he needed to ask to make sense of this. "You're not a gentleman's son." Of course he wasn't. Lawrence ought to have known that any son of a proper English gentleman wouldn't take kindly to being targeted with flying books or addressed in terse profanities. But then what was the man doing as a secretary, a position generally held by the third sons of impoverished vicars?

Now Turner was regarding him with a look Lawrence recognized as exasperation. "I'm not a gentleman, full stop. And I don't know why I'm telling you this, except that I don't expect you care." He looked strangely thoughtful now.

This was why it was safer to communicate in scowls and monosyllables. Safer still was to avoid people entirely. He put his foot wrong as soon as he started a conversation. He ruffled feathers without even knowing he had encountered a bird.

"No more talking," Lawrence muttered. "I'll send another message." This time he transmitted the alphabet. No more waistcoats, no more friendly conversation.

The alphabet transmission took bloody near forever, but it went through without a short circuit. Tomorrow he would try with longer wires and see if he could replicate this small success. Perhaps if he were farther away from Turner, everything would return to normal.

Just then, an ungodly noise came from outside, shouting mingled with what sounded like the death cry of a wounded animal. "What the devil is that?" he asked.

Turner was on his feet and at the window in a flash. "It looks like a cart got mired and overturned. The driver and your cook are unhitching the horse and—lord, she's giving him quite the dressing down. She has a lot to say about the man's intellect and parentage, and something about 'in broad daylight,' although I can't imagine she'd prefer a cart to overturn at midnight. I almost feel bad for the poor bastard. Do you think you could go and help them set the cart upright?"

Lawrence managed to choke out a rough, "No." His heart was louder than the horse's panicked neighing, louder than the cook's scolds. Damn it. Curse his blasted brain. It was only noise—jarring and incessant but only noise. For God's sake, nobody liked the cries of a wounded animal, nobody liked the distressed shrieking of a woman, but as far as Lawrence knew he was the only one who was provoked into fits by these commonplace disturbances.

Instinctively, he dropped his hand to his side, groping for Barnabus, who seemed to have an instinct for knowing when he was needed. But the dog was in exile this afternoon, Turner having insisted that one errant wag of Barnabus's tail would result in all three of them being killed and Penkellis burning to the ground. Lawrence struggled to fill his lungs with air.

Turner still watched the show out the window. "I understand that it's beneath you, but really I only have the one pair of boots, and I'm not ruining them. Besides, you're nearly twice my size, so you'd be of more use to them than I'd ever be."

"I said no," Lawrence ground out. "I cannot."

Turner looked over his shoulder and appeared to notice what kind of condition Lawrence was in. His eyes went wide. "No, I don't suppose you can." He stepped away from the window. Likely he'd come up with a pretext for leaving. But instead, he crossed the room and crouched beside Lawrence's chair.

Lawrence didn't dare look up. He felt a hand on his shoulder, just the lightest touch, but so unexpected and so unfamiliar that it sent him careening closer to absolute panic. "Are you all right? No, that's a silly question, of course you aren't. What do you usually do when you're, ah, discomposed?" Turner's voice was as cool as ever, as if there was nothing alarming about being in close proximity to Lawrence. As if this was all totally normal and Lawrence wasn't having an episode right here in front of his secretary.

Lawrence shook his head.

Turner squeezed Lawrence's shoulder. Surely the gesture was simply meant to be reassuring, and it might even have worked on someone whose world wasn't already tilting off its axis.

"I need to lie down." He stood up immediately, intending to shut himself in his bedchamber until he felt reasonably sane. But because he could not manage the simplest blasted thing without disaster, he knocked over his chair and lost his footing. He was going to crash into the table, ruining days of work. Suddenly he found himself supported by a pair of wiry arms.

All Lawrence's thoughts dissolved into a sea of Turner's confounded scent and the warm puff of the man's breath against his neck.

"Whoa, there," Turner said. "Steady now." His grip shifted to Lawrence's arms, the hot trail of his touch plunging Lawrence into further confusion.

Lawrence should have looked away, stepped away, done anything to get away, but he bloody obviously wasn't thinking straight that morning. Instead, as he righted himself, he found himself gazing down into the other man's face, close enough to see the shadow of a beard on Turner's jaw. What was that expression—not pity, not annoyance. Concern?

Lawrence suddenly felt a flush of heat. He slid his fingers under the collar of his shirt, trying to free his burning skin. He ought to have gone outside to chop firewood or mend a fence minutes or hours ago. Hell, he ought to be locked in an institution where he could quietly go mad without anyone to bear witness.

Turner pressed one of his hands against the small of Lawrence's back, steering him towards the sofa. There was more strength in the secretary than he might have expected in such a slender man. *Not a gentleman,* he remembered, but he was too rattled to think about what that meant.

"I'm fine," Lawrence said, a bald-faced lie.

"Quite," Turner agreed, gamely playing along. "Sit anyway."

Lawrence sat.

And then he felt a gust of fresh air, a blessed relief. Turner had opened a window.

"There we go." Turner's cool, clipped London voice came from across the room. "And how about this one too? Your cook has everything under control, and there's no more commotion." More cold air as Turner threw the remainder of the windows open.

It took him a few seconds before he remembered to breathe, before he could make himself believe that this moment would pass—at least this time. In the future, he'd be carried away by stray feelings and dangerous notions as surely as his father and brother had been, and it would end the same for him as it had for them: madness, followed by death.

He tried to watch the motes of dust caught in the breeze that blew through the open windows. He forced himself to listen to something other than the drumming of his heart— the crows calling to one another outside, the wind whipping through the bare branches of the trees around Penkellis, the ivy scratching against the windows. Beneath his clammy fingers was the familiar rough, pilled damask upholstery of the sofa. After some time, his heart resumed something like a normal rhythm and his thoughts slowed down.

Slumping, he tipped his head against the back of the seat. "Damn," he said.

"Indeed," Turner said. He was somewhere nearby, a slim silhouette off to the side, but Lawrence did not allow himself to look. "Do loud noises bring on these episodes? Or is it something else?"

Lawrence shook his head. Noise was only the beginning. "I need things to be predictable," he said, all too conscious of how pathetic that must sound. But Turner only nodded and looked thoughtful. "You ought to leave," Lawrence said. "Go back to London."

Silence. "Am I being sacked?" There was an edge in the man's voice.

He ought to say yes, and he might have, but for some reason he didn't want to insult Turner. "No. What I mean is that you're free to leave. I'm not safe to be near. Surely you can see that for yourself."

"What I see is a man who had a moment of...I don't rightly know what. Nothing remotely unsafe, though."

Lawrence could have laughed at the man's naïveté. "Go home, Mr. Turner."

Turner snorted, such an unexpectedly rude noise from the polished and tidy secretary that Lawrence turned to look at him before he could remember that it was a bad idea. The man was leaning against the wall between the two open windows, his ordinarily smooth hair ruffled by the wind.

"Oh, how nice to be an earl," he said, "and not have to worry your tangled head about how other people keep body and soul together. I was counting on this position, my lord."

"You'd rather stay here and be killed?" Lawrence challenged.

For some reason this made Turner laugh. "Are you planning to kill me?" Bland unconcern, not a trace of fear. "Somehow I doubt it."

Lawrence stared at him. "I threw a book at you before I had known you even a quarter of an hour."

"Oh, you'll have to do better than that. Where I come from people stab one another when they're serious about doing harm. My own father was in the habit of throwing chairs when he didn't get his way—when we had chairs, which wasn't often by any means. The rest of the time he threw empty bottles of gin. A book? Six inches clear to the left of my head? Either you have pathetically poor aim—and it can't be that, since you manage an ax competently enough—or you only wanted to pester me."

Pester? *Pester?* Lawrence stood and crossed the room in two easy strides. His sense of panic from earlier was quite gone, replaced by the urgent and inane need to prove that he was a threat to his secretary's safety. "You've heard of my brother? My father?" He saw recognition in the secretary's expression. "I am from the same stock. The same blood. The same brutish body, the same dangerous mind. You ought to go to London, I tell you."

Turner arched a single elegant eyebrow. "They say your brother murdered his mistress and disposed of her body and that he somehow contrived to kill his wife. Are you in the habit of murdering women?"

Lawrence shook his head in frustration. "No, but—"

"Men?" Turner asked, and surely it was Lawrence's imagination that the man's voice went silkily suggestive on that single syllable, as if he were not talking about murder but something else entirely.

"I'm not in the habit of murdering anyone, for God's sake."

"Do you wish you were?" Turner's tone was now conversational, as if he were asking whether Lawrence took his tea with lemon or milk.

"Of course not, but you're missing the point." With a single, menacing forefinger, Lawrence touched Turner's chest. He had meant for the gesture to be intimidating, but it felt strangely intimate. Before he knew what had happened, Turner had taken hold of Lawrence's large, calloused hands in his own fine ones. Lawrence didn't know if the man was motivated by kindness or self-defense, but he found that he was holding hands with a person for the first time since he was a child.

"Here's how I see it, my lord." Turner's voice was cool and unconcerned. "You're not quite cut from the same cloth as most people. But you're hardly mad or dangerous."

Not cut from the same cloth? The sheer understatement ought to have been amusing. Lawrence tried to focus on the need to get through to Turner, but all he could think about was the warmth of Turner's skin against his own. "You yourself pointed out that the telegraph and battery could kill us." Which may have been a lie Lawrence made up to keep his secretary's hands off the device, but it also served the purpose of convincing Turner that he was employed by a dangerous lunatic.

Turner rolled his eyes. "Please. This time of year, men go about the countryside shooting pheasants and acting like it's perfectly normal when one of them comes home peppered with shot. Nobody calls those fools mad."

"You've been here a week." Lawrence tried to master himself despite the light pressure of his secretary's fingers against his wrists. "You can't possibly think this household is normal."

"Of course it isn't normal. You eat nothing but ham and apples, for God's sake. You dress like a stableman. And your house is a shambles. But if none of that bothers you, then it doesn't bother me."

"*Bothering* doesn't enter into it, damn you—"

"And I suppose if that's what it takes for you to accomplish everything you've done, then so be it."

"Accomplish?" God damn it, Turner was stroking the inside of Lawrence's wrists with his thumbs. And for some reason Lawrence seemed to feel this touch in his cock. Was there a nerve that went from the wrist to the prick? Another sign of incipient madness, then.

"Your inventions. The communication device."

The telegraph. God yes. He tried not to think of how badly he wanted it to work, to have a way to remain in his refuge but perhaps not be quite so isolated. "Nearly all my servants have quit," he said, returning the conversation to the solid ground of his lunacy.

"Yes, well, that *is* interesting," Turner said. "I've been wondering about that. Did you notice they left without pocketing any of your valuables?"

"What?" Perhaps it was the way Turner was leaning against the wall, looking up at him through a thick fringe of lashes, that made Lawrence's cock feel so heavy.

"I assure you, the standard procedure when taking leave of a violent and despised employer is to nick a candlestick or, at the very least, a couple of teacups." Turner's voice was only loud enough to be heard a few inches away. "But that didn't happen here. There's such a quantity of dust and cobwebs around the house that one would see straightaway if anything had been removed, and it's quite clear that nothing has been disturbed."

"What on earth does that have to do with anything?"

"If you're such a dangerous monster, such a trial to serve, then why wouldn't a servant help himself to a bit of silver? In the name of justice, naturally."

"Justice?"

"That's what they'd tell themselves, you understand."

He certainly did not, but gathered that Turner did. *Not a gentleman,* Lawrence repeated to himself. *Perhaps not a secretary either.* "Even so, all but a handful of my servants quit over a month ago."

"Two. You have two servants left. A cook and a maid, both thoroughly indolent. Sally Ferris and a girl named Janet."

Sally Ferris. Lawrence's mind reeled. Of all the people to willingly stay under this roof. Good God. He'd have thought she'd be the first to leave under any pretense. "You'd do best to follow the example of the others. Most of them grew up nearby and know more than you do about the madness in my family," he managed to say.

"Precisely," Turner said. "I intend to figure out what exactly they know and why they haven't taken so much as a teaspoon."

Lawrence twisted his hands out of Turner's strong grip, placing them flat on the wall next to the secretary's head. He took a step closer, caging the smaller man in.

"Do you not understand what I mean by danger?" Lawrence growled. "To hell with candlesticks and to hell with telegraphs. I'm talking about you and me. Do you not realize that I'm nearly twice your size?"

Turner made a noise at the back of his throat. His lips were slightly parted, his breathing fast. Was that fear? If so, good. It was about time.

They were so close. If Lawrence took another fraction of a step, his hardening prick would press into Turner's belly, right against the brightly embroidered waistcoat that had started this trouble.

"I could murder you without breaking a sweat, if that's what I wanted to do," he said.

Ducking out from under Lawrence's arm, Turner shot him a wry look that he couldn't make heads or tails of. "But that's not what you want to do to me, is it?" he asked, heading for the door. He threw a look over his shoulder, one side of his mouth curved into a sly grin. "Not even close."

CHAPTER SIX

A stream of obscenities came from the table where Radnor assembled his machine.

"Another short circuit, my lord?"

"God damn it, yes, and you fucking know it."

Radnor had added more disks to the pile and for some reason the result was a series of short circuits and a very surly earl.

"If I may say so, my lord, I seem to recall reading that another gentleman encountered this very problem." Georgie had discovered that the earl hated any suggestion of deference or servility, so he heaped it on thick when he wanted to provoke a display of snarling profanity.

"I know that, damn you, but I can't remember what he did about it."

"Oh dear," Georgie said, biting his lip. "If only you had a secretary who had organized all that information for you."

"Out with it, you swiving bastard."

Georgie tilted his chair back towards the shelves that lined the wall, effortlessly retrieving the volume he sought. "My lord," he said, presenting it with a flourish.

"You're showing off," Radnor said, flipping through the pages.

"I'm afraid so." Georgie felt that he was quite justified in his smugness. He had not only organized the study, but he had become sufficiently familiar with the earl's work to offer assistance. This was no mean feat for a man whose only formal education had been sporadic at best, and he found that he wanted to be acknowledged for his work. That was new. Usually Georgie's efforts were, of necessity, invisible. Now he wanted Radnor to know just how good Georgie was. He wanted Radnor to admire him.

To *admire* him? That was absurd. Total nonsense. He wanted Radnor to do a good number of things to him, none of which involved admiration, unless it was Georgie admiring the earl's bare torso.

But try as he might to feel otherwise, Georgie was proud of his work for Radnor. He felt as if he were a vital part of something important, something almost magical.

Something he was going to steal in order to wheedle his way back into a life of crime.

No. Something he *needed* to steal in order to keep a dangerous man away from the people he loved. Yesterday he received a letter from Jack, informing him that Sarah was safely at Oliver's sister's house and that Jack was looking into ways of bringing Brewster around. This was not terribly reassuring, because it meant that Brewster's manhunt was in full effect.

It also meant that Georgie was still without a way to return to his life, to his brother and sister, unless he double-crossed the man who currently stood before him, brows furrowed, furiously paging through a scientific journal.

Georgie's pigeonholes were in chaos.

Radnor flung the journal onto Georgie's desk, opened to the page that showed the diagram he needed. "He put it sideways, blast the man."

They spent the rest of the morning producing what Radnor called a trough battery. The problem with the vertical pile, Georgie gathered, was that the weight of the disks caused liquid to be squeezed out of the quilt pieces and to leak down the sides, causing a short circuit. By laying the pile on its side, they could add more disks but take the pressure off the electrolyte.

Late in the afternoon, Georgie heard the painstakingly soft footsteps outside the door, signaling a delivery of the inevitable ham, apples, and bread. His stomach turned. Even if he had to forage in the woods he would have a decent meal tonight.

"Do you know," he said thoughtfully, "I don't think I can see myself through another supper of ham and bread."

Radnor bent over his battery, not paying attention.

Georgie rose to his feet. "Two weeks of ham is quite enough. I'll have a proper dinner or I'll know the reason why." He headed for the door.

"No, damn it, we're working."

"You can carry on without me. You got along perfectly well before I came, I'm sure," he said, knowing it was a lie and hoping Radnor did as well. "I'll be back in a tick."

"You're my secretary, damn you." Oh, Georgie had his attention now. "You can't mean to saunter off like this."

"I assure you, that's precisely what I mean to do. Although I'm gratified to know that my presence means so much to you."

Radnor looked like he wanted to smash something. But he didn't, and Georgie thought that restraint might amount to something close to a compliment.

"Sod off, then," the earl said, returning to the box he was insulating.

"No." Georgie put extra acid into his voice. " 'Sod off' is not the correct response when somebody has gone to a great deal of trouble and spared you a headache. While I'm gone, reflect on what you actually meant to say." He took his top-coat and hat off the hook and swept out of the room.

Radnor didn't even look up, damn the man.

Georgie hadn't meant to lose his patience. But Radnor could guess again if he thought he was going to keep Georgie on prison rations and not even properly thank him.

Stepping out onto the crumbling ruin of a terrace, he pulled his topcoat more tightly around him, guarding against the wind that blew in from the sea. He headed towards a lane that he hoped led to the village and threw a glance over his shoulder at the looming bulk of Penkellis. There was something altogether unsettling about a house that was unlocked, unguarded, and unrobbed. The locks—when there even were locks—were the sort that any enterprising child could pick. Even now, Radnor's dog, who Georgie had put outside earlier that afternoon, was attempting to push his way back in through one of the flimsy garden doors. Georgie gave him even odds to force the rusted hinges, even without the use of any hands.

He must have watched the house a second too long, because the dog stopped his housebreaking efforts and came bounding towards him, evidently mistaking eye contact for an invitation. The mongrel—he was so shaggy and so extremely large that Georgie refused to believe he could be a proper breed of dog—proceeded merrily along the lane like they were old friends, keeping an appointment.

"Bugger off back to the house," Georgie tried. The dog regarded him with a lolling tongue that Georgie supposed was a counterargument.

And really, the dog had the whip hand in this situation, because there wasn't a damned thing Georgie could do, unless he wanted to go back to the house and get the earl to fetch his monster of a dog. If Georgie returned now, he'd quite ruin all the work he had put into making a dramatic exit. It was one thing to work for a temperamental bastard, quite another to work for an ungrateful one.

Georgie needed to step away before he found himself trying to seduce his employer. He had noticed Radnor's flushed cheeks, his darkened eyes, the way his entire body seemed to prickle with awareness every time their hands accidentally brushed. Getting hanged for sodomy was not going to improve his current situation, Georgie reflected grimly.

In the village, he posted a letter to Jack, saying that Lord Radnor was rude and awkward but hardly seemed mad, and reassuring his brother that he had no intention of returning to London quite yet. He had meant to get supper at the inn, but when he approached that establishment, he looked back to see Barnabus gazing at him wistfully. Oh, sod it all. He shouldn't care about whether the dog would have to wait outside in the cold.

All the same, he walked back towards Penkellis. There was more than one way to get a hot meal. He approached a cluster of cottages, probably the homes of farm laborers. At the nearest cottage, a woman stood in the doorway, scattering feed for the chickens that clucked around her. Georgie fished a shilling out of his pocket.

"Good evening," he called, doffing his hat and fixing an innocuous smile on his face. Not wanting to alarm her, he stayed a good two yards outside the weather-beaten wooden fence that enclosed the garden. Barnabus eyed the chickens with a hungry gleam but didn't move any closer.

The woman looked up from the chickens and eyed him warily. Then she saw Barnabus and her expression darkened. She looked to be about forty, maybe a few years older. Even in the fading sunlight, Georgie could see how worn her dress was, how dingy her apron. It had been a hard year across the country, and he guessed these people hadn't had it any better than most.

"And what do you want?" she asked, folding her arms across her chest.

"May I trouble you for some eggs or cheese?" He played with the coin in his hand so she'd be sure to see it, a gesture that suddenly made him homesick for the streets of London.

The woman's gaze traveled from Georgie to the dog. "You come from the castle?" Her Cornish accent was so thick, Georgie had to strain to understand.

"From Penkellis? Yes. I'm his lordship's new secretary."

With one hand she shielded her eyes from the sun that hung low in the sky behind Georgie's head. "Have they no eggs at Penkellis?"

"Not that I've seen."

A man stepped out of the cottage and looked back and forth between the woman and Georgie. "Any trouble, Maggie?" The words were addressed to his wife but the message was for Georgie: this woman was under his protection, and anyone who insulted her or caused her grief would pay the price.

"He says he comes from Penkellis and wants to buy eggs," Maggie said. "Says he's the earl's secretary."

The man looked directly at Georgie with open skepticism. "And would these eggs be for the earl?"

Barnabus began to make a low growling sound. Georgie, without taking his eyes off the couple, started to pet the dog's scruffy head in what he hoped was a reassuring manner. "No," he said. "They'd be for my supper."

"Radnor has his servants fend for themselves, does he?"

"I fancied something different from his usual fare."

"And you want Maggie's eggs." More skepticism.

"I'd settle for anything that wasn't bread, ham, or apples. That's the only food I've seen since I came here."

The couple exchanged a glance. "Sixpence for half a dozen eggs," the man said, a barely suppressed smirk on this face.

That was an outrageous price, but Georgie would let himself get fleeced for a good cause. "I'll make it a shilling if you'll also let me have some cheese, butter, and maybe a couple of mushrooms." Georgie had seen a basket of mushrooms hanging on a peg near the door.

A minute later a girl of ten or twelve came out of the cottage with a parcel wrapped in cloth. "Mama put an onion in too," she said, fingering the shilling as if she had never seen one. And maybe she hadn't. "Do vittles cost so much where you come from?"

They certainly did not, but he was paying for something other than food. He was hoping to purchase goodwill, and maybe information. Because even though he had assured Jack that the earl was in his right mind, there was something else going on at Penkellis, and he didn't want to leave until he knew what. "They look to be very fine eggs," he said.

The girl shrugged and made as if to go back inside, but then turned a questioning face up at Georgie. "Is he a real devil?" she whispered.

"The dog?" Barnabus was enthusiastically rolling around in chicken shite. "He's much the same as any other dog, only larger."

"No, *him*." She tilted her chin in the direction of Penkellis.

"The earl? No, he's only different. He's also very large."

The girl tugged at one of her braids. "He stole Betsy's caul."

"Her what?" Was this a bit of colorful rustic vocabulary?

"Her caul," she said, exaggerating the pronunciation, as if that would help the matter. "From when she was born," she clarified. "He stole it."

Oh, a *caul*. Good God. Georgie had never thought of a caul as something that anyone would want to steal. "How…unexpected."

"It went missing before Mama had even finished drying it." The girl's tone suggested that this added to the infamy of the crime. It certainly added to its unsavoriness.

"Did he steal it away with his own hands? How"—he searched for a word suitable for a child's ears—"dastardly."

She seemed to need a moment to think about this. "I don't reckon so. I never heard that he came here, only that the caul went missing. Mrs. Ferris said the earl took it. Who else would do such a thing? And a caul is a handy sort of thing to have if you're doing witchcraft, Mama says."

So, Radnor's servants were spreading tales, were they? "Well, I can tell you that I've never seen a caul in the earl's study." If he had, he wouldn't have recognized it. And if he had recognized it, he would have thrown it in the fire.

The cottage door creaked open and a very small child stuck her head out. "Mama says you're to come in or you'll catch it."

Both children went inside, and Georgie whistled for Barnabus, eager to reach the kitchens before the sun was completely gone from the sky.

When Turner flounced out of the room, Lawrence was relieved. He was quite determined on that score: he was relieved to finally have some peace and quiet, and in no way did he miss his meddlesome secretary. Turner could be an exhausting fellow, forever tidying and rearranging, asking too many questions and taking endless notes, to say nothing of how his very existence was a distraction. He served as a fine reminder of why Lawrence preferred solitude in the first place.

Worse, he served as an incitement to the very sort of madness Lawrence found most tempting. Every time Turner came close, Lawrence was assailed by images of that lean body underneath his own bulky form or over him, alternately compliant and masterful. His imagination was evidently capable of infinite variety where Turner was concerned.

But *was* that desire truly part of his madness? He was aware that his conviction on this point was sadly unscientific. He was relying on an unreliable source—the rantings of his deranged father and a couple of passages in a holy book he had never paid much attention to anyway. He had only a paucity of data, his own experiences in pleasures of the flesh being sadly limited. Perhaps this desire was a commonplace thing. Perhaps it had nothing to do with madness.

This left Lawrence as unsettled as if somebody had demonstrated that electricity was caused by fire sprites. Because if his desire for fellow men wasn't madness, then perhaps none of his other oddities were madness either. As that seemed grossly unlikely, he hardly knew what to think about anything at all.

He stood and paced across the study, trying to sweep his mind clear of its tangle of lust and confusion, but all he could think of was Turner and the disappointed look on his face when he had left. It seemed that after two weeks of working together all hours of the day and night, Turner's absence was even more distracting than his presence. He kept looking over at Turner's desk, expecting to see a dark head bent over tidy stacks of papers, expecting to hear the methodical scratch of Turner's pen.

As pacing was doing precisely nothing for his state of mind, Lawrence attempted to work instead. He sat at his desk and absently reached for the latest letter from Standish. Somehow, the paper was where Lawrence meant for it to be, exactly where he put his hand, even though Lawrence was quite certain he hadn't put the letter there himself. Usually, finding Standish's latest letter involved a great deal of tedious weeding through unrelated correspondence, if he even found it at all. It was Turner's doing. Turner always knew what Lawrence required and saw that it was done.

And wasn't that just the worst of it, how the man had made himself indispensable. Turner really was a very good secretary, even though Lawrence was doubtless unpleasant to work for. All his fussing and interference resulted in Lawrence being less frustrated. Calmer, even. Certainly more productive. Which was somehow even worse than if Turner were simply a shiftless nuisance.

He found himself dreading the day when Turner finally realized what a bad idea it was to live in close quarters with such a man as Lawrence. Because the fellow eventually would realize it, and then Lawrence would be less productive, less calm. *Alone.*

It was a mystery how a man like Turner had found his way to Penkellis in the first place. Surely he belonged in London, among men who were fashionable and powerful, among ladies who would properly appreciate his good looks and fine manners. Then again, perhaps fashionable, powerful men didn't care to employ secretaries with dubious backgrounds. Likely Lawrence ought to object as well, but he found he didn't care in the least where Turner came from.

The fact that Lawrence was now willing to do what it took—including grovel, apologize, or throw himself at Turner's feet—to keep him at Penkellis meant Lawrence was no better than his father or brother. They had always put their whims ahead of all else, including the safety of innocent people. Lawrence was determined not to be mad in that particular way. He would make it easy for Turner to leave Penkellis, and he would delay the onset of madness for just a bit longer.

"Never in all my years." Mrs. Ferris shook her head. "I never thought I'd see the day when a gentleman interfered with my kitchen."

"I'm not really a gentleman, if that makes a difference." Georgie unloaded the contents of his basket onto the broad, scarred table. "I fancy an omelet and figured I'd make it myself rather than put you to any trouble."

Mrs. Ferris clucked disapprovingly. "If you'll put those eggs down, Janet will see to them."

Janet made a sound of protest.

"Tsk," Mrs. Ferris scolded. "When was the last time you lifted a finger?"

Georgie took a knife out of the block and tested its sharpness on his finger. It was sharper than he would have expected in a kitchen that saw hardly any cooking. Someone had taken this blade to the whetstone. Likely the same someone who kept this kitchen in an immaculate state of cleanliness.

"I know it's most irregular, but it'll take a quarter of an hour, and I'll scour the pans myself," Georgie said, arranging the mushrooms before him in a straight row. "I just can't face another ham sandwich."

Janet snorted, and Mrs. Ferris glared in her direction. "I can't blame you," the cook said. "It's no way for a man to live. Never a hot meal, always the same thing day after day."

It occurred to Georgie that the earl's insistence on an endless succession of ham sandwiches meant these women might not get much else to eat either.

He felt the older woman's gaze on him as he placed the onion on the chopping block and started to peel off its papery skin. On a hunch, he cut the onion into several oddly sized chunks. Before its pungent aroma had even reached his nostrils she was by his side.

"No, no. What are you about? Chop the onion fine, like this." She took the knife from his hand and held up a paper thin slice of onion for his edification. "Each piece the same as all the others. Janet, melt the butter in that saucepan. Mr. Turner, you slice the mushrooms."

Mrs. Ferris took charge of the operation as if she had been longing to oversee the preparation of a meal. If she had gone into service intending to be a proper cook, she might be bored off her chair in a house where there was nothing to do but bake bread and slice ham. No wonder the kitchen was spotless.

Twenty minutes later, the three of them shared a mushroom omelet in Mrs. Ferris's parlor.

This was the coziest room Georgie had yet seen at Penkellis. There was neither dust nor mice, the windows were reasonably clean, and a fire burned high in the little hearth. On the chimney piece was a row of carefully arranged knickknacks—a braided lock of hair, a small whittled animal of some sort, a sketch of a very young man.

"Who's the woman in the whitewashed cottage with all those yellow-haired children?" Georgie asked. "She's the one I bought the eggs from."

"That'd be Maggie Kemp," Janet said around a mouthful of eggs.

"What's this about Lord Radnor stealing her caul?"

Mrs. Ferris paused with her fork halfway to her mouth. "You know how these people are," she said. "Superstitious." Georgie noticed that she avoided meeting anyone's eyes.

"Of course," Georgie agreed. He didn't mention that the child had said Mrs. Ferris herself had blamed the earl for the theft. Instead he decided it was time to ingratiate himself with the servants. "It seems a waste to keep an experienced cook and not have her do any cooking."

Mrs. Ferris sighed. "His lordship wants his ham and bread and won't hear otherwise. That's the way he is. Of course, I told him, years ago, back when he still came down to visit the kitchens, that a man needs more than that to live, but he's set in his ways. So it's ham and bread, and apples when they're in season."

Georgie realized that if the walnuts he had seen Mrs. Ferris shelling on the night of his arrival were not intended for Radnor, they must have had some other purpose. Presumably she sold them and kept the proceeds for herself. It seemed strange that Mrs. Ferris would profit from the sale of Penkellis's walnuts but not avail herself of the fortune's worth of silver and china littering the house. But Georgie knew the lines people drew for themselves. Stay on the right side of the line, and it wasn't *really* wrong. Georgie had those lines too, only they never seemed to stay in the same place for long. One moment he felt quite above reproach, and the next he was telling young Ned Packingham that he ought not let his aunt invest in a certain fictitious canal company.

Georgie tried to steer his attention away from the swamp of regret and shame that was the Packingham job. "Does he not let you clean?" he asked Janet.

"His lordship doesn't like to be disturbed," Janet said primly. "Getting on his bad side is more than our lives are worth."

"Is that why the other servants left? Because they feared getting on his bad side?" Georgie had a hard time imagining

Radnor actually harming anyone. This morning Georgie had watched in astonishment as Radnor rescued a spider that Georgie had wanted to kill.

The women exchanged a long look. "There was an explosion—a very small one, nothing to fuss over—but they got it into their heads that they'd be blown to bits."

"Now, I wonder why they'd think that," Georgie pondered. He kept his attention on Janet, figuring her as the one more likely to accidentally reveal something. "Radnor owns mines elsewhere in Cornwall, does he not? I take it the powder and fuse he developed were for use in these mines? It seems odd that the villagers, who surely must have some relations who work in the mines, wouldn't understand that."

Georgie, after two weeks spent elbow-deep in Radnor's papers, knew perfectly well that the earl had invented a safety fuse that was meant to make work safer for the miners. By all rights, the local people ought to regard him as a hero.

"Well," Janet said slowly, "the folk around here think he's some kind of devil worshiper. Can't imagine why."

"Janet!" Mrs. Ferris chided.

"Well, they do. Like Mr. Turner said—"

"Call me Georgie, please," he said, bringing out his best smile.

"Like Georgie said, Maggie Kemp has been going on about that poxy caul for years now. How old is Betsy? Three? Three years that she's been telling everyone who darkens her doorstep that Lord Radnor is using her Betsy's caul to summon devils or whatnot."

Mrs. Ferris pushed some stray bits of onion around her plate. "There's no harm in him. I always tell them so."

Georgie wondered what else she told them. He would have bet almost anything that she was at the heart of the rumors and suspicion that surrounded Radnor, but he couldn't see why.

"The lad in the sketch." He gestured with his fork at the drawing that sat on the chimney piece. "Is he your son?" he asked Mrs. Ferris.

By the time the kitchen clock chimed ten, Georgie had learned that Mrs. Ferris's son was a midshipman in the navy. He knew Janet was Mrs. Ferris's cousin's daughter and also a Ferris. This, Georgie noted but of course did not remark on, likely meant that Mrs. Ferris was really a *miss*. And yet, she had somehow managed to get her child a commission.

He could have done this routine in his sleep. Ingratiating himself was what he did best. He hadn't done it with Radnor, though. He hadn't needed to—he was genuinely intrigued by the earl's device, even more so by the man who had invented it. Instead he provoked and irritated Radnor as much as he pleased. That was not how he treated marks. It was not even how he treated his friends.

No matter how hard Georgie tried to keep his mental pigeonholes sorted, he could not seem to keep Radnor where he belonged.

CHAPTER SEVEN

Lawrence needed to apologize to Turner. It was the right thing, the sane thing to do. He knew this because it was the exact opposite of what his father or brother would have done after behaving boorishly to a servant. He would do something else his father and brother had never thought to do: he would offer to let the man leave, even paying his wages through the next quarter. He would make that offer because he wanted Turner to stay, damn him, and he was operating on the vague sense that when in doubt about the correct course of action, he ought to consult his desires and behave contrary to them.

Candle in hand, he headed to the wing that housed the only inhabitable bedchambers. He didn't know which one had been assigned to Turner—or indeed who could have done the assigning in the first place—but unless the man was bedding down in the stables he couldn't be far from here. But the west wing was utterly silent. There was no sign of life, no smell of wood fire, no rustling of bedsheets. All he could hear was the familiar nighttime scurrying of mice and the wind whistling through a cracked window.

He opened each door along the corridor, unleashing cloud after cloud of dust. For the first time, he realized what it meant to live in a house with essentially no servants. Soon this wing would go the way of the crumbling east wing. The furniture would molder and rot. Small leaks, then larger ones, would spring in the roof. Eventually it would cave in and the walls would fall. Small weeds would grow in between the toppled stones.

He could see it with perfect clarity: Penkellis gone, eradicated from the face of the earth. The bloodline of the Earls of Radnor would end with Lawrence, and all that was left was to wait for the house itself to crumble. It brought him a small mote of joy to think that this place, with all its evil and sorrow, could be done away with. But at the same time he knew it had to be slightly mad to fantasize about one's own ancestral home being reduced to rubble.

That was why he had to hold fast to any sane impulse that got into his head, like a ship's captain leaning hard on the wheel during a storm. He needed to throw his weight into choosing not to be mad, while he still had a choice. He would not go the way of his father and brother, letting himself be governed only by his madness, only by his pleasure. Not yet. Not while he still had a choice.

But it was all too clear that Turner was not to be found in this part of the house. Lawrence returned upstairs, to the tower that housed his study and bedchamber.

Rounding a corner, he saw Barnabus lying outside the door to what had once been Lawrence's own dressing room. The dog sleepily thumped his tail, but made no other move to greet his master. Lawrence bent to scratch the animal behind his ears.

"Stay," he whispered, pushing open the dressing room door. In the darkness, he could barely make out the silhouette of a man lying on the sofa.

He ought to shut the door and tiptoe out the way he had come. Turner was sleeping. Of course he was sleeping. It was likely past midnight. This was not the time for apologies, Lawrence realized belatedly. He ought to be in bed himself.

Instead he stepped further into the room. He assumed there was some good reason for Turner to be sleeping here but didn't bother taxing his mind with a question when the answer didn't matter. Much more interesting was the fact that Turner slept with his hands folded under his cheek like a child, his knees tucked up close to his chest.

Even more interesting still was the fact that Turner slept without a shirt. The coat he was using as a blanket had slipped down, revealing a shoulder that was burnished to a pale glow by the faint moonlight.

Lawrence placed the candle on an empty table and took a step closer still. Turner looked very young and unsophisticated while he slept, his beauty unrelieved by the sharp edges of urbanity and archness. Dark eyelashes rested against smooth cheeks in obscene extravagance. Lawrence was disconcerted to see the man like this, all sleepy innocence.

As he watched, a spider crawled across the secretary's face. Turner's nose twitched in unconscious discomfort. Instinctively, Lawrence reached out and brushed the creature off Turner's cheek.

Instantly, Turner's eyes sprang open, and Lawrence found himself being shoved to the ground.

"Who sent you?" Turner asked, his voice raspy with sleep.

What the hell kind of question was that? And what kind of life had Turner lived to wake up in such a fashion?

"It's Radnor," he answered, slightly stunned by the force with which he had hit the floor. Turner was kneeling over him, one knee on his chest, his hands pinning Lawrence's wrists to the bare floor. If that was what he could do while still half-asleep, Lawrence didn't want to find out what he was capable of at his best.

It occurred to Lawrence that perhaps Turner *hadn't* been menaced by any of Lawrence's theatrics. He could defend himself against a man of Lawrence's size, which was certainly not a skill typical of a secretary. But Lawrence already knew that Turner was no ordinary secretary. What the devil he actually was remained unclear.

"Radnor," Turner repeated in confusion—and was that relief?—taking his knee off Lawrence's chest so he now was kneeling astride Lawrence. "What the devil are you doing in here?" His voice was hoarse, tired.

"I could ask you the same thing," Lawrence pointed out. There was just enough light to see Turner's black eyes, his sleep-tousled hair falling across his forehead as he leaned over Lawrence. Lawrence let his gaze drift over the other man's chest, lean and wiry.

Neither of them moved. Surely one of them ought to, but it wouldn't be Lawrence. The mere proximity of this man was doing dangerous things to his already chancy grip on self-control.

"I take it we're even now." Turner's mouth, alarmingly close to Lawrence's own, crooked up in the ghost of a smile.

"Even?" Lawrence, frantically trying to persuade his cock that now was not the time to get ideas, was not following the other man's logic.

"Now we've both nearly killed one another after being startled from our sleep."

"I'm very sorry about—"

"What a pretty pair we make." Turner was looking down at him with an expression that Lawrence couldn't read, but which his prick seemed eager to interpret.

Still neither of them moved.

Lawrence might go the rest of his life without ever being this close to another person again, without feeling his body stir, without absorbing heat from another man's touch. Even this simple contact, Turner's hands pressed against his own, might be something he would never know again. Perhaps that was why he made no effort to get free of Turner's grip.

But that didn't explain why Turner didn't let go.

Lawrence squeezed his eyes shut. He had come here to behave decently, to act with whatever shreds of sanity he could muster, not to nurture lascivious thoughts. "If you choose to leave, I'll pay your wages through the next quarter and write you a character." Another moment, another rising and falling of chests. "You're a very good secretary. I should have told you that earlier."

"That's why you came to my room in the middle of the night?" There was amusement in Turner's voice. "To praise my secretarial skills?"

"Technically, I came into my own dressing room."

"I'm not quitting my post."

Lawrence flung open his eyes. "But—"

"As you said, I'm a good secretary." Turner's dark eyes sparkled even in the dimness. "I don't think you have any malice in you."

"I—you don't know what I'm capable of."

"Stop." Turner's hands closed tightly around Lawrence's much larger ones. "Stop," he repeated. He shifted on his knees in a way that couldn't help but cause his thigh to brush against Lawrence's cockstand.

Ripples of sensation coursed through Lawrence's body, causing want as sharp and needful as thirst. His hips wanted to buck upwards, and he had to exert all his will to keep them decently against the floor.

But then Turner shifted, and they brushed together again. This time Lawrence couldn't help but let his hips move, seeking relief that he would never—could never—achieve.

He waited for the inevitable moment when Turner would recoil in disgust and alarm. But that moment never came. Instead they remained half-tangled together in the silence and darkness.

"You should go." Lawrence groaned. "Or I should."

Another shift of their bodies, another fleeting ripple of pleasure. "What if I don't want to?" Turner's voice was arch but with a hint of huskiness.

The only response Lawrence could make was a guttural grunt.

"Make me."

"Pardon?" Lawrence managed to say.

"If you want to leave, you'll have to make me let you go."

Lawrence wrested his hands free of Turner's grip and rolled the other man onto his back. Turner lay on the floor, Lawrence crouching over him.

Only then did Lawrence realize that Turner hadn't put up a fight at all. He was letting Lawrence manhandle him. Lawrence refused to let himself understand the meaning of this.

Turner licked his lips. Lawrence forced himself to stay perfectly still. But when Turner twisted one of his hands out of Lawrence's grip, he didn't try to stop him. And when Turner brought that hand around Lawrence's neck and tugged him down, he didn't stop that either. He only closed his eyes, because he didn't think he was equal to watching whatever was about to happen. His other senses were already overwhelmed and overtaxed.

He felt Turner coming closer, felt the other man's breath on his face, heard the rustle of limbs being rearranged. Almost, almost he could taste—but he wouldn't let himself think of mouths and tasting and the slow pink flick of Turner's tongue when he had licked his lips.

Then a warm hand rested on his cheek. He heard a sigh, and then the hand was gone. "Up you go, Radnor."

Lawrence stood. Looking down, he saw Turner pass a hand over his mouth and heard him sigh again.

Lawrence hesitated at the door, resting one arm against the door frame. "You ought to get back to sleep." Turner did not respond.

Instead of heading next door to his own room, Lawrence went downstairs to the kitchen. It had been months, perhaps longer, since he had traveled these corridors. The kitchen was silent and dark. "Sally?" he called. To think of Sally Ferris still at Penkellis. Why would she have stayed here? Hadn't he offered to set her up somewhere else? Well, she had endured far worse than Lawrence, and this was the only home she had ever known, so perhaps she had simply chosen the devil she knew. Maybe that was why Lawrence was still here too. "Mrs. Ferris?" he amended, remembering the passage of years.

A figure in a dressing gown and cap appeared. "Good heavens, is that you, Master Laurie?" She looked startled and tired but not afraid. "My lord, I mean to say."

"I'm so sorry to trouble you," Lawrence said, attempting some semblance of courtesy despite the late hour. "But could you see to it that the blue bedchamber is aired and cleaned, and a fire lit there for Mr. Turner?"

"Now, my lord?" She looked so much older than the last time he had seen her. That was how time worked, he reminded himself. She was likely thinking the same about him.

"No, no. Tomorrow. And thank you."

When he returned to his tower, he paused outside the dressing room door. Barnabus was fast asleep, but he heard rustling inside the room. Lawrence didn't dare go next door to his own room. Instead he crossed to his study and lit a lamp.

Georgie rubbed his eyes and sat up. Only the faintest light was streaming through the window, but strange sounds were coming from the corridor outside the dressing room door. In any decent house, early morning rustling would be no cause for alarm, nothing more than servants going about the mundane business of lighting fires or carrying up trays of tea. In this house, it was more likely to be wild animals prowling for food.

He dressed in haste and opened the door, intensely conscious of his stubbly jaw and creased cravat, but if ever there was a place to let personal standards fall by the wayside, it was Penkellis. Down the length of the corridor ran a rope of twisted wires. At one end, Radnor knelt by one of the trestles of his communication device.

"Over there, Turner," the earl said, as if they were already in the middle of a conversation. "Take hold of the wires and keep them steady while I fasten the ends to this trestle." His voice was rough, and he avoided looking at Georgie.

Georgie had already decided that he would proceed as usual, as if he hadn't come within a hair's breadth of kissing the man. As if he hadn't lain awake for hours thinking of the way Radnor's hard-muscled body had pressed him into the cold floor. Flushing, Georgie put that thought aside for the moment, something to be taken out and enjoyed later.

"I trust that I'm not to be shocked to death?" Georgie asked, but he held the wires without waiting for Radnor's response. The earl might be eccentric, but nothing Georgie had seen suggested recklessness.

They proceeded in this manner for most of the morning, Radnor ensuring that each wire was properly connected to the trestles, and Georgie stealing furtive glances at the earl. Georgie watched how Radnor absently rubbed his beard when he was thinking, and how he pushed his hair off his face in such a way that pulled strands haphazardly out of his queue. With his hair at sixes and sevens and his beard covering the lower part of his face, only Radnor's eyes and nose were really visible. His nose was nothing special, perfectly unobjectionable as far as noses went. But his eyes were an eerie, almost luminescent blue. Georgie couldn't think of anything quite that shade, not even a gemstone or a pricey bit of Italian glasswork, but he knew that if he ever came across anything that precise hue, he wouldn't be able to stop himself from thinking of Radnor.

He didn't like the idea that he wouldn't be able to shake the memory of Radnor loose from his mind, even after he was miles away, years into a future that now seemed bleak and lonely. He had always appreciated being able to start fresh with each new job: a blank slate, his misdeeds wiped clean away. But this time he wouldn't be able to do that; he'd carry the memory of Radnor with him, along with his knowledge of whatever harm he did the man.

Only when they heard footsteps coming up the tower stairs did they pause in their work. Or, rather, Radnor paused, going utterly still, as if the footsteps might belong to a marauder instead of a servant bearing the usual ham and apples. But Radnor was usually holed up in his study at this hour, and Janet simply left the tray outside his closed door. Today, he would have to actually encounter the girl.

Georgie stood and went to the top of the stairs, intending to act as ambassador between the girl and her master. Passing Radnor, he whispered, "Her name is Janet," but he wasn't sure if the earl heard, or if he even knew what he was supposed to do with that information.

"A fine morning, Janet." Georgie reached for the tray. "Let me take that," he offered. "It's wires and whatnots all over the place, and I don't want you to trip."

She cast a wary glance at the wire cutters and bits of the broken glass tube they had dropped earlier. It likely looked very ominous to an outsider. Georgie felt a totally unexpected rush of pride that he was not an outsider—he and Radnor were two of a handful of people who knew that this device was even a possibility.

"Mrs. Ferris told me to ask you down for tea," Janet said.

"No," Radnor barked, appearing from around the corner. Both Georgie and Janet stared at him. "He'll take his tea with me. Send up whatever is needed. Biscuits or..." He gestured vaguely. "Muffins," he said decisively, before turning to go back to his work. Then he paused, halting his step. "Thank you, Janet," he said, without looking back.

"Well," Janet said on her way downstairs. "I've been here three years and that was the first time he's spoken to me, let alone thanked me."

"He's making an effort," Georgie said, realizing it was true. Radnor was trying to be a good employer. A good man. The realization was like a blow to the gut. Georgie could hardly suck in his next breath.

"I think he's fond of you," Janet said. "Tea. Whoever would have thought?"

Oh, hell. A good man, fond of Georgie. Georgie wanted to hide under the covers of his bed—some other bed, far away from Penkellis.

He didn't deserve this. Neither of them did. Radnor didn't deserve to be deceived. Georgie didn't deserve anything like fondness, not from a good man, not from anyone at all. Radnor's kindness felt unearned. Stolen.

Georgie left the tray in the study and rejoined Radnor in the corridor. The earl was bent over the place where the wires twisted together.

"It's nearly ready." Radnor spoke without looking up. "You send the first transmission, and I'll send something back in return." The point of today's work, Georgie understood, was not only the greater distance between the two trestles but also seeing whether whatever Radnor had done to the battery would prevent short circuits.

Georgie watched the earl disappear around the corner, his strong thighs straining the buckskin of his breeches, his overlong hair barely contained in a queue, and felt a strange sort of unease, as if he wanted to keep the man in sight. Which was nonsense, of course. Radnor wasn't anything to him, and he wasn't anything to Radnor, interesting midnight interludes notwithstanding.

Last night, Georgie had stopped himself just in the nick of time. Another instant and he would have pressed his body fully against Radnor's, letting the other man feel the force of his desire. Radnor wanted him, that much had been abundantly clear. Equally clear was that he had no intention of acting on his desire. And Georgie wasn't in the habit of coaxing potential lovers into being free with their favors, not when the world was filled with people who weren't afraid or ashamed of what they wanted.

"Now, Turner!" Radnor bellowed from around the corner.

Oh, bugger it all. Georgie had never been good at resisting temptation. He sat on the floor before the trestle and tapped out his message before he could think better of it.

During the next few silent minutes, he started to worry that he had badly miscalculated, that he had gone too far. But then the bubbles started to rise. He picked up his pencil to write down each letter.

Georgie's transmission had been short, modeled after the earl's own transmission the previous week: *Thatbeard*. If Georgie's waistcoat was fair game for telegraphic scorn, then so was Radnor's blasted beard.

He looked at the paper on which he had transcribed the earl's return message. *Whatofit*. What of it? His heart beat faster, not only because his message evidently hadn't annoyed the earl, but because the device was working. Here they were, having a conversation several dozen yards apart, by way of wires and tubes and bubbles. This wasn't something he had even contemplated two weeks ago, and now he was witnessing it. And it was Radnor, for all his eccentricity, who had done it.

As quickly as he could, he sent his next message. *Soft*.

He waited. Had he gone too far? Had the machine failed? A full minute passed, more than enough time for his message to have gone through.

He heard the sound of heavy footsteps approaching him. Radnor's massive boots came to a stop inches away from where Georgie sat. Just for the thrill of it, Georgie let his gaze travel ever so slowly, decadently, up Radnor's massive frame. The earl's ensemble was as deplorable as ever today, but there was something to be said for worn buckskins on a man built like Radnor. Looking up further still, he only allowed himself the briefest glance at the placket of Radnor's breeches. He had felt enough last night to know that what was behind that placket would not disappoint. And then there was his shirt, threadbare and overlaundered and barely concealing muscular chest and arms. Radnor's waistcoat had apparently gone on holiday with the man's coat. Georgie found he couldn't complain.

"We need a question mark." Radnor's voice was gruff.

"Pardon?" Georgie wasn't following. He was too busy thinking of what other articles of the earl's clothing he'd like to see vanish.

"Your transmission. I can't tell if it's a question or a statement. We need to add wires for punctuation."

Soft. He had meant it as a question: *Is your beard soft?* "It was a question. I don't have enough data to make a definitive statement." He looked Radnor directly in the eyes. "Unfortunately."

Radnor shook his head. "You can't go on like that. I...you don't know what you're doing. If you knew, you wouldn't say such things."

Georgie ignored this. "Really, Radnor, today you ought to be celebrating." He rose to his feet and took a step closer. *No harm in trying,* he reasoned. "Your machine has succeeded. You've done what no other man in England has even attempted."

Radnor briefly squeezed his eyes shut, a helpless little gesture that Georgie was amazed to discover he found endearing. "You don't understand."

"I understand perfectly well. You're brilliant. You're talented." Georgie let those words drop out of his mouth in much the same register as he'd say *you're so big and hard* in another context. And why not, when Georgie's desire was being wound up by Radnor's mind as much as it was by any other part of his anatomy. Tentatively, as if reaching out to pet a strange dog, Georgie lifted his hand and lightly touched the earl's beard.

"Perfectly soft," Georgie murmured.

Radnor grabbed Georgie's wrist and held it away from him. "Stop," he growled. "You cannot know what you're doing to me."

Could the man really not see how Georgie felt? He was being as overt as he possibly could without actually jumping on him. "Why don't you tell me?" Georgie purred, trying to make it obvious for him.

"I..." Radnor swallowed. "I have perverse tastes." He winced, as if it physically hurt to speak those words aloud. "Deviant inclinations." He must have mistaken Georgie's silence for confusion, because he went on. "Men. Criminal."

"I understand," Georgie said quickly, to spare Radnor from the pain of further elaboration, and also because he didn't want to hear his own desires painted in such a shameful light.

"I choose not to act on my urges. Anymore. But, still, you wouldn't touch me if you knew what I felt when you did. You would keep your distance, as would be right." He closed his eyes and took a deep, shaky breath. "You have nothing to fear. You're in my house and under my protection, and I won't do anything to lead you astray."

Georgie stood perfectly still. Whatever he had thought Radnor might say, it wasn't this. Protection? Georgie hadn't been protected by anybody since he was a child. If anyone in this musty corridor needed looking after, it was Radnor himself, especially since, in addition to his odd habits, he was apparently awash in shame and humiliation.

Pity, like a hard lump, sat in Georgie's belly. He suddenly felt a wave of gratitude that, whatever hardships he had faced, he had managed to figure out that people simply liked what they liked, and that embarrassment didn't need to figure into it.

All the same, Georgie was touched by the man's care. "Don't worry about me," he said gently. Georgie cleared his throat. "You were married," he ventured. Of course he knew that some men who enjoyed the company of men also sought pleasure with women. Georgie himself found that his desires were pretty evenly split between men and women. But there was something about the way Radnor had spoken of his desires that made Georgie think that he believed *all* his desires to be forbidden.

Radnor laughed, bitter and short. "Briefly. I'm no fit husband. Isabella ran off with some blackguard and died in Italy. I can hardly blame her. She couldn't very well spend the rest of her life in a place like this. With a person like me."

Georgie knew from Jack that Radnor had gotten married before he was of age and that a child had been born. Presumably the child had died in Italy with the mother.

"Never?" Georgie asked.

"Pardon?" Radnor said, his voice hoarse.

"You never act on your…impulses?"

"Not since I was a young man."

"You're not yet thirty. That's no way to live, Radnor." Georgie could hardly stand the idea of Radnor alone, ashamed, turning away from companionship and pleasure. Life was too short, too cold, too bloody hard as it was, without making it worse.

Georgie would make it easy for the earl. It was a small thing he could do. It would not be a hardship at all. He felt his mouth curve into a smile and watched Radnor's eyes go wide in answer. Not a hardship in the slightest.

CHAPTER EIGHT

Lawrence leaned on his shovel and wiped the sweat from his brow. Halliday had come by earlier to tell him he ought to hire laborers to do this sort of job. "Spread the wealth," the vicar had pleaded. "Throw some money around and endear yourself to your tenants."

Lawrence hadn't any answer to that kind of nonsense. He could offer any sum and still nobody would come to work at Penkellis ever again. And thank God for it. Less noise, fewer people, and Lawrence could cling to the last bits of his sanity for a while longer. If he had known that blowing up the conservatory would bring him such peace and quiet, he would have done it a decade ago.

This trench ought to have taken two full days to dig by himself. But after this morning's damnable conversation with Turner, he had needed fresh air and physical exertion, and now he had a ditch running nearly the length of the castle. With any luck, he'd have the wires safely encased in an insulated pipe and buried in the trench by tomorrow evening, and then he could test the device under those new conditions.

With a grunt, he buried the shovel in the earth and lifted out another mound of soil, tossing it onto a hill with the rest of the dislodged dirt and weeds. His muscles ached but his head was clear. Tonight he would fall into bed and sleep easily. Last night he hadn't even tried, not after grappling on the floor with Turner.

That thought sent unwanted sparks of desire through his body, like so much electricity coursing through copper wires, only more dangerous. He looked over his shoulder to check the progress of the sun, to see how much daylight he had left, how much time he had to burn off this restless energy.

But there, leaning against a tree, was a slim, dark figure. Turner. And the way he was standing—legs crossed easily at the ankles, arms folded across his chest—suggested that he had been there awhile.

When he saw that Lawrence had noticed him, Turner pushed off the tree and came closer. "Digging graves for your enemies, my lord?"

Turner only bothered with *my lord* or even *Lord Radnor* when he was being facetious. "What do you want?" Lawrence asked, deliberately rude.

"My bedchamber," Turner said, and for a long moment Lawrence's thoughts couldn't get past the tantalizing intersection of Turner and bedchamber. "It's very clean. Thank you."

Lawrence turned back to his work, hefting another mound of earth. "Thank the girl," he said, panting. "She did the work."

"At your request, I don't doubt."

"Can't have you sleeping in my dressing room." Lawrence would never have any peace of mind knowing that a single door was all that stood between him and a half-naked Turner. He lifted another shovelful.

Turner didn't say anything, but Lawrence felt his gaze. Usually Lawrence preferred silence—so much less potential to get things wrong, so much bloody *quieter*—but there was something about this that wasn't right.

"Why aren't you talking?" Lawrence demanded.

"I'm quite enjoying watching, to be perfectly frank."

Lawrence went still, shovel poised midair. "I told you not to talk like that."

"No, you told me that if I talked like that I'd cause you to have unnatural desires, or however stupidly you phrased it. And I don't much care about that, so I'll talk how I please, thank you."

Lawrence felt his cheeks heat. He didn't respond; words didn't exist that could give voice to the confusion of desire that swirled through his mind. He buried his shovel deep in the earth, savoring the clarity of his muscles' ache.

"Is that why you avoid people?" Turner asked.

"What?" Lawrence panted.

"Do you think your…tendencies disqualify you for human company? That simply by being around another man you'll contaminate him? Because if it is, I'll let you know that isn't how it works at all." A beat of silence, during which all that existed were Turner's laughing, dark eyes. "More's the pity."

Lawrence laughed mirthlessly. "Of all the qualities that disqualify me for companionship, that's not even in the top three."

"Tell me about the top three, then."

"Madness." He hefted a shovel heaped with dirt. "Madness." Another shovelful. "And more madness."

"I've been here for two weeks, and I'm still waiting to see evidence of this madness." Turner's voice was clipped, ironic. If he had displayed the faintest trace of sympathy, Lawrence would have found it easier to dismiss his words as so much charity or flattery. "I have to say, I'm fairly disappointed. I had hoped for some good old-fashioned howling at the moon, and all you do is build ingenious inventions and eat too much ham."

Another shovel, and another. Lawrence felt rooted in the pain that traveled down his back, through his arms. "My father was stark raving mad. My brother was not only mad but murderous, to boot."

"But *how* were they mad? Madness isn't like a fever, where one can figure out what's wrong by putting a hand to a patient's forehead. I've asked Janet and Mrs. Ferris, but they only look at one another darkly and refuse to talk."

Lawrence turned around, startled. "Don't plague Mrs. Ferris with talk about my family." He'd tell Turner whatever he wanted to know as long as he didn't pester Sally. "My father used to spend weeks at a time in bed, generally quite drunk. He was a miserable sod. One day, I came home from riding and found him dead in the stables. We told everyone he died while cleaning his gun, but he left a note. I burnt it." The old man had been buried decently in the family crypt, as if he had ever acted with the slightest concern for the fate of his soul.

"Do you ever spend weeks in bed?"

"No—"

"Do you ever wish to kill yourself?"

No, he didn't. He had found his father's body and wouldn't wish that experience on anyone. But how to explain that it didn't matter whether he wanted to or not, because one day the madness would take him? "I hope I never kill myself."

Turner was silent a moment. "And your brother?"

Lawrence lifted and tossed another heaping shovelful of dirt. "You mean when he wasn't imposing himself on the servants or beating his mistress?" he asked, his voice ragged with exertion. "He died a few years ago in a riding accident in the shires. I suspect he was drunk."

"And then you inherited and promptly closed the house up."

"Yes." More dirt. More pain. If Turner kept up his inquisition, Lawrence would have the trench complete before nightfall.

"I don't mean to make light of your concerns, Radnor. And to have lost your father in such a way—I really can't imagine what that was like for you." Turner fell silent for long enough that Lawrence began to hope this ill-advised conversation had come to an end. "Your mind isn't typical—"

Lawrence snorted.

"No, I'm serious." Turner's voice was earnest, pleading, devoid of the detached cynicism that was usually there. "Listen. Your mind isn't like other men's minds, and I know it can't be easy for you. But you don't seem anything like your father. As for your brother, it seems to me that nobody would have thought him deranged if he were a commoner. He was a villain, not a madman."

Lawrence felt certain that most people would think his own tinkering with explosives and electricity stranger than mistreating a mistress, but he wasn't going to argue the point.

Turner was close behind him now. Lawrence buried his shovel in the ground and stepped on it to keep it in place. He couldn't work with Turner this near. Too dangerous.

"I've been thinking about what you told me. Do you completely deny your urges, or do you think about them in private?"

Lawrence swung around, whacking his arm against the upright handle of the shovel. "What the bloody—"

"Oh, you've cut yourself."

Turner was right. There was just enough light to see the line of blood trickling from where Lawrence had scraped his forearm on the metal handle. Before he could protest, Turner had taken out his handkerchief and wrapped it around the cut, holding the makeshift bandage into place with both his hands in a way that made Lawrence feel like an oversized brute.

"What I was going to ask," Turner murmured, "was whether you—"

"I know what you were asking. What the hell kind of question is that?"

"Well, I was curious. I've never been partial to shame and self-denial, and I was wondering how far you take it. I mean, sometimes you just have to scratch an itch."

Lawrence hoped it was dark enough to conceal his flaming cheeks. "Are you seriously asking about that? Good God, man. I thought I was the one without any manners." And then he felt one of Turner's hands come to settle against his cheek.

"It really *is* soft," Turner murmured.

Surely Lawrence ought to protest, but he couldn't find the words, and he didn't want to find them anyway. Instead he settled for somehow not rubbing his cheek against Turner's palm like a cat.

"Listen," Turner said, his voice silky. "I'll spell this out for you. I want you badly. I won't try to persuade you to do anything you might regret, but I also won't hide how much I want you."

Turner didn't step any closer. He left a sliver of space between their bodies, and Lawrence knew that was for him. Turner gave him that space to do with as he pleased. Lawrence could leave that space empty, for the cool night breeze to blow between them, or he could close the gap. Neither choice would be wrong.

Lawrence didn't know whether it was nerves or desire that was causing his pulse to thunder so, but surely Turner could feel it. Good God, the man could probably even hear it, it pounded so loudly in Lawrence's ears. But Turner stood still, his only movement the slow and rhythmic stroking of his thumb along Lawrence's cheekbone.

It could have been a minute that passed, or maybe it was an hour. The sun was quite set by the time Lawrence got used to the idea of Turner's touching him, when the proximity of the other man's body seemed…not quite comfortable, but not dangerous either. Christ, but he wanted this. And however much he feared that this desire was madness, Turner didn't seem in the least deranged, and that seemed enough to hold on to.

Perhaps some things were simply easier in the dark, because when he felt Turner's stance shift, tilting ever so slightly towards Lawrence's own body, he knew it for an invitation, and didn't move away. He felt the other man's breath on his face, soft against his beard. Turner's hand slid to the back of Lawrence's head.

And then it was only a matter of Lawrence leaning mere inches forward, skimming his mouth against lips that were already there, waiting for him.

Georgie felt Radnor's soft exhale. Not capitulation but agreement. He pushed up onto his toes and wrapped both arms around the earl's neck.

Their lips met, a whisper of flesh against flesh. It was more the suggestion of a kiss than an actual kiss, but Radnor gasped anyway. Georgie forced himself not to ask for too much, not to plunge his tongue into the earl's hot mouth, not to grind their bodies together. This had to be at Radnor's own pace or not at all.

Slowly, tentatively, Georgie brushed his lips across the other man's mouth. The scratch of the earl's beard sent a shiver of desire coursing down Georgie's spine. Radnor must have felt it too, because Georgie felt the man's huge hands clamp down hard on his hips. Taking that as assent, Georgie teased his tongue along the seam of the earl's lips.

He found himself being steered backwards, then pressed unremittingly against the tree trunk. One of Radnor's arms was braced on the tree near Georgie's head; the other hand grasped Georgie's hip.

Georgie groaned in pleasure, and Radnor abruptly stilled.

"Damn it." The earl's voice was rough but gentle and Georgie felt his heart clench. "Did I hurt you?"

"No," Georgie managed. "Don't stop." Please, he wanted to say, please press me into every tree and wall in the kingdom. He ran his fingers through Radnor's long hair, tugging the other man's head down to meet his own. He kissed the corner of the earl's mouth, sucked on his soft lower lip.

Radnor growled and one of his hands slipped lower, cupping Georgie's arse and drawing him close. Georgie gasped at the pressure of the other man's jutting cock. They were outside, in the dark, utterly alone. They were two men with nothing to worry about but a pair of rampant cockstands.

Georgie allowed his tongue to slip into the other man's mouth, probing, teasing. Radnor tasted of cider and salt, smelled of sweat and dirt. Georgie moved his hips in the hint of a rhythm, nothing fast or hard enough to bring relief, only enough to let Radnor know what he was thinking. To let him know it was an option.

"Fuck," Radnor growled into Georgie's mouth.

Radnor crowded Georgie's body, one of his massive legs coming in between Georgie's. Georgie dipped his head to kiss the other man's neck. He ran his tongue along the soft skin where neck met beard, and Radnor must have liked it because Georgie felt an alarmingly hard cock being pressed into his hip. He managed to get a hand between them and grasp Radnor through his buckskins.

"Do you want me to—"

Radnor grabbed both of Georgie's hands and pinned them to the tree on either side of his head. That would be a no, then. But this, being held in place and—oh *yes*—kissed ruthlessly, relentlessly. This would do very well. Now it was Radnor's tongue slipping into Georgie's mouth; it was Georgie gasping and writhing in pleasure.

The bark of the tree bit deliciously into the backs of Georgie's hands. Radnor's grip was bruisingly tight on his wrists.

Being held against the tree by such a large man had a lot in common with being crushed by a ton of bricks. An almost painful surge of want hit Georgie when he realized Radnor was finally owning his desire. He was letting himself go, just a bit, but Georgie wanted to be there when Radnor let himself completely off the leash. He wanted to get to his knees and take that thick cock into his mouth; he wanted Radnor to bend him over the nearest desk or table or fence and—

"Wait." Georgie wrested his mouth away. There was a sound that didn't belong out here in the still, bleak Penkellis garden. For the briefest moment he thought he heard wheels crunching along the badly graveled path.

Radnor stopped immediately. He was breathing heavily, his chest rising and falling against Georgie's. "What do you want?" It might have sounded rude if Radnor's mouth weren't against Georgie's ear, if his voice weren't low and needy, raspy with desire.

"Listen," Georgie whispered. "Is that a cart?"

Radnor let go of Georgie's hands, then stepped away. The night air felt bitterly cold as it came between them. "I don't hear anything."

Georgie didn't hear it anymore either. But he had heard something similar the other night when he was prowling about the house. After a lifetime of skulking about at night, Georgie knew better than to doubt his hearing. He also knew better than to ignore his instinct about something being amiss, and there was something decidedly amiss at Penkellis.

CHAPTER NINE

It rained all bloody night and straight through into the morning. When Lawrence woke he threw back the curtains and saw his trench filled with water. It would drain, but not today. After a good night's sleep, he was doubting the wisdom of burying the wires after all. Perhaps there was a better way to have wires span a great distance. Or perhaps this project was doomed. Standish certainly seemed to have his doubts about its practicability. But Lawrence wanted to hold out hope. He didn't know if it was because having Turner here had given him an inkling of what life would be like with a little less loneliness, but he found that he needed this device to work. He was prepared to spend the day puzzling over that matter, when he pushed open the door to his study and discovered Turner at his desk.

Somehow he had thought the man wouldn't show up after last night, that he would have vanished, like a dream. Like a madman's delusion.

But instead, he was sorting a stack of papers.

"I found this under the sofa, Radnor," Turner said, waving a sheaf of papers, "along with a ham hock. Although Barnabus was delighted to discover the bone, I was less pleased to discover the correspondence. Some of it dates from months ago."

There was nothing in the secretary's voice to suggest that twelve hours earlier they had been in one another's arms. Turner sounded as casually caustic as ever. Lawrence was unspeakably grateful. He knew—more or less—how to treat a secretary. He did not know how to act with a lover, or whatever it was Turner was now. If indeed he was anything.

"Burn it all," Lawrence suggested. "If any of it matters, they'll write again."

"Oh, a fine secretary I'd be." Turner held up a thick sheet of creamy paper. "There's also a letter from an Admiral Haversham, thanking you for some unnamed service to your nation and asking about your progress with the telegraphic machine. Quite official looking too. All manner of seals and whatnot."

Lawrence grunted. "That's for the powder." Browne's Improved Black Powder, useful in mines but even better at destroying ships.

"I see." Turner tilted his head to the side. "Do you have any other accomplishments or accolades you'd like to share?"

Lawrence thought about it. "No."

Turner was giving him a strange little smile, the sort of smile Lawrence's late wife used to give the men who flocked around her. Was Turner flirting with him? Well, if so, he was quite on his own. Lawrence shouldn't be thinking of flirting at all. Not when last night had put him into such a muddle, not when he had felt—

Lawrence couldn't complete the thought without a rush of blood to his prick. Right here in his study, in broad daylight too.

But perhaps he hadn't behaved too disgracefully last night, because Turner wasn't treating him like a fool or a degenerate. Instead he was behaving quite unremarkably. Except for that smile. Did he even realize he was smiling like that?

"What's that letter?" he asked brusquely, pointing at the topmost paper in the pile Turner was sorting. He let his hand drop to the table next to Turner's, so close their little fingers were a hair's breadth apart. He didn't move his hand away, and neither did Turner.

"Oh, that's our friend Standish again. He never runs out of questions, does he?"

Lawrence snorted. "He needs things explained in minute detail, often with sketches." This was a part of their process; once Standish could successfully replicate Lawrence's invention, Standish handled the business end of things. It was Standish who arranged for the safety fuse and the black powder to be patented and widely produced, and presumably he would do the same with the telegraph.

Turner tapped his pen on the desk. "I'm surprised you indulge him. I understand what he stands to gain from this endless correspondence, but what's in it for you, Radnor?"

Radnor hadn't thought of it in those terms. "It isn't everyone who takes an interest in explosives and electricity. When he asks one of his questions, I sometimes have to work through the answers in my own mind. And he's better at implementing ideas than I am. I cobble something together, and he refines it." That was more or less how they had stumbled onto the safety fuse. Lawrence, as an aside in one of their letters, had mentioned that he was working on a fuse that would burn more slowly and more predictably, to make it safer for miners. Standish had suggested coating the fuse with various substances, and several explosions and dozens of letters later, they had a safety fuse.

Their letters were prone to that sort of digression. Standish would mention some problem he had encountered in installing new water closets, and Lawrence would sketch out a solution. After a few years of correspondence, Lawrence felt they had established a sort of friendship.

"And the money?" Turner inquired.

"Standish deals with it." Business was not something that amused Lawrence, but evidently Standish enjoyed it, so Lawrence let him have his way. Lawrence already had enough money—Percy died before he managed to run through the entire Radnor fortune—so he didn't pay much attention.

A long moment passed, during which Turner regarded Lawrence curiously. "I see," he finally said. "I don't suppose you've met Standish?"

Lawrence turned his head to fully face his secretary and raised his eyebrow. He didn't meet anybody, and Turner bloody well knew it.

"I didn't think so," Turner said.

Lawrence looked to where their fingers nearly met and saw that the back of Turner's hand was scratched, red scrapes livid against the secretary's pale skin. Lawrence took the man's hand in his own, fingering the angry marks. He felt his heart drop. "Is that from—"

"The tree."

"I'm so sorry." He ought to have guessed that he was too big, too rough. He had no business even touching a man like Turner, smooth and polished and fine. "If I had known I was hurting you…"

"I liked it." Turner's voice was low. "I liked everything about it, actually."

Lawrence felt his cheeks heat, and when he looked at Turner he saw an answering flush on the other man's face. "Sometimes I fear that it's part of my madness," he murmured.

"Desiring men?" Turner's voice was steady, his hand still in Lawrence's own.

Lawrence nodded, avoiding the other man's gaze.

"I'm not mad. Nor are any of the men who've been my lovers. You aren't mad either, but even if you were, this"— he squeezed Lawrence's hand—"would have nothing to do with it."

Last night, under the tree, he hadn't felt mad in the slightest. Kissing Turner had felt like the suddenly obvious answer to an equation he had been trying to solve for years. Hell, every minute he had spent *not* kissing Turner seemed evidence of an unsound mind.

Georgie knew a swindle when he saw one. He would have bet his life that Radnor was being duped by this Standish bastard. The man was using all the tricks Georgie himself would have used: asking too many questions, paying too many compliments, insinuating his way into a mark's life.

He was outraged by the idea of Radnor being cheated, even though he had hoped to do precisely that. Outraged, as if there were a swindlers' code of professional ethics, for God's sake. But he was absolutely certain that any proper confidence man ought to be ashamed of stealing from such a complete innocent. Radnor had spent too long in isolation to develop the sixth sense that alerted most people to fraudulence and connivance.

Hell, if he had any sense he wouldn't trust Georgie. Georgie hardly trusted himself at this point. He didn't know whether he was more annoyed with himself for wanting to deceive Radnor or for taking so long to do it. And it wasn't simply that a couple of kisses had clouded Georgie's judgment. No, his judgment had been dangerously fogged to begin with and had been for months. Time with Radnor had obfuscated it completely.

He took out a clean sheet of paper and wrote a letter to Standish, or whoever he was, purporting to keep the fellow apprised of Radnor's latest experiments and making sure to get all the details catastrophically wrong. With any luck, the bastard would shock himself to death if he tried to recreate the device. At the very least the man's plans would be useless, and it would buy Georgie a little bit of time.

Time for what, though? Georgie hardly knew. Time to put the device through another series of tests? Time to get to the bottom of village gossip about stolen cauls, time to figure out why Penkellis hadn't been looted? Time to kiss Radnor some more, time to feel the press of those strong hands? God, but he wanted that time. He wanted to ignore the rest of the world, everything that had ever mattered to him, and instead crawl into bed with Radnor, just to find out what it would be like.

But he knew what it would be like, didn't he? Radnor, strong and demanding, on him and in him and making him crave things that were best left alone.

No. Georgie steeled himself, forced himself to think with the part of his brain that had seen him through cold nights and hungry winters. He doubted whether Radnor's device alone would be sufficient to purchase Mattie Brewster's clemency. But now, if he were clever, he might be able to trade information about Standish as well. Brewster hated competition. He liked to have his hands in all the right pies. That was why he had acquired Georgie's services, after all.

"Radnor!"

"In here." Radnor's voice was faint, coming from behind the heavy oak door that separated the study from the earl's bedchamber.

Georgie moved to stand by the door. "What are you going to do with the telegraph when it's complete?"

There was silence from behind the door.

"Radnor?"

He heard the ominous sound of water dripping. The last thing this shambles of a house needed was a leak in the roof. He pushed the door open, which he knew to be rude, but manners as he knew them didn't seem to exist at Penkellis.

There was no evidence of a leak in Radnor's bedchamber. Instead Radnor stood by the side of a great old-fashioned tin bathing tub, his hips wrapped in a sodden piece of linen toweling that left nothing to the imagination.

Georgie made a sound that was mortifyingly like a squeak.

"Oh God," Radnor said.

Georgie didn't even bother trying to feign composure. The earl was every bit as gorgeously massive unclothed as he was fully dressed, of course, only the sheer fact of his size was harder to ignore without the distraction of clothes. Georgie didn't know where to look first. There seemed too many options, too much acreage of exposed skin. His eyes traveled up, over narrow hips and ridged belly, over a thickly haired chest and broad shoulders, until he reached the earl's face.

"Your lips are blue." Georgie could almost feel the chill on his own lips. "Did you just take a cold bath?" There was a heap of clean-looking shirts on the clothes press, and he handed one to the earl.

"The water had gone cold by the time I had finished carrying it up here." He started to put the shirt over his head.

"No, stop that. You're still wet. Dry off first, or you'll catch a chill." He started dabbing at Radnor's chest with a dry length of toweling. Radnor's nipples were pink and hard, and Georgie wanted to take each of them in his mouth and find out whether the earl preferred having them bit or sucked.

Radnor took the cloth out of Georgie's hand and scrubbed roughly at his hair.

"Next time, have a servant carry up hot water," Georgie admonished.

"The girl was busy."

Georgie raised an eyebrow and gave Radnor a pointed glance. "This is why most people have more than one housemaid."

"Maids are loud. Forever clattering around, opening and closing doors, and yammering their heads off. I'd be in Bedlam by Christmas."

"You don't mind me yammering my head off." There was a bead of water trickling down the center of Radnor's hard chest, and before Georgie knew what he was doing, he had brushed it away, tracing its path with his finger.

Radnor froze, then took a half a step backwards. "Yes, well, if I had a household of servants like you, I'd have other troubles. Wouldn't get anything done at all."

Then Radnor flashed him one of his rare smiles, and Georgie felt simultaneously like he had been given a precious gift and like he had been hit in the head with a shovel.

And the earl thought *he* was likely to go to Bedlam. Georgie was halfway there already. As soon as he got out of the bedchamber, he stood with his back to the closed door, trying to catch his breath and collect his thoughts. What the devil had gone wrong in his brain? He had wanted to know whether the patents to Radnor's inventions were in his own name or Standish's or someone else entirely—that way he would know exactly how big a swindle he was uncovering, and how much value the information would hold for Brewster. Instead he had been distracted by an eyeful of hard muscle and then was put even more absurdly off course by the prospect of the earl's getting a chill.

A chill, for God's sake. He wanted to smack himself in the face. A man as rugged as Radnor wasn't going to waste away by taking too cold a bath. And even if he did, what of it? All the lords and ladies in Britain could drop dead and it shouldn't make the least difference to Georgie. It was an embarrassing error, a raw novice's mistake, to care about a mark. It was one thing—bad enough, really—to let one of them take him to bed. It was quite another to start worrying about them as if they mattered.

He didn't have the luxury of fine feelings, nor the time for compassion. He had lived his whole life on the knife's edge of survival, and now he had a chance to earn his way back to the only place on earth where he thought he might belong. He was a swindler, born and bred; a creature of back alleys, smoke and mirrors, whispers and lies. He didn't know any other way to be.

Chapter Ten

Turner was being devilish slippery. One minute he was holding Lawrence's hand, and the next he was sliding away whenever Lawrence got too near. Which just went to show that Lawrence would never understand how other people worked. Machines had the decided advantage in predictability, even this bloody machine, which had just suffered its third short circuit of the afternoon.

"Bugger and fuck," he muttered. "Shite."

No reaction from Turner's desk, not even a flash of the impertinence Lawrence had come to look forward to.

There was a coughing sound from the doorway, and Lawrence turned to see Halliday.

"What do you want?"

"A friendly visit, Radnor." The vicar's voice had that irritatingly soothing register that people used on invalids and children. And fully grown madmen, apparently.

"Not interested." Lawrence went back to his work.

"Perhaps I'll see the vicar out?" That was Turner, taking any opportunity to put distance between himself and

Lawrence. "I have to speak with Mrs. Ferris about tea, anyway. She's sending up enough scones and muffins for a score of people, and while they're delicious, I thought that she could perhaps send a basket over to the Kemps instead."

Lawrence thought he heard Halliday repeat "scones and muffins" in tones of incredulity, as if it were so very remarkable that such items were present at Penkellis. Just because Lawrence preferred the same foods every day—it was one less thing to think about, and a very sensible practice he was surprised more men didn't adopt—didn't mean he was a stranger to the notion of variety. Even if he *had* forgotten about it during the first weeks of Turner's employment.

But as he got used to having Turner around, the habits of ordinary life gradually returned to him. At first he felt like he was remembering details from a book about the customs of a foreign land, vague and unfamiliar. People ate at regular hours, so he had Mrs. Ferris send proper meals for the secretary. People's living quarters were generally not festooned with cobwebs, so he had Janet tidy up the blue bedchamber. People—at least wealthy people—had baths drawn in their bedchambers, instead of washing at the pump, so Lawrence hauled bathwater up three flights of stairs.

Turner had gotten slippery immediately afterwards. Lawrence had now endured two days of painstaking efficiency and indifferent cordiality. Gone was the man who had asked appalling personal questions. Now the secretary moved silently about the room, writing things down, putting things away. Every piece of furniture had been turned upside down and inside out, its contents cataloged and labeled in Turner's neat copperplate hand. He was invisible and efficient, and exactly the sort of secretary Lawrence might have wished for a month ago.

Lawrence was well and truly sick of it.

"Excellent idea. Capital," Halliday agreed, and he and Turner left together. Barnabus trotted alongside, because he was a wretched turncoat and eight years of loyalty meant nothing compared to the fact that Turner kept bits of muffin in his coat pocket.

To hell with all of them. Lawrence liked being alone. This notion he had gotten into his head about enjoying Turner's company was nothing more than a delusion. He was mad, and mad people had strange turns of mind. That was all. It would be much more remarkable if he did *not* have episodes of delusion, all things considered.

Then why did he feel like he was lying to himself? Surely not. Did Turner's dispassionate, straightforward argument that Lawrence was not in fact mad really amount to anything but the pretty speech of a man much accustomed to giving pretty speeches?

Now that was a thought. Lawrence pushed away the cursed battery and leaned back in his chair. What made him so certain that Turner *was* skilled in flattery? Perhaps because it had been Isabella's stock in trade, Lawrence had learned to detect a honeyed tongue.

Perhaps because Turner, like Isabella, only wanted to get close to Lawrence for a reason.

Now, as to what that reason might be, Lawrence could only speculate. Isabella had found herself pregnant and in need of a husband. Lawrence hadn't seen any reason not to oblige her. Oh, he had been very, very young and shockingly naive. But at least he had gotten Simon out of the bargain, for however brief a time.

Too late, he remembered to tuck that thought away with the rest of his memories of Simon.

But why was Turner here? What did he need from Lawrence? It was time he gave Turner's motives serious consideration. Secretaries didn't have dubious upbringings and they didn't know how to wrestle men nearly twice their size. And even if they did, a secretary of Turner's competence didn't volunteer for a post miles from any civilization.

After Turner had made that comment about Penkellis being filled with items a person might find worth stealing, Radnor had half expected the secretary to disappear with an assortment of treasures. But he was still here, and so were all the things that might be stolen. At least, he assumed they were. It wasn't as if he took an inventory of the place. But he had to suppose that Mrs. Ferris would mention any significant theft.

Wouldn't she? It wasn't as if Lawrence had encouraged his servants to speak to him. Quite the contrary.

It had been a quarter of an hour since Turner left, more than enough time for the man to have finished his business in the kitchen. Lawrence could safely venture forth without worrying about running into him in the corridors and having to watch the man make an excuse to slide away.

Just to be safe, he took a winding route to the back of the house. His path took him through what had once been the portrait gallery. Strictly speaking, it still was the portrait gallery, even if the portraits were draped in cobwebs and covered in a film of dust and soot. His ancestors appeared to be regarding him from behind a mist.

How many of these Earls of Radnor had been mad? In pride of place was a portrait of Father and Percy, and it might have looked like the portrait of any other father and son, if you didn't know that Percy, at the time he sat for the portrait, was making a habit of raping the kitchen maid. Father was too drunk to notice or too proud to care. But they looked quite respectable in the painting, as did all the rest of the earls and countesses and assorted Browne family hangers-on who were captured in oil and canvas.

Radnor caught his own murky reflection in a clouded window. He didn't even look respectable. He looked positively disreputable, like a well-fed medieval hermit, only worse. His beard would not have been out of place on a prison ship. He had put on a jacket so as to avoid embarrassing Sally—Mrs. Ferris, he reminded himself—but still managed to look like a castaway.

Good. Quite right for the outside appearance of a man to reflect his inner character. This way, anyone would know straightaway to keep their distance. That was safer for everybody. Turner had the right idea in staying away. They had been getting closer than any madman deserved, sharing kisses and confidences like a pair of courting lovers.

The other night when he had visited the kitchens, they had been cold and dark and quiet. Now, poised on the top step, he could hear women laughing and smell meat roasting. If one didn't know better, one might think this was an ordinary kitchen in an ordinary house. He descended a few more steps and picked up bits of conversation.

"He hasn't laid a hand on me or said a single improper word. And more's the pity."

"Janet!"

"Well, who can blame me? He's handsome as sin, and even if he weren't, I don't think I'd care."

Mrs. Ferris laughed, a warm trill of laughter that Lawrence hadn't heard since he was a child sneaking down these same stairs to steal jam and cakes. "No better than you ought to be."

"Bugger 'ought.' I'm too bored to be good. I've half a mind to crawl into his bed and see what happens."

"And what would his lordship think if he knew he was harboring such a jezebel under his roof?" But the cook's voice was indulgent.

"Pffft. His lordship would have to leave his precious tower in order to know about it."

When Lawrence cleared his throat, the women snapped their gazes to where he stood. "Mrs. Ferris," he said, interrupting a flurry of curtsies and *my lords*. "Have there been any attempts at theft at Penkellis?"

Mrs. Ferris's expression didn't falter, but Lawrence saw the maid flick a wary glance in the cook's direction. "No, my lord," she said.

"Where are my mother's jewels?"

"I took the liberty of having all the countess's jewels sent to the bank in Falmouth for safekeeping."

He ought to have thought of that himself, but he hadn't been in any state for practicality after Percy died and the estate passed to Lawrence. "Quite right." He nodded. "Thank you."

Mrs. Ferris tucked a strand of hair into her cap. "The Browne silver is locked away in the pantry, but I didn't bother with the lesser pieces."

"Why has nobody stolen the, ah, lesser pieces?" This year's harvest had been abysmal. It would be a hard winter. Why had nobody thought to nip into Penkellis and help themselves to some of what Mrs. Ferris considered mere lesser silver?

"I daresay they didn't want to cross you, my lord," Mrs. Ferris said, not meeting his gaze.

"Ha! They have no fond feelings for me, and well you know it."

Janet made a noise that could have been a giggle or a gasp.

"Out with it, Janet," he commanded. She stared at him in open-mouthed dismay. "We can stand here all day and look at one another. I have nothing better to do in my precious tower," he said, and watched with satisfaction as the maid flushed with embarrassment.

"They're all afraid you're going to hex them, m'lord." Her words came out in a high-pitched rush.

"They're rustic people," Mrs. Ferris interjected. "You know how they are."

"I know nothing of them at all." He hadn't ever thought to learn anything about them. He had thought it better if they forgot about him entirely. But Halliday had told him of salt sprinkled on windowsills, herbs gathered at midnight. "They think I am like my father and brother. That I will harm them."

"Certainly not," Mrs. Ferris protested. She knew all about dangerous lords. She knew altogether too much about lords who took advantage of their servants, and wasn't that what Lawrence had been contemplating doing to Turner? "You're nothing like either of them. They were evil, if you don't mind my saying so, my lord." She had to know damned well that he didn't mind, because she didn't pause for his objection. "And you ought never to have heard anything about village gossip." She glared at Janet.

He leveled his gaze at Mrs. Ferris. "How is Jamie?" That was Mrs. Ferris's son.

Lawrence's nephew.

"Quite well. He's a midshipman aboard the *Lancaster*, thanks to your lordship's—"

"Enough." He wouldn't have her thanking him for trying to make right what Percy had made wrong. But as he climbed the stairs, Mrs. Ferris's words echoed in his mind. *Nothing like either of them.* Turner had said much the same thing. And for the first time, Lawrence wondered if they might be right.

"**I**'m glad to speak to you alone, Mr. Turner." The vicar's voice was stuck on a note of apologetic solicitude. No wonder he didn't seem to be a particular favorite of Radnor's. "I hate to put you to the trouble, but I wanted to know how far you've gotten in your inquiries."

Georgie could have said that it was no trouble at all. He had been longing for an excuse to get away from the earl, and passing the time at the Fiddling Fox with Halliday was as good an escape as any. Georgie didn't trust himself not to leap on Radnor at the first opportunity. He didn't trust himself to do what needed to be done instead of worrying about Radnor.

He also didn't trust himself not to hurt Radnor along the way, but that was of no importance, he told himself. He had to keep his priorities straight.

Georgie took a measured sip of his ale. "Lord Radnor is a man of unusual habits," he said in a voice that made it clear the fault lay with anyone who took issue with the earl's habits. "He is certainly scatterbrained and inclined to keep odd hours, but no more so than other men of a similarly scientific bent." Georgie had no idea if this was true but it sounded plausible. Weren't geniuses infamously eccentric?

"Oh," said the vicar, dragging it out to more syllables than strictly necessary, each of them soaked in unwanted concern. "I've heard two people say they saw Lord Radnor stealing a sheep."

Georgie nearly spit out a mouthful of ale but managed to keep his expression neutral. "I fail to see how Radnor could possibly be going about stealing sheep when he never leaves the grounds of his estate. He hardly ever goes farther than the garden."

"And yet, David Prouse swears that he saw the earl lead away a sheep. I heard him tell his cousin."

Georgie knew perfectly well that people saw what they wanted to see. He had depended on that very suggestibility many times during his swindles. "And what does Radnor want with your Mr. Prouse's sheep? Surely if he has a fancy for sheep, he can afford his own."

"This sheep...oh dear." Halliday now seemed ready to expire from awkwardness. He was gripping his own glass of ale so fiercely that Georgie feared it might shatter. "Lord Radnor is supposed to have used the sheep for some kind of...ensorcellment." He downed half the glass in one go, which was rather coarser behavior than Georgie might have expected in a vicar. "I gather it was an unusual sheep," he added, with a shrug of helpless bemusement.

Georgie goggled. How the hell special could a sheep possibly be? Never in his life had he been so glad to have been raised in London by proper criminals rather than left to the care of rustics in a backwater like this. "Mrs. Kemp's caul," he said, rubbing his temples. "I daresay that was intended for another round of hexes or some such."

The vicar made a plaintive sound. "Precisely."

"Do you not have a Sunday school where people can be disillusioned of this nonsense?"

Halliday muttered something to do with money and time.

"In case any further members of your addlepated flock come to you with tales of the earl's dark arts, do let them know that I have turned his lordship's quarters inside out without finding anything even remotely suggestive of the occult." He let each word drop with acid crispness.

"Ah yes." The vicar shifted in his seat. "Quite."

"Was this spate of dark magicks"—Georgie rolled his eyes—"what motivated you to have the earl's mental competence looked into? I gather he's been in much the same condition for years, so what precipitated this sudden interest?"

"Well," the vicar stammered. "I received a letter."

"A letter," Georgie repeated, dread pooling in his stomach. "What kind of letter?"

"It would seem that an, ah, interested party—a connection of Radnor's heir—might seek to have the estate put into a trusteeship."

"To have Radnor declared incompetent and seize his property, you mean."

"I'm not certain, but that's my fear."

That would destroy Radnor. A loud, unfamiliar court-room would be hellish for him.

"This is quite beyond what I'm capable of investigating," Georgie all but spat. "If you were concerned for his lordship's well-being, you ought to have called in a doctor. You ought to have had Radnor engage a solicitor."

"He would never have consented to any of that," Halliday protested.

"True," Georgie conceded, but he was still furious. At the vicar, at this unknown relation of Radnor's heir, at Jack for having sent him here in the first place. At Radnor, for making him care.

"I daresay even a warlock's money is as good as anyone else's, so we'll try to solve this problem in the usual way. I need men to drain the gardens on the east side of the castle. His lord-ship needs a dry trench, and right now he has what looks more like a canal. I don't know what the going rate is, but I'll double it." He trusted that double wages would tempt even the most superstitious souls, especially in a year that had seen such a bad harvest. "If the tenants like him, that will go some distance in stopping gossip and perhaps silencing this relation of his."

The vicar nodded his assent, and Georgie took his leave as civilly as he could.

Outside, the sun had nearly set. They were in the first week of December, and the days were getting short. The cres-cent moon was hardly visible through the fog, and Georgie had to pick his way carefully to the lane.

So somebody was out to make Radnor look like a villain. That really was the only explanation Georgie could come up with that didn't involve widespread lunacy. Somebody had decided to take advantage of the local belief that the Earls of Radnor were a bad lot and mix it all up with a dose of superstition. But who, and why?

Mrs. Ferris knew something, and likely Janet too. He could wheedle the secret from Janet in the usual way— compliments, caresses, promises that would never be fulfilled—but he didn't have the heart. She was harmless. Hell, she was becoming a friend.

There went another one of his pigeonholes, toppled over into complete chaos.

The lane was still muddy from the other night's rainfall, and Georgie was going to have a devil of a time cleaning his boots when he got back to his room. Even marooned in Cornwall, he wasn't going to go about in soiled boots. He tried to stay on the edge of the lane to avoid the wheel ruts and lessen the damage.

Penkellis loomed in the distance. Lit from behind by the setting sun and reduced to a silhouette, it didn't look half as bad as it did in daylight. The ruined wing was hardly visible, and it was too dark to count the boarded-up windows. Straight and tall, Radnor's tower looked almost noble.

He must have gotten distracted and forgotten to watch where he was going, because he had wandered off the lane, and the next thing he knew he had landed arse first in cold water.

"Bleeding buggering Christ!" He must be in Radnor's trench. That sodding ditch had been waist deep, and now he was sitting in it, wet to the shoulders in muddy, freezing water. Now what the hell was to become of his boots, to say nothing of the rest of his clothes? It wasn't like he could nip over to the tailor and equip himself. Not likely in bloody Penkellis, where he couldn't even guess the direction of the nearest actual town. "Fucking fuck—"

"Turner!"

Why the bloody hell was Radnor out here to witness his humiliation? Could he not be left to his muddy misery in peace? "What do you want, Radnor?"

"To fish your skinny arse out of my trench." And with that, Radnor stepped into the ditch and lifted Georgie against his chest, with one arm behind the knees and the other arm around Georgie's back, as effortlessly as if Georgie were a newborn kitten. "Stop wriggling. There's nothing about Penkellis that would be improved by the corpse of a secretary. Let me get you out of here."

Georgie might not be a great brute of a man like Radnor, but he was soaked to the bone, and his sodden topcoat alone had to add a stone to his weight. Nonetheless, Radnor climbed out of the trench without breaking stride. In any other context, Georgie would be content enough for the earl to demonstrate his strength upon Georgie's person as much as the fellow liked, but being rescued from a ditch in such a sorry state was a bit much for his pride to take.

"Hold on to my neck," Radnor ordered, his mouth terribly close to Georgie's ear.

"Like hell I will. Put me down."

Radnor did so immediately, and Georgie landed on the ground with a revolting squish in his boots. He made a sound of disgust but kept walking.

"Wait." He noticed where the earl had brought him. "Why are we heading towards the kitchen door?" He wanted nothing more than to strip, climb into bed, and mourn the loss of his clothes. "Don't tell me you're suddenly concerned about the state of your carpets."

"So you can dry off."

"I can dry off in my own bedchamber, please and thank you." His teeth were chattering, which made it hard to speak with the necessary sangfroid.

"Aye, but I need to tell Janet to bring you a hot bath."

"What?"

"You told me that was the proper procedure. The housemaid brings hot water for a bath lest one catch a chill." Even in the dark, Georgie could tell that Radnor was having fun with this, the bastard.

"Quite. That's the procedure for earls, not for the rest of us." Any acerbic dignity he was trying for was quite lost in the chattering of his teeth.

"Doesn't matter." He held open the kitchen door and gestured for Georgie to enter.

Georgie found himself turned over to the care of Mrs. Ferris. She took his coat and boots, promising to return them to some semblance of presentability. Janet was dispatched with pitchers of hot water to carry upstairs to Georgie's bedchamber.

When he turned around to thank Radnor, he found that the earl was gone.

CHAPTER ELEVEN

Georgie soaked until the water turned cold, trying to wait out the ruinous urge to towel himself off and promptly climb naked and uninvited into Radnor's bed. It was tempting, the idea of Radnor's warm body covering his own, pressing him heavily into the mattress.

No, it was more than tempting. Apple tarts were tempting. New waistcoats were tempting. Stealing a gentleman's hat was tempting.

Radnor was disastrous.

It was as if after a quarter of a century of blithely not giving a damn about anybody, he had accrued a surplus of damns to give. First, old Mrs. Packingham, and now the earl.

Right now, at the very moment he ought only to be thinking of how best to secure his own future and his family's safety, he was instead so stupidly touched by the earl's thoughtfulness in having a bloody bath drawn for him that he couldn't even manage to wash himself without feeling that it was somehow Radnor's hands rubbing the soap along his limbs, rinsing the mud out of his hair.

Even now that the water was cold, he didn't want to get out of the tub because this bath had been Radnor's doing. The sad truth was that Georgie's policy of not giving a damn had gone both ways. He knew how to charm and wheedle his way into almost any society, but once there he kept his marks at arm's length; he kept his secrets and lies and any other vulnerabilities safe within a hard shell of indifference.

And then Radnor had come along and turned his shell to mush, and his brain right along with it.

As much as Georgie hated to admit it, it was, after all, pleasant to have somebody who wished to carry one out of a muddy mire, to ensure one was warm and cared for.

Fucking pathetic, it was.

Sighing, he toweled himself off and quickly stepped into a pair of loose trousers. No sooner had he pulled on a shirt than the door creaked slowly open behind him. He spun around, assuming it would be Janet come to fetch the bathwater, and for one mad moment hoping it was Radnor.

Barnabus, tongue lolling, trotted through the door and hopped onto Georgie's bed.

Georgie snapped his fingers. "You. Out." But the dog continued digging through the bedding. Moving to the doorway, Georgie patted his leg and whistled. That earned him a bored look from Barnabus, who arranged himself on the bed in a shaggy circle.

"You've left no room for me." As if the mongrel could be reasoned with. Force was out of the question, because Georgie couldn't lift an eight-stone dog who didn't want to cooperate. He took hold of an edge of the coverlet and tried to tug, but Barnabus only shifted to the exposed sheet, leaving Georgie with an armful of blanket and still no place to sleep.

"Well, that didn't work," said a voice from behind him. It was Radnor, leaning against the door frame, one hand jammed into the pocket of his dressing gown and the other carrying a stack of books. "This is what happens when you make a practice of bribing a dog with bits of muffin. You earn yourself an acolyte."

"I'll take an acolyte over a ravening beast any day." Georgie had been fairly certain that if he kept the dog stuffed to the gills, he wouldn't become the mongrel's next meal.

"He's harmless," the earl said unconvincingly. His dressing gown was parted at the neck, revealing a triangle of dark hair.

Georgie suddenly felt exposed. Unlike the earl, Georgie was not accustomed to going about in shirtsleeves. But Radnor's gaze drifted downward and lingered at Georgie's chest, and then lower, as if he liked what he saw.

And god damn it, but Georgie's nipples went hard. A shiver of awareness traveled through his body.

"You're cold," Radnor said, a wrinkle appearing between his eyebrows.

"Oh. Yes. Quite." It wasn't a lie, even though cold had nothing to do with Georgie's shiver.

Radnor deposited the books on a table, then poked the fire and added a log. "This room is drafty."

"The entirety of Penkellis is drafty, my lord. That's what comes of not having the windows replaced or the chimneys repaired in a century or two."

The earl shrugged. "I don't feel the cold as much as you do. It's a matter of surface area. I have less surface relative to mass compared to you."

Georgie raised his eyebrows. "Indeed you do." He let his gaze rake up and down over some of that surface area. And who could blame him?

"With the result that less heat escapes through my skin than does through yours."

Really, it wasn't possible to listen to this kind of talk with any semblance of equanimity. Surface area, mass—bugger it all to hell. There was no reason all this learned flimflam ought to go straight to Georgie's cock, but it did so anyway.

"Perhaps you could extract your dog so I can sleep in my bed." Georgie's voice was sharp, with no finesse whatsoever.

And Radnor did precisely that. He didn't need to be told twice when it came to Georgie's comfort, did he? With one fluid movement and a ripple of flexing muscles visible through his threadbare dressing gown, he scooped the dog against his chest and headed for the door.

"Oh, before I forget," Radnor said over his shoulder, "I brought you some books."

"Books?"

"You were disappointed to find that the books in the library are unreadable. I found some novels in my own collection." He gestured to the pile of books he had placed on the table.

"How did you know I like novels?" And who would have guessed that Radnor had a collection, of all things?

"A guess," Radnor said. "Good night."

"No." Georgie winced at the stupidity he was about to commit. "Stop. Put Barnabus by the fire."

Radnor regarded Georgie over the dog's head. "I hadn't realized you had taken a fancy to the dog, Mr. Turner. Hear that, Barnabus? Your affections are returned, you lucky fellow." He crouched to set the dog on the thin rug that sat before the hearth. "I was out walking with him when he saw you tumble into the ditch, you know. It was too dark for me to see, but when he saw you fall he gave a howl and ran off towards you." He was still crouched, petting his dog, and looked up at Georgie with the faintest hint of a smile. "I'm afraid he scarpered when he realized he wouldn't get any biscuits."

"Quite right," Georgie managed, trying to put some acid into his voice just for show. "If he had come whimpering for sweeties, I would have pulled him into the ditch beside me."

"Mean-spirited of you." The earl was now smiling outright, a curve of soft lips set in his beard, and Georgie shivered again as he remembered the feel of both against his skin. Radnor's unearthly pale blue eyes were in on the joke, crinkling warmly at the corners. "You still look cold."

Georgie shook his head. "I'm not bloody cold, Radnor."

"Oh? You look—"

"I'm not cold." The man didn't know enough to distinguish cold from arousal, and Georgie could not let that stand. "Come here."

"Pardon?" He rose to his feet, plainly bewildered.

"I'm going to show you that I'm not cold."

Understanding dawned across Radnor's face. His eyebrows flew up, but he didn't come any closer. "Are you, now?"

Peeved, Georgie folded his arms across his chest. "Well, if you'll let me."

"Over the last few days you haven't acted like someone who wanted me within ten yards of him, let alone—"

"I've been awful, I know." Georgie ran an anxious hand through his damp hair. "I don't have my head on straight when it comes to you, to be frank."

"I see," the earl said, his voice a trifle hoarse. He clenched his fists, his body rigid.

"Come here," Georgie repeated, knowing he was on the verge of disaster and proceeding anyway.

The room was small and Radnor crossed it in two strides. Georgie could feel the heat coming from the bigger man's body. And then Georgie was being hauled against the earl's chest, and he had never felt as safe and totally imperiled as he did at that moment.

So Turner liked being pressed against trees and walls and what have you. Lawrence could do that. He could and would press the man into any surface the fellow pleased. He shoved Turner against the closed door of his shabby, drafty bedchamber. Turner's mouth opened for him, or maybe it was his own mouth opening for Turner, but regardless, the end result was a hot slide of tongue over tongue, and a whimper from the other man's mouth.

But that whimper didn't mean pain, or if it did, Turner didn't seem to mind, because he kept on.

Lawrence let his hands roam over the other man's back, tugging Turner's shirt up by the handful to reach cool, smooth skin. The sight of his secretary in a rare state of dishabille, an elegant hand on one slim hip, arguing with a sleeping dog, had charmed Lawrence to the core of his being. He wanted to touch and admire every inch of the man, and was about 90 percent certain that this was exactly what Turner wanted as well, that what they were doing was right and sane and good. But that remaining 10 percent was terrifying.

That balance of uncertainty was where Lawrence's madness lay, whatever wires in his mind were prone to short circuits. But Turner seemed to understand that, because a second later his shirt was simply gone, and he tilted his head to the side, presenting Lawrence with an expanse of soft neck to kiss. Lawrence complied, pressing his lips against the curve where neck met shoulder. Turner sighed, and Lawrence let his mouth drift upwards, to the soft underside of the other man's jaw, surprisingly rough with stubble. He licked the place where the stubble began and heard a faint gasp.

Against his own hip, he felt the pressure of Turner's erection. Oh, thank God. He had been feeling like a rutting dog, walking around with a full cockstand scarcely concealed by his dressing gown, but if Turner was in the same condition then it could hardly be objectionable, could it?

Lawrence lowered his hands, cupping Turner's arse and pulling him higher and closer, letting him feel how hard Lawrence was. Then Turner's legs were wrapped around Lawrence's waist, and he was pinned between the wall behind him and Lawrence's own oversized frame in front of him. But he seemed to like it—he was responding to Lawrence's tentative thrusts with his own.

"Just like this," he gasped.

Lawrence felt his dressing gown being pushed out of the way, and then the press of skin against skin, chest against chest. Turner's deft hands were everywhere, as if he were trying to learn the topography of Lawrence's chest by touch alone. He felt his secretary's efficient fingers trace the outline of muscles in a way that sent desire spiraling down to his cock. Then—oh Jesus—Turner's index finger drew a circle around one of Lawrence's nipples.

"Fuck," Lawrence ground out.

Turner let out a breathy laugh that Lawrence felt against his neck.

Lawrence pulled Turner away from the door, intending to steer him towards the bed. But without the door to hold them up, they both sank to their knees. Turner pushed him down to the ground and kissed him, hard and sweet.

The bare floor bit into Lawrence's shoulder blades as Turner's fingers dug into his biceps. Lawrence felt a hot mouth press a line of kisses from his jaw to his neck to his chest, and then—

"Holy God!" He arched off the floor when he felt the light press of teeth on his nipple.

"Good or bad?" Turner murmured, looking up at Lawrence with dark, dark eyes.

Good hardly seemed adequate, so inadequate as to almost be dishonest. He took hold of one of Turner's hands and dragged it to the bulge in Lawrence's breeches.

Turner grasped Lawrence's cock through the fabric. Lawrence bit back a curse.

"Radnor," Turner said, and to Lawrence it sounded like a plea.

"No," Lawrence said abruptly. Hearing his title—his father's and Percy's title—from a man whose hand was wrapped around his cock was altogether wrong. "Call me Lawrence." He watched as a look of surprise flitted across the other man's face, as if he hadn't expected the intimacy. "Or don't…"

"Lawrence," the secretary agreed. "You'll call me Georgie?" Without waiting for an answer, he began unfastening Lawrence's breeches and tugging them off. At the first touch of fingers—fingers that were *not his own*, after so long—curling around him, Lawrence's eyes flung open. This he had to see. Georgie was kneeling over him, black hair tumbled over his forehead. With his thumb he spread moisture over the head of Lawrence's throbbing prick. And with his other hand, he—God help him—he was unfastening his own trousers. When Georgie bent his head and flicked his tongue over the tip of Lawrence's cock, Lawrence thought his heart might actually stop.

"I want…" Lawrence started, before realizing he couldn't reach the right words. "Come here," he tried, pulling Georgie up and then reaching for the fall of the other man's trousers, where he could just see the head of the other man's cock. "Give it to me," he managed, his voice hoarse. The man's cock, when Lawrence touched it, was silky and hard and already wet at the tip. Experimentally, he stroked it the way he would stroke himself, long leisurely pulls, rubbing his thumb along the slit.

The noise Georgie made, a desperate and shuddering sigh, made Lawrence's cock jump. Then Georgie bent over him, taking one of Lawrence's nipples in his mouth, and Lawrence groaned. It was too much, too good. He was feeling too many things at once, but he still wanted more.

He twined his fingers in Georgie's still-damp hair, pulling him up, seeking out the relative familiarity of Georgie's mouth. Georgie kissed him back, hard and urgent. When Georgie took both their erections in one hand and began stroking them together, Lawrence bit him on the lip. He was ready to apologize, but Georgie moaned into his mouth and kept kissing him even harder, so he figured he hadn't gone too terribly amiss.

Georgie's back was smooth and warm under Lawrence's hands, his arse taut with thrusting. "I need to…" Georgie said, his voice thick and needy.

"I want to watch," Lawrence rasped out. "Show me."

Georgie knelt back and Lawrence watched him, both cocks held tight in Georgie's fine-boned hand. And then Georgie was shuddering, his seed spilling over Lawrence's belly.

The sight of Georgie's face as he spent was all it took to push Lawrence over the edge. His climax felt torn out of him, wretched and blissful and confused all at once, simple pleasure a mere fraction of the experience.

Georgie collapsed onto Lawrence's chest, seed and sweat mingling, Georgie's hair falling all over Lawrence's neck. They lay together for a few breaths before Georgie rose, graceful as always. With economical movements he made use of the towel and bathwater to clean himself off. His lean muscles glowed in the firelight.

Lawrence sat up, meaning to do as Georgie did and tidy himself. But Georgie came to kneel beside him and wiped Lawrence's belly with a wet cloth. He felt the muscles in his abdomen clench at the unexpected cold, at the strangeness of being touched by somebody else, the even more foreign sensation of being looked after by somebody else.

The strangeness started to spread over his body, a seeping sense of unbelonging. He did not know what to do, what to say, where to go. *Not now.* He cursed whatever forces made his chest feel as if it were constricted by iron bands, his lungs unable to take in nearly enough air.

But Georgie took care of that with the same matter-of-fact nonchalance he always adopted when ordering Lawrence about. "I'm for bed," he said, extending a hand to Lawrence.

Lawrence grasped Georgie's hand and rose. "Bed," he agreed, and gathered that he was meant to leave. He could do that. He dropped Georgie's hand, gathered up his clothes, and headed for the door.

His progress was checked by a hand on his elbow. "This bed, Radnor. Lawrence," he corrected.

Lawrence turned and saw Georgie looking up at him hopefully, maybe even a little embarrassed. His usually sleek hair was tousled and disordered, his cheeks red from where they had rubbed against Lawrence's beard.

Lawrence nodded.

The bed was scarcely big enough for one person, let alone two, one of whom was fourteen stone. But it turned out not to matter, because Georgie pushed Lawrence down onto the bed and climbed nearly on top of him, resting his head on Lawrence's shoulder. Lawrence shut his eyes, and nothing existed beyond the scent of clean hair and the feel of sinewy limbs tangled with his own. They fit in the bed like this, Georgie molded to Lawrence's side, hardly taking up more space than Lawrence alone. It was an alien sensation, being this close to another person, unfamiliar but not unpleasant, something Lawrence could imagine finding agreeable, given enough time.

"Are you all right?" Georgie asked, as if following Lawrence's thoughts.

"I am," Lawrence answered, and it was almost the truth.

CHAPTER TWELVE

Georgie hadn't meant to fall asleep, but his eyes shut almost as soon as he settled in the crook of Radnor's arm. When he opened them again, the first fingers of light had already appeared in the sky outside his sooty bedroom window. Carefully, he tipped his head to look at the man sleeping beside him. Radnor radiated heat, and at some point during the night one of his arms had landed heavily across Georgie's middle. It was like sleeping against a wall of hot muscle, which ought to have been uncomfortable but was, in fact, the first time Georgie had been properly warm since arriving at Penkellis.

With a sigh of resignation, Georgie slid carefully out from under Radnor's arm into the cold and made his way towards the north tower. He couldn't stay here another day, that much was all too clear. It was a terrible nuisance, having a conscience. A year ago he would have cheerfully filled his valise with Penkellis treasures, stolen the earl's secrets, and spared Radnor nary a thought on his way back to London.

But now, after so many years of working and scheming, with no purpose but to ensure that he would never have to face the grinding, dirty poverty of his youth, he was prepared to leave Penkellis empty-handed and with nowhere better to go. And all because of a heap of fine, useless feelings.

He was fairly disgusted with himself, but no matter how he turned the matter over in his mind, he couldn't let Radnor—*Lawrence*, he thought with a rush of warmth—be a part of any swindle. He felt nauseated to think how close he had come to actually stealing the telegraph plans. And worse—he might have put Lawrence in harm's way by exposing him to Brewster.

When Georgie pushed open the door to the study, he found the room cold and dark. He set about lighting the fire and a candle to work by. He took his time cutting a nib, refilling the inkwell, and arranging the paper so it was precisely aligned with the edges of the blotter. This was not a letter he wished to write, but after a lifetime of disappearing like so much smoke, he found that he couldn't leave Radnor without a word.

But there were no words to convey what he felt, likely because he didn't want to put a name to it. Any word he could come up with felt like stolen property, something that rightly belonged to a decent person, not Georgie Turner.

Instead, he set about the task of cataloging the earl's notes. Over the past few weeks he had become familiar with Lawrence's bold, scrawling hand and with the abbreviations and symbols he employed. Georgie took each stained, ripped, dog-eared sheet of paper and wrote a short synopsis of the experiment in his own much more legible hand. It was satisfying, this process of sifting through the products of Lawrence's brilliant mind, and translating them into understandable prose.

Four pages in, he came across a paper that did not belong. It was a letter, still folded and sealed and addressed in shaky writing nearly as illegible as the earl's. Georgie tore it open and read it, as he did all the earl's correspondence.

And then he stared.

"Radnor?"

Lawrence heard his name being called, sound traveling through bedcovers and the fog of deep slumber. He ignored it and tried to fall back asleep.

"Radnor!" The voice was closer now, harder to ignore. A moment later, and it was accompanied by hands roughly shaking his shoulders.

Lawrence woke with a jolt. He was in a strange bed, a strange room, everything out of place. The mattress hit his back in all the wrong spots, the faint sunlight came in at a disconcertingly unexpected angle, and the fire was on the opposite side of his head from where it ought to be. Barnabus, who habitually slept behind Lawrence's knees in an apparent effort to make as much a nuisance of himself as possible, was absent.

When he recalled that he was in Turner's room, Turner's bed, not a stitch of clothing on his body, he did not feel relieved.

It was Turner who had been calling him, shaking him. It could hardly have been anyone else. Lawrence's skin still felt alive with Turner's touch, and his head still swam with the strange wonder of last night. He rubbed his eyes and propped himself up on his elbows, trying to resist the urge to cover his chest with the sheet.

Turner was waving a piece of paper in Lawrence's face. "You have received a letter from your *son*," he said, making it sound like an accusation. Turner was usually so equable, too languidly decorous to make a fuss. Lawrence felt himself greatly out of his depths. "And *such* a letter, my lord."

"Why?" Simon never wrote. His aunt had insisted on caring for the child after Isabella's death. "He's at Harrow."

"Quite! For the next week, at least. Then he's coming here for his holiday."

"Impossible." Lawrence got to his feet and pulled on his trousers. "He stays with his mother's family during his holidays."

"Well. He writes that"—Turner glanced at the paper—"Cousin Albert and Cousin Genevieve have the measles, so he humbly requests to visit you. To *visit* you." He poked Lawrence's bare chest with a single finger. "Radnor, I was under the impression the child had died with his mother, or lived on the Continent, or…" His face wore an expression of blank confusion. "I don't know why I assumed any of those things. But you never speak of him."

Lawrence disregarded everything but the essential fact he knew to be true. "He cannot come here. Write to the school and explain that he will board through the holiday, until next term."

"I bloody well will not." Turner looked so furious as to be hot to the touch. His hands were clenched by his sides, one of them clutching Simon's letter.

"I fail to understand—"

"You fail to understand so damned many things, Radnor, but I will explain as clearly as I can that you must not refuse to let your child visit you. *Visit*, for God's sweet sake."

"Of course I can." He pulled his dressing gown tightly around him. "The last time Isabella's daft sister refused to take him, he went to stay with a schoolmate."

Turner's eyes were bright, his cheeks flushed. "Refuse... take..." He shook his head. "This child is your heir. This is his house. You are his *father*. Radnor—hear me now—he signs his letter 'Your Simon.'"

"My Simon," Lawrence repeated, and it felt like the floor was evaporating under his feet. "Mine. Good God. He should be glad he is not."

"Whatever nonsense you have in your head, get rid of it," Turner spat. "He's yours, he's coming, and we have at most ten days to get this house into some semblance of habitability. Do you not understand? He has been with his aunt. He has been with his schoolmate. He will know how things are done and how they are not done, and the way we live at Penkellis is decidedly *not how things are done*." He poked Radnor's chest on each of those words, brandishing the letter like a weapon.

Lawrence grabbed Turner's wrist, stopping the assault. "I've made myself clear. He is not to come here. This house is no place for a child. I'm no company for a child."

"Company? This is no question of company, my lord." He twisted his hand free but didn't step back. "You are his father."

"No, I am not."

Turner opened his mouth as if to protest but snapped it shut again.

"Isabella was with child when I married her. That is *why* I married her. She, for reasons you are well acquainted with, found me an unsatisfactory husband and Penkellis a highly unsatisfactory house. She took Simon and ran off with her lover. When she died, her family fetched the child from Italy and raised him."

Turner's mouth set into a grim line. "And you have not seen him since?"

"No."

As Lawrence watched, Turner composed himself, his brow smoothing, his mouth flattening into a firm line. Lawrence had the sensation that Turner was resuming a mask, only Lawrence had not realized there had been any mask in the first place.

"Does he know?" All the usual cool polish had returned to Turner's demeanor.

"Know what?"

"That he is not your natural child?"

"I should damned well hope not."

"You prefer for him to believe that he has been abandoned by his own father, then. I see." Turner's voice was glacially cold.

"I prefer for him not to have anything to do with this place, or with me. The best thing I could possibly do for him is to keep him away from Penkellis and its master."

Turner's eyes opened wide. "No. You are wrong there. I have told you so many times that you are not mad. But what you have just said is the closest to madness you have ever come. You are…" He gestured with his hands, as if physically grasping for a word. "You are a fine man. You will do admirably as a father."

Lawrence gaped at his secretary's wrongheadedness. "You have no idea what you speak of."

"Do I not? I was raised by…not a good man, although I dare say he did his best, for what little that's worth." From the way Turner pressed his lips together, Lawrence inferred that it was worth very little indeed. "My mother died when I was an infant, and my brother and sister worked, so I was mainly left to my own devices. My father was always late with the rent, and once I came home to find our rooms empty and my father gone. It took me days to find him. He was drunk and penniless, but I was so relieved because I had nowhere else to go, and even if he were bedding down on the street, I could at least be with him." He paused to take a deep breath, his eyes flashing darkly. "And you, with all your money and all your many rooms, will not do as much for a few weeks? A few weeks, Lawrence."

Maybe it was the sound of his name that made his resolve crumble. It had been so long since anyone had called him that, and it was patently absurd for anyone on earth to be speaking to him in such a way. Not because it was improper—which of course it was, but hardly the most improper aspect of this scenario, and Lawrence had given up on propriety years ago anyway—but because it implied an impossible level of intimacy. He didn't have friends, for God's sake. His mind was a thicket of thorns and weeds and nobody could get in far enough to achieve anything resembling friendship.

"A few weeks," he repeated.

"Even if you were as mad as a hatter. Even if Penkellis were filled to the rafters with evil, a few weeks would not harm the child, and being sent away will harm him very much." He spoke with such conviction, Lawrence could not dismiss him. Lawrence was unmoored and unhinged, sure of absolutely nothing, and here was his secretary, his lover, so utterly confident and sure. Lawrence wanted Turner's confidence to be enough for both of them.

He let out a sigh. "Fine."

Turner looked like he might sag with relief, but he simply nodded.

Lawrence made to leave, to retreat to the safety of his study.

"Wait," Turner said. "I need your authority to make the necessary accommodations for the child. I'll have to go to Falmouth to engage servants and tradesmen and purchase supplies. I'd hire local people but there isn't enough time to win them over. I'll return the day after tomorrow. Will you write to your bankers and give me that authority?"

Lawrence nodded. "You'll have whatever you require." He might agree to anything as long as he did not have to look at the raw earnestness that had momentarily returned to Turner's face.

Chapter Thirteen

Lawrence flung down his pen when the pounding started anew. It was impossible to string two coherent thoughts together in these conditions. There was a disturbingly arrhythmic banging that he could feel vibrating through the floors and walls as surely as he could hear it. It was a wonder the castle was still standing.

Furious, he threw open the study door. "Stop that at once!" he bellowed, but there was no chance he had been heard. The noise, it seemed, was coming from downstairs. He descended the stairs two at a time and stalked towards the racket.

There were no fewer than half a dozen men in the drawing room, all strangers. One was shouting something up the chimney. Two others were using crowbars to pull up a rotten piece of floorboard. Another pair sawed lumber.

Through the threshold that led to the small parlor, the room where the ladies of Penkellis had once practiced the harp and worked on their samplers, he could see a man with a bucket of paint and three women scrubbing the floors. The drapes and carpets were gone from both rooms, and the windows had been cleaned to a shine.

Lawrence had become accustomed to his house having a muted, blurred-around-the-edges appearance due to the accretion of filth and the spread of decay. He wasn't used to this gleaming, glowing space. The house even smelled different, of sawdust and whitewash, lemon and lavender.

In the middle of it all, lit by a shaft of light, stood Georgie Turner, his hands on his hips.

"What the devil is going on here?" Lawrence roared over the noise, when what he really wanted to do was fall to his knees and thank God his secretary had come back. He ought to have returned days ago, and Lawrence had almost given up hope. It occurred to him that he had missed Turner. That was an unexpected novelty; he hadn't thought himself capable of missing anyone. He hadn't thought he'd ever have a chance to do so.

The racket abruptly ceased, and a score of fearful eyes turned to look. Not at Lawrence, but at Turner. There was no doubt as to who was giving the orders here.

"Good afternoon, your lordship." Turner bowed slightly, with a mildly ironic air that sent a jolt of happiness through Lawrence's body. Lord, but he really had missed the man. "Carry on, carry on," Turner said to the workers, while gesturing for Lawrence to follow him through a set of doors into the library. This was where Lawrence's father had met with his man of business. It was also where he had summoned Lawrence for regular whippings. He shuddered. There were reasons he didn't traipse about the house. Too many memories, none of them good.

Perhaps some of his unease showed on his face, because Turner looked up at him and continued straight out the French doors and onto the terrace.

Lawrence closed the doors behind them, but cracked glass was not enough to muffle the noises from within. There was even more chaos outside: somebody was hacking away at the kitchen garden, another man was raking gravel smoothly across the drive.

"The improvements are well underway, my lord."

"I cannot imagine how you expect to fund this nonsense," Lawrence snapped, mainly because he was feeling disagreeable.

Turner narrowed his eyes and sucked in a breath. "My lord, you wrote a letter giving me authority to do what was needful to ready the house."

"I thought you meant airing the bed linens, not refurbishing the entire ground floor."

"It is not the entire ground floor, but only a suite of five rooms that will, I hope, create the illusion of this being the home of a gentleman. The rest of the house will be quite the same, less a few squirrels and mice."

"What will it cost?" Lawrence was unfamiliar with the cost of paint and lumber. "A hundred pounds?"

Turner cast him a pitying look. "Quite a bit more than that, my lord. But you can well afford it. I've seen your books. I've *kept* your books. You had no books until I came."

This was a gross exaggeration, as Lawrence was quite certain that his steward—a fellow who was far too canny to pester his employer with anything more than a quarterly report—must have some records that could be referred to as books.

"And if you make a fuss when the bills come due," Turner went on, "I'll pawn every last gewgaw in this house."

Lawrence growled. "You are driving me out of my mind."

"Oh?" Turner, who had been studying his fingernails, looked up idly at Lawrence. "You concede that you were previously in your right mind?"

"Turner, I cannot abide this racket. Or with any of the rest of it." He rubbed his temples and squeezed his eyes shut. "I swear that I heard some sort of carpentry going on outside my window well before dawn."

"Nonsense, the carpenters could hardly have worked without light."

"Turner. Georgie, I'm begging you. Do something."

The silence stretched out, and when Lawrence opened his eyes he saw the secretary regarding him carefully, all traces of irritation and feigned boredom quite gone. "All right. Go for a walk. Barnabus is in the kitchens and could use a run. He has much the same opinion of carpentry as you do, Lawrence." He froze. "My lord," he corrected.

Lawrence wanted to say that he preferred the sound of his own name on Turner's tongue, not the title or honorific that had been his father's and brother's. He wanted to say that it filled a spot in his heart that he hadn't known was there, a spot he full well knew he didn't deserve to have filled.

"To hell with 'my lord' and 'Radnor.' Call me Lawrence or nothing at all. I want you, Georgie." Lawrence watched the man's dark eyes grow momentarily wide. "To *work*, damn you. I need you. I had a thought about zinc—oh never mind. I need you helping me, not scrubbing floors and mending things. I can't get on without you." He hardly knew how he had managed before Turner came here.

"Speaking of mending." Turner's gaze raked up and down Lawrence's body. "I need you to try on your new clothes."

"Absolutely not." This was the outside of enough. "My clothes are fine."

"No, they are not. They are the opposite of fine. They are coarse and ill kept. Your son—do not look at me like that, Radn—Lawrence—your *son* will be embarrassed to see you so badly dressed. You need a valet—"

"Stop this!" He must have shouted, because Georgie went still, and the noises outside momentarily quieted. "I apologize," he said in a normal tone of voice. "I had a valet, but he left."

"I daresay he did, if you insisted on dressing like a convict and growing a beard."

Lawrence unthinkingly raised a hand to his chin. "I was under the impression you liked my beard." The man had rubbed his face against it, for heaven's sake. As if Lawrence were in danger of forgetting such a thing.

"So I do." A hint of arch amusement, but nothing more. "But it's just the thing to strike terror into the heart of a schoolboy. When?"

"Pardon? When what?"

Turner cocked his head to the side. "When did your valet leave?"

"I can't rightly say. Two years ago? I noticed one day that he had gone."

"You noticed one day…" Turner glanced away, brushing a strand of raven-dark hair behind his ear. He hadn't had a haircut since coming here, and now the ends touched his collar. "How long would it take you to notice that I was gone, my lord?"

"That's a stupid question. You know perfectly well that I mark every moment you're with me." They were standing quite close in order to hear one another over the din of the sawing and hammering and gravel-raking. Beneath the smell of sawdust and cleaning polish, Lawrence could detect Turner's scent, and he focused his mind on it as desperately as a drowning man might cling to a rope.

"I don't know anything of the sort," Turner said, his eyes flashing darkly.

Lawrence shook his head, dumbfounded that Turner hadn't caught on. "I can't help but notice you being there, so you'd damned well best believe I notice when you aren't. The last few days when you've been away...I've noticed." He let his voice drop on those last words.

"Because you prefer being alone, no doubt." Turner looked up at him with an expression that did not belong on his cool, calm face. He looked young, raw, vulnerable.

"That's not it." It ought to have been, but it wasn't. "I didn't...I wanted you back. I..." Lawrence was on the verge of telling Turner that he had missed him, that every moment without him was the pointless ticking of a clock that didn't even keep proper time. But he had already revealed too much, to Turner and to himself. "As I said, I need your assistance."

That strange expression dropped from Turner's countenance, replaced by his usual *froideur* and then some. "My absence was for a good cause, my lord."

"Leave off this 'my lord' gammon, will you?"

"Oh, you're in a charming mood. As I was saying, my absence was for the very good cause of making your house suitable for your son."

"You don't understand. This house will never be suitable for Simon or anyone else." Including you, he wanted to say. "I had hoped to spare Simon the sight of this place." He had hoped to spare Simon the sight of himself.

Turner regarded him speculatively. "You have memories of this place that the child will not share."

"And thank God for it."

"My point is that to you, Penkellis is a horrible, evil place, because you have seen and known horrible, evil things here." Somehow Turner knew this without Lawrence ever having said so. "The child doesn't share that understanding."

"He'll hear of it all soon enough if he spends any time here. He'll hear about what his uncle and grandfather were. He'll hear about me." None of them were truly the child's blood relations. The Browne legacy of evil and madness wasn't Simon's future, but he didn't know that. "It would have been better for him to stay away."

"Shove it."

Lawrence instinctively drew himself up to his full height and raised his chin. "Excuse me?"

"Oh, it is very amusing how lordly you are when you choose to be. I might be intimidated if I didn't know better. But you can shove it, nonetheless. Try and put yourself in the child's place. He's never been asked to visit here. Perhaps he's already heard whispers of the mad earls from whom he believes he has descended. Surely you can see that he will be afraid. That is why we will make this house—and its master—as normal and friendly as we can. We will make it so he wants to come back."

"No!"

"But he will come back, Radnor. Even if it's half a century from now, when you're dead and buried. He'll come back. This will be his home. This is his future, and you need to make sure he is not afraid of it."

Lawrence let out a breath he hadn't known he was holding. "Damn you."

"Quite. Still, Radnor, you understand that I'm here to help you get through this, don't you?"

Lawrence swallowed hard. Then he moved to clap Turner on the arm, whether in thanks or acknowledgment or dismissal, he did not know. But at that same moment Turner stepped towards him, and the result was that Lawrence's hand skimmed down Turner's back. It might have been unremarkable, but for Turner's slight shiver. Lawrence couldn't help but grin wolfishly. Turner's lips were slightly parted, and if it weren't for the fact that the house and grounds were crawling with people, Lawrence might have bent his head and kissed the man.

God, he wanted more. The other night, that frantic coupling on the bare floor of Turner's room, had been a revelation.

Sodomites had been a favorite subject of his father's rage-fueled tirades, in which he lumped it in with other crimes against nature, such as Catholicism and being French. When he noticed—or thought he noticed—his younger son looking at the curate in an unnatural way, he had locked Lawrence in his bedchamber for a fortnight and prohibited him from attending church indefinitely. When Lawrence suffered one of his spells—heart racing, palms sweating, the abiding urge to hide—the old earl had declared it all part of the same madness that had the boy ogling clergymen. He had refused to send Lawrence to school, on the grounds that madness and depravity ought to be concealed. Lawrence's one feeble protest had been met with threats of madhouses.

"Radnor?" Turner asked. He had a bit of plaster in his hair, and Lawrence reached out to brush it away, letting his thumb linger overlong on his ear.

"It isn't mad to want to touch you," Lawrence said, his voice hoarse.

Turner sucked in a breath. "No, indeed. I'm glad you know that."

One of the French doors cracked open and the yellow-haired housemaid stuck her head out. "Mr. Turner, the mason is here to see about the front steps."

"If your lordship will excuse me?" Turner spoke in a cordial, businesslike tone that Lawrence knew was meant for the housemaid's benefit, so he didn't complain about the honorific.

"Very well," he said.

Lawrence watched him pass through the library and into the drawing room beyond, his slim figure silhouetted against the bright light that shone through the freshly cleaned windows.

"Surely there's no need for all those extra servants, Mr. Turner." Mrs. Ferris's brow was furrowed as she looked up at the ladder where Georgie attempted to wrangle the new drapes into submission. "Another girl would have been more than enough, maybe a woman from the village to come help on laundry day. His lordship hates being disturbed, and with all these servants and workmen bustling about he'll be in a terrible state."

"I'll see to his lordship," Georgie said. "Leave him to me." As far as Georgie cared, Lawrence could sod right off if he dared complain again about the preparations for this child's arrival. Rendering the house habitable for a child who was legally and—as far as Georgie cared—ethically the earl's own son was the damned least Lawrence needed to do. Even if Lawrence had only married the boy's mother out of kindness, even if he had only been twenty when he had taken on the responsibility, it was his responsibility nonetheless.

Georgie couldn't remember the last time he had thought in terms of responsibility. Or ethics, of all things. He felt like he was in a strange land, trying to make his way through a new city in a foreign language. But here he was, regardless, and he was nothing if not adaptable.

For God's sake, he had even stripped to his shirtsleeves and set to work himself. He was likely filthy. They were running out of time.

"One more thing, Mrs. Ferris. If there are any local people you think ought to be engaged as servants, please do so. That's within your purview, and I'm afraid I overstepped by taking on that task myself." He had hired servants in Falmouth to go beyond the reach of whatever superstitions afflicted the villagers. But if Mrs. Ferris could persuade some tenants to serve at Penkellis—and he dearly hoped she would, because anything to gain the goodwill of these people could only help—then those servants could simply join the ranks of those Georgie had hired. It wasn't as if there was any shortage of work to be done.

Mrs. Ferris appeared slightly mollified when she went back to the kitchens.

"She'll come around," said Janet, who was holding the ladder in place. "Can't have the little lad sleeping in his papa's workroom, can we? He'd blow himself up, or get into whatever mischief his lordship conducts up there."

"He'd also believe his father to be stark mad, living in one tower out of a house this size. No, you're right, Janet. We have no choice but to get this wing into a state of tolerable readiness." He glanced around, suppressing a wave of dismay. The glaziers had not finished replacing all the cracked windows; the furniture had been taken away by the upholsterers, revealing badly worn parquet. The smell of paint and hartshorn lingered noxiously in the air. "There's nothing to be done about the worst of the damage, not with such short notice. But we can have the place habitable for him."

Janet looked skeptical. "Seems a strange thing, for a child not to know his own home."

Of course young gentlemen were sent off to schools, nothing out of the ordinary there. It was no different from young boys from regular families being sent off as apprentices, or girls sent off to work as servants. For that matter, it was a hell of a lot better than being sent out to pick pockets, with the clear understanding that one must not return home without something to show for the day's work.

But all those apprentices and servants knew they had a place where they belonged, people who claimed them as their own. Simon Browne, bounced between the homes of his schoolmate and his aunt and reduced to writing a pathetic letter to the stranger who was his father, might not even have that.

Georgie climbed down from the ladder. A patch of plaster landed at his feet. He sighed and kicked it away before carrying the ladder to the next window.

In Falmouth, Georgie had spent more money than he had over the course of his entire life. He had acquired everything from beeswax candles to the servants who would light them. He ransacked his memory for every convenience and ornament a gentleman's house ought to have.

Georgie was determined that the poor child—which was how he persisted in thinking of this heir to an earldom—feel like he was welcome and wanted.

Extending a warm welcome to a young lordling ought to be the last thing in the world Georgie gave a damn about, but the necessity of making things right for this child was also the only thing Georgie knew to be an immutable truth, so he clung to it with both hands.

He needed things to be right for young Simon Browne. More than that, he needed Lawrence to get it right.

CHAPTER FOURTEEN

Returning from his walk, Lawrence found Georgie in the study, tacking bolts of cloth to the walls.

"What the—"

"This felt will muffle the sound and give you some peace," Georgie called over his shoulder.

Lawrence trailed a finger over the lengths of coarse dark material that now lined his walls. It was true; he could hardly hear the commotion downstairs.

"Thank you," he said. "Thank you for thinking of it." *Thank you for knowing*, he wanted to say. He shouldn't be surprised that Georgie knew how much Lawrence valued his silence.

Georgie spared him only a glance by way of recognition. "The maids will clean this part of the house on Wednesday afternoons, during which time you may make yourself scarce or scowl silently or whatever pleases your lordship. Regardless, I will be present to ensure that none of your more lethal equipment is interfered with."

This was less tolerable, but still Lawrence grunted his assent.

"When the child comes, dinner will be served in the dining parlor at six o'clock."

No. "To hell with this—"

"It's a meal, Lawrence. Not a ritual sacrifice. Just sit there and bear it. There will be one footman present. If you play your cards right, the only people you'll have to see all day are your son and one or two servants, both of whom will be instructed not to be alarmed if you act like a perfect savage."

Lawrence shut his eyes and drew in a breath. He did not want to be forced out of his sanctuary; he did not want to sit at a long table and endure the stares of servants. He couldn't conceive of a single sane thing he could say to Simon, and the very idea of seeing the child he had last held as an infant threatened to short circuit his brain. "And you," he said.

"Pardon?"

"I will also see you."

Georgie looked startled, which was to say that his usual mask of cool composure slipped for the merest instant. "I thought you didn't mind me. Not two hours ago it was 'I need you, Georgie,' unless you only said those things to be gallant?"

Lawrence was so astonished by this image of himself being gallant that he let out a crack of laughter. And then he saw the answering smile on Georgie's face, lighting it up like a candle.

"You caught me out," he said, trying for a light tone, "telling falsehoods to flatter everyone around me."

Something shifted in Georgie's expression. "No, I daresay falsehood and flattery are not *your* abiding sins." He returned his attention to the felt.

There was an emphasis on the *your* that made Lawrence want to say that it was all right, that Georgie's secrets didn't matter, whatever they were. But he still didn't know the exact nature of the man's secrets, and he was afraid that by asking he would ruin everything between them, so he said nothing. Instead he came up behind Georgie, resting a hand on his shoulder.

"I'm glad you're doing the right thing," Georgie said, putting his hand over Lawrence's. "That's all." Suddenly, he pivoted, and his arms were around Lawrence's neck, his lips against Lawrence's cheek. Lawrence was too startled to do anything but put a steadying hand to Georgie's hip.

"What was that for?" Lawrence asked, his mouth almost touching the secretary's ear.

"A kiss for luck."

"Only for luck?" Lawrence asked, bringing his other hand to Georgie's face. The man looked weary. He had dark smudges under his eyes. Lawrence bent his head to kiss one, then the other. As Georgie's eyes fluttered closed, a puff of air escaped his lips. "You're done for the day. Go to bed. That's an order."

"I can't," Georgie protested, sinking against Lawrence's chest. "My bed is covered in bolts and bolts of fabric. It was the only place I could think where they wouldn't get dusty. And none of the other bedchambers are clean yet." He glanced up at Lawrence in a way that seemed to ask a question.

"I have a perfectly good bed. Right over there, in fact." He gestured with his chin towards his bedchamber while tugging Georgie closer with both hands. "Big, too." It was large enough for them to sleep without even touching, if that was what Georgie had in mind. But even now Georgie was unbuttoning Lawrence's coat, so it looked like that was not what he wanted after all. Lawrence took hold of Georgie's hands, pulling them away from his coat.

"You don't want to…" Georgie's voice trailed off in some confusion as Lawrence spun him so he was leaning against a wall.

"Oh, I want to, all right." He went to his knees, watching Georgie's eyes darken.

Lawrence kissed the length of him through his breeches. Ever since he had felt Georgie's mouth on him the other night, his filthier imaginings had been focused on the need to bring Georgie pleasure, to watch and feel him come unraveled under Lawrence's hands and mouth.

"By all means, then," Georgie said, sounding a trifle hoarse. "I certainly shan't stop you."

Georgie watched Lawrence flick open his trouser buttons with more deftness than he might have expected from someone with such large hands. But he had seen those thick, calloused fingers build batteries and telegraphs and other things he hadn't even known existed a month ago, and now they were working with the same deliberate precision on Georgie's trousers. Lawrence's gaze was similarly focused, as if Georgie's cock were as worthy of study as a stack of electrodes or a tangle of wires. The intensity of his expression was something Georgie could almost feel on his flesh.

The last button was undone, and Lawrence raised his eyes to Georgie's face, as if asking permission.

"Please," Georgie whispered, hearing a neediness in his voice that he wished weren't there. But that ship had sailed around the time Lawrence had fished him out of a muddy ditch, if not even earlier.

Lawrence's hands went to Georgie's hips, tugging the trousers down a few inches, just enough for his cock to spring free. He was already hard, had been almost from the minute Lawrence had knelt. And now Lawrence's hands were on the bare flesh of Georgie's hips, his fingers splayed, his thumbs resting on the crease where belly met leg. He was staring at Georgie's cock as if it were a puzzle that needed solving. Georgie could feel the heat of Lawrence's breath on his sensitive flesh.

Lawrence licked his lips, and Georgie let out a choked noise.

"Never done this before," Lawrence muttered.

"I'm sure you'll muddle through, somehow," Georgie managed. "Cocksucking, you know—it's right there in the name." He knew he was babbling, but he was desperate and didn't care.

Then, finally, finally, Lawrence leaned forward and kissed the head of Georgie's prick. Just a soft kiss, but lingering. Georgie hissed when he felt the tentative touch of a tongue. He spread his palms on the wall behind him, wishing there were something to grab, but needing to stop himself from taking hold of Lawrence's hair and pushing into his mouth.

Lawrence traced a line of open-mouthed kisses down to the base of Georgie's cock, each kiss soft and wet and maddening. Then he slid his hands back, so they were cupping Georgie's arse, and kissed the places where his hands had been—the bones of his hips and all the ridges and furrows around them. Georgie had never thought of those places as being in the least sensitive, but the feel of Lawrence's lips, the tip of his tongue, the scratch of his beard, all combined to make him feel like he was being turned inside out.

And that was all before Lawrence paid any serious attention to his prick. The instant Lawrence's mouth closed over that aching tip, Georgie swore. He felt Lawrence give an experimental pull, a gentle suck, one hand wrapped around the base of Georgie's cock and the other clamped firmly to his arse.

Georgie groaned. "More. Please. Take more of it." And Lawrence did, tentatively at first, then sucking him nearly all the way down. Lost to all reason, Georgie threaded his fingers in Lawrence's hair, gave a little tug, a little push. And Lawrence, far from being put off by this small aggression, actually moaned, a contented hum, around Georgie's cock.

Georgie couldn't take his eyes off Lawrence as those soft lips encircled his cock, moving up and down in a rhythm they were both figuring out as they went. But when Lawrence cast his gaze up at Georgie, his misty blue eyes dark with lust, Georgie couldn't take it anymore.

"Stop. Please."

Lawrence stopped. Of course he did. Georgie knew at that moment that he could have asked Lawrence for a thousand pounds or a specially commissioned incendiary device or permission to host a gathering of circus performers at Penkellis, and Lawrence would agree. Georgie was not the only one who was utterly lost.

"I want you in my mouth," Georgie said, tugging Lawrence to his feet and steering him backwards to the sofa. "I need to taste you." When the backs of Lawrence's legs hit the seat, he collapsed, sprawled out on the sofa, legs spread. Georgie dropped to his knees, unfastened his lover's breeches, and had the head of Lawrence's cock at the back of his throat in a heartbeat.

Christ, how long had he wanted this? Since Lawrence had pressed him up against the wall that first day, probably. Maybe longer, somehow. Maybe Georgie had always wanted to kneel before a man he adored with every mote of his being, maybe he had always wanted to love a man with his mouth and his tongue and all the rest of him, and he had just never admitted it to himself.

Calloused fingertips caressed his ear; a rough baritone murmured absolute nonsense. Georgie took his own straining prick in his hand and gave it a few tugs. Lawrence must have seen, because he growled, "Yes, do that. Do it for me."

Georgie nearly whimpered. He stroked himself, he sucked Lawrence, and any composure or reserve he had ever possessed was quite gone. He was lost; he was as helpless as a ship tossed by the waves. When he felt Lawrence's cock harden by another impossible degree, when he heard something that sounded like a garbled, obscenity-laced warning, that pushed him over the edge too, and he was spilling his desire into his hand at the same time Lawrence came in his mouth.

He kept up his sucking and stroking until he felt strong hands on his arms, pulling him up, so that he was sitting on Lawrence's lap, being kissed fervently. Reverently, even.

Georgie knew then that he would go back to London, or wherever the next part of his life took him, and this man, this thing that was growing between them, would be the standard by which he'd judge the rest of his days. And it would all come up short, because this was the best and happiest and safest a man like him could ever possibly feel. And if he were half as clever as he thought he was, he'd run like hell.

He didn't, though. Instead he kissed Lawrence back, searching kisses that weren't about pleasure so much as contact. They were sweet and slow, the sort of kisses that weren't supposed to be for men like Georgie, men who were crooked and wrong to the very core.

And then Lawrence took him to bed and peeled off his clothes with a care that brought tears to Georgie's eyes, and held him until he fell asleep.

CHAPTER FIFTEEN

The carriage arrived without any warning while Georgie was fussing over the arrangement of knickknacks on the chimneypiece and Janet was still sweeping out the great hall. At the sound of wheels on the freshly graveled drive, they exchanged a wide-eyed look.

"Run to get his lordship," Georgie told Janet. "You"—he gestured to one of the new footmen—"go outside and hand the boy down from his carriage and attend to his luggage." He fished coins out of his pocket and handed them to the footman. "And pay the driver."

Georgie heard voices coming from outside, but Lawrence had still not come down. Finally there came the sound of footsteps from the direction of the tower, too light and fast to belong to the earl.

Janet entered the hall, breathless and flustered. "He sent me away," she panted.

"He's not coming?" Georgie asked, more to himself than to Janet. Bewildered, he looked searchingly around the hall, as if he could lay his eyes on something that would make this scenario better. "You told him the carriage arrived?"

Janet squeezed his arm. "Never you mind him. We'll get the little lad set up with some tea and cakes, and his lordship will come around."

Or he won't, Georgie thought. Or he'll hide in that tower for the next fortnight. God knew he was capable of it, damn him.

"Quite right," Georgie said, more for Janet's benefit than because it was true.

The door swung open without so much as a squeak, since Georgie had the workers rehang it and oil the hinges. As if all the well-oiled hinges in Cornwall could make up for an absent father. John the footman entered, holding the door open for an impossibly small child. He was eight years old, Georgie knew, but he was so thin and little he could have been much younger. Perhaps young gentlemen at pricey schools didn't have a much better time of it than the apprentices and pickpockets he had been comparing them to the other day.

Simon was pale, a washed-out, porridgey shade that spoke of illness or exhaustion or both. His hair was a colorless hue that reminded Georgie of nothing so much as used bathwater. This unprepossessing specimen was Radnor's heir, the person for whom Georgie had spent the last ten days working his fingers to the bone. This scrap of a child was listed on the pages of Debrett's as "Simon Browne, Viscount Sheffield." For all his confused parentage, he had a courtesy title that was rightly his, and Georgie had instructed the servants to call the child Lord Sheffield, as was his due.

Georgie had envisioned a strapping, hearty lordling. The sort of fellow who would, in a couple of years, pinch housemaids in stairwells and carouse drunkenly in London. It was a type he knew all too well.

As Georgie watched the boy shift awkwardly from foot to foot, he felt a rush of affection sweep over him.

"Lord Sheffield," he said, the title sounding preposterously overblown for such a wisp of a boy. "I'm George Turner, your father's secretary. Would you like some cakes?" Georgie had planned to have a footman serve the child and his father tea in the parlor, but he couldn't very well put the boy into the parlor by his lonesome; besides, Simon looked like he would vanish into the vastness of that grand room.

The child nodded, glancing timidly up at Georgie. "I like cakes," he said in a thin, overbred accent.

"Of course you do. Janet—this is Janet, the head housemaid, and she's been looking forward to your coming—will you run ahead and tell Mrs. Ferris that we'll join her in the kitchens for some of her special cakes?" Janet, bless her, had the presence of mind to smile reassuringly at the lad before leaving. "And this is John, whose job is specially to look after you," Georgie said with a pointed look at the nearest footman, who he hoped would understand that he had just been assigned a new duty. "Please bring Lord Sheffield's valise up to the bedchamber across from mine, and make a bed for yourself in the adjoining room." There was no way this child was going to be consigned to the lordly suite of rooms Georgie had readied. He might still have nightmares. God knew he looked like he did.

Georgie kept up a stream of meaningless chatter as they made their way to the back of the house. He asked about the long journey from school and received single syllables in answer. Good God, how would this child and his father manage a conversation, if neither of them were inclined to actually speak? Georgie would send a note over to the vicar, begging for his company at dinner. Georgie too would take his dinner in the dining parlor, even though he supposed it wasn't quite the thing for secretaries to dine with the family. Anything would be better than a painfully silent dinner; if nothing else, he and Halliday could blather to one another.

What if Lawrence didn't even come down for dinner? Georgie refused to consider the possibility. He had specifically told Lawrence that dinner was at six, and even Lawrence couldn't imagine that it would be acceptable to miss the child's first dinner at Penkellis. Not that Lawrence had ever given a damn about acceptability. But surely he had to understand the importance to Simon. To Georgie.

No, he would not let his thoughts head down that path. He would not try to divine Radnor's feelings towards him, not when his own feelings towards Radnor were disastrous enough.

"Oh, I smell the cakes," Georgie said unnecessarily as they approached the kitchens. "Mrs. Ferris has been baking for days." And so she had. Equipped with two new maids, she had been every bit as busy as Georgie.

The cook spun around when she heard footsteps in the doorway.

"Oh my stars, you're the spit of your mother." She clapped a floury hand to her cheek. "She was a little bird. And to think, you're only a few years younger than my Jamie, and him twice your size."

Georgie winced. This was not the line of conversation to pursue with a smallish young man. He knew this, having been a painfully skinny child himself. "Perhaps Lord Sheffield would like some cakes?" he suggested.

The child nodded. "My aunt and cousins call me Simon," he said, hardly audible. "And Uncle Courtenay calls me Simon in his letters. At school they call me Sheffield, but I…" His voice trailed off, and a flash of something like pain crossed his face.

"Well then, Simon, let's sit here and eat these cakes, and then we can explore."

At that last word, the child perked up for the first time since his arrival. Georgie had nearly said "get you settled," but then remembered that even the quietest eight-year-old would dread the prospect of being settled. Besides, Penkellis was good for nothing if not exploration. There were corners that Georgie hadn't even seen yet.

"We're near the sea," the child said.

"It's less than a mile," Mrs. Ferris interjected, setting plates of cakes and hot cups of tea before them.

"I like the sea."

"Then we'll walk over to the cliffs today," Georgie said. "And if you like tall ships, we can take the carriage to Falmouth tomorrow."

Simon's mouth curved into the beginnings of a thin smile. "Before Mama died, we lived with Uncle Courtenay in a villa in Italy. We could see the sea from Mama's bedchamber window." He seemed to be watching Georgie carefully, waiting for a reaction.

Of course. The child was accustomed to the mention of his dead mother provoking scandal and censure. Georgie was no stranger to having parents whose names could only be mentioned in embarrassed whispers, even years after their death. But Simon's mother had achieved notoriety on a grand scale by leaving her husband's home to run off with some kind of artist or poet. The "Uncle Courtenay" Simon mentioned was his mother's brother, a figure so depraved there had once been a ballad written about his exploits.

"Eat the cakes before they get cold," Mrs. Ferris admonished. "You could both do with fattening up."

The cakes were flat, like oatcakes, doused in butter and studded with raisins. There was also a slab of cheese, which Georgie had long since discovered that Mrs. Ferris considered a crucial component of every meal. When she brought over a dish teeming with biscuits, Georgie nearly asked her to desist, but then he noticed that Simon's plate was empty. He had eaten his cheese and cakes and was cheerfully tucking in to the biscuits. The boy was plainly ravenous. What in God's name was going on at that school if the child was half-starved?

"Eat up, lad," Mrs. Ferris said, returning to the long kitchen table where Georgie and Simon sat at one end. "There'll be more where that came from at supper."

When Simon finally finished, they bundled into their topcoats and headed for the sea. Georgie cast a look over his shoulder towards Lawrence's tower, but the curtains were drawn.

The door flew open, slamming into the wall behind it with a bang that shattered Lawrence's nerves.

"You are not dead, I see." Georgie glared at Lawrence. "Or indisposed. I hardly know whether to be relieved or disappointed."

Lawrence nearly said that Georgie looked neither relieved nor disappointed, but furious. Instead he raised an eyebrow and returned to his book.

"In the event that you wondered, your child arrived alive and well. No," he said, as if struck by an insight, "*well* would be an exaggeration. He's half-starved. Do they not feed children at these schools?"

Lawrence doubted that Harrow starved its students, and recalled Percy returning home for holidays as stout as ever. "I hardly know. I didn't go to school. My father didn't see any purpose in educating a mad second son."

That seemed to take some of the wind out of Georgie's sails, because his expression softened for a moment. "Is that so? The more I hear about your father, the sorrier I am that he's dead, because I'd dearly like to kill him myself." And from the hard gleam in Georgie's eyes, Lawrence didn't doubt that he meant it.

Thinking to steer this conversation away from his failure to attend Simon's arrival, and also because he liked seeing Georgie rise to his defense, Lawrence said, "He was afraid that my madness would embarrass the family."

"As far as I can tell, your father and brother did a damned fine job of embarrassing the family without your help, but you're keeping up the Browne tradition of appalling behavior with today's performance."

So much for trying to change the topic. "About that—"

"I had a place set for you at dinner. Did you even wonder who would dine with Simon if you weren't there?"

Of course he had not. He had other things to worry about besides dinner arrangements. "Judging by your attire, I'd say you had dinner with the child, which seems only right, seeing as how you were the one who insisted on his coming here." Lawrence would have liked to linger over the sight of Georgie in narrowly tailored evening clothes. "I've decided not to see him."

"I gathered as much." Georgie shook his head, his lips pressed into a tight line. "It's a cruel plan."

"What would be cruel would be for him to meet me and form an attachment."

"Rubbish."

"I'm not right in the head—"

"Oh, I see we're having this conversation again."

"I'm not, Georgie. I know it. You know it too. I don't want Simon"—he stuttered a bit over the name—"to come to know me, only to watch me get worse."

"Why do you think you're going to get worse?" Georgie perched on the arm of the sofa, and Lawrence tipped his head against the back of the seat to better see him. "Has something happened?"

Only that he was petrified by the idea of leaving his study, or meeting new people, or being assaulted by too much noise, or really doing anything that took him out of the cocoon he had created for himself. But Georgie was already all too aware of those deficits, and remained unconvinced. "My father got worse and worse until he killed himself. Percy…" He snorted. "He started out bad enough, and I hardly need to tell you how things were at the end."

"And you have nothing to do with either of them. I'm bored of this conversation." He languidly extended a hand to examine his fingernails, such a transparent attempt to feign indifference that Lawrence nearly smiled. Only the slight furrow between his eyebrows betrayed that this was a topic that he even cared about in the slightest. Lawrence wanted to pull him close and kiss that wrinkle. "We've had it at least twice before. You aren't mad, and even if you were it wouldn't be in the same way as your abominable brother and father. You aren't living their lives, and you don't need to atone for their sins."

"That's not what's happening here," Lawrence protested. "I know that I have nothing to atone for." As he spoke, he knew it to be the truth. Whatever the state of his mind, he wasn't like his brother or father. This knowledge had been creeping up on him for weeks, and now he had no choice but to confront the possibility that he would not wind up like either of them. He might have an entire life stretching before him, and he didn't know what to do with it.

Georgie regarded him with a shrewdness that made Lawrence feel that his thoughts were as visible as a specimen in a glass jar. "I wonder what will happen when you realize you aren't mad. So much of your life hangs from that one supposition. It's like the story you were telling me about that Italian fellow who thought electricity was inside the dead frog—a lot of his science was rubbish because of that one error. What will you do with yourself when you grasp that your mind is only different, not deranged?"

This so closely mirrored Lawrence's own realization that he was momentarily startled. So instead he tried to turn the tables. "You won't be here to find out what happens then, will you? You'll have finished your business at Penkellis and moved on."

Georgie opened his mouth, and for a moment Lawrence thought he would confide in him. Instead he slid off the arm of the sofa and swung a leg over Lawrence's lap, straddling him and looking him levelly in the eye. "I will always be glad to have known you, Lawrence." He brought a hand to Lawrence's jaw and stroked his beard. "I want you to remember that. When I'm not here, I want you to know that wherever I am, however we part, I'll be better for having…" He hesitated, then touched his own heart before bringing his hand to rest on Lawrence's chest. "For having had you as a friend," he said.

Lawrence took hold of Georgie's hand and trapped it on his chest, partly so Georgie could feel the way his heart pounded, partly because he hadn't the faintest idea how else to respond. All he knew was that he needed to hold Georgie close and keep him safe and spend the rest of eternity enumerating his every quality. He realized with disorienting certainty that this was love. Judging by the bleak tenderness in Georgie's dark eyes, he knew it too. But what they had felt so fragile and out of place, built of blown glass on unstable ground in the middle of a hurricane. Beautiful, but never meant to last.

All Lawrence could think to say was, "Stay, then. Don't leave."

Georgie wriggled his hand free and took hold of Lawrence's shoulders. "I don't stay," he said slowly. "It's the nature of my line of work."

Confess, he wanted to say. *Tell me the truth. Tell me why you're here, so I can know that I love you despite it, and you can know it too.* Instead he raised an eyebrow and said, "Being a secretary, you mean."

Georgie returned the raised eyebrow. "Being a secretary," he said firmly, but Lawrence thought he saw a flicker of surprised amusement in the other man's eyes. This wasn't quite honesty, but more like leaving the door open to the truth. The truth was something they could both see out of the corners of their eyes, lurking in the shadows of an adjacent room. If they didn't look right at it, they could pretend it wasn't there.

"Anyway," Georgie went on, "I meet a good many people, but I try not to get close to them. Not to care about them."

"I see," Lawrence said solemnly. "It's probably best for secretaries not to get too close to their clients."

Now Georgie laughed. "Yes, damn you. My point is that…" He broke off and leaned forward to brush a kiss onto Lawrence's lips, and when he spoke again his expression was serious. "It's no way to live. I find myself…" His eyes grew bright, and he blinked quickly, as if trying to hold back tears. "I find myself quite alone, and without any prospect of that changing. I wish I had gone about things a bit differently, but there's no use wringing my hands about that now. But you can do better. Meet your son. Know him. Let him know you. Let him love you, Lawrence. I know it's hard. But I know it's the right thing."

"And why should I trust that you know what is right?"

"Touché. Perhaps because I've found it out by the process of elimination?" Another kiss. Every time they got closer to acknowledging the shadowy truth, Lawrence felt the delicate, fragile thing between them grow stronger, the ground beneath it less shaky. "But truly, Lawrence, I've tried living the other way. So have you, for that matter. It's no good to be alone. Don't let Simon be alone."

Lawrence wished he could be so sure.

CHAPTER SIXTEEN

"That one looks good, I think?" Georgie asked hopefully.

Simon threw him a pitying look. "Not nearly big enough."

Georgie had no idea how they were supposed to get the mistletoe down from the tree, and even less what they were meant to do with it once they got it back to the house. But Mrs. Ferris and Simon both insisted that vast quantities of greenery were instrumental to any proper Christmastide, and Georgie was hardly in any position to argue. His own understanding of Christmas was that it was a particularly good time to pick pockets, so many people having an extra shilling or even a new watch. But he could hardly suggest larceny as an alternative to boughs of holly.

He and the child had bundled into their coats and scarves, equipped themselves with kitchen shears and an alarming-looking handsaw, and prepared to divest the Penkellis woods of all manner of ivy, holly, and mistletoe, maybe even a few fir boughs. Basically, if it was green at this time of year, it was fair game for plunder.

They had lingered in the hall for a while after midday, waiting to see if Lawrence would come down. Even now, Georgie cast a glance over his shoulder to see if he could discern a figure heading towards them.

"He isn't coming," Simon said, resting a tentative, mittened hand on Georgie's arm. "It's all right."

It wasn't all right, not even close. Last night, sitting close together, hands intertwined, he thought he had gotten through to Lawrence. But obviously he hadn't. He wondered if Lawrence even wanted anyone in his life at all. Maybe he really was happier alone in his tower, seeing no one, caring about no one.

"No worries," Simon continued, a sympathetic note in his voice, as if Georgie were the one whose feelings needed soothing. "I don't even remember him."

Georgie desperately tried to blink away tears. Crying in front of the child would only make things that much worse for both of them. "That isn't the point."

Simon regarded him, his nose red with cold. "Uncle Kemble says Lord Radnor isn't my real father anyway. So it's only natural that he can't be bothered."

"Uncle Kemble can sod right off, then," Georgie said promptly, before recalling that this language was not suitable for an eight-year-old's ears. "Damn!" No, that was no improvement. Simon's eyes were wide. "I'm sorry. But your uncle is a thoroughgoing bastard if he says that sort of thing to you."

Simon gave him an appraising look. "He's not my favorite."

"And your aunt?"

"She is…better."

"A ringing endorsement."

"Ha. They don't like me much, and they aren't as jolly as Uncle Courtenay, but they aren't bad, not really." Something about the child's tone suggested that he knew what kind of behavior might constitute "really bad." Georgie didn't like that one bit. But they were supposed to be having a festive afternoon, gathering holly and ivy and whatever the hell else country people needed for Christmas, and he didn't want to spoil it by asking too many unpleasant questions.

"If I lift you, do you think you can climb the tree and get that big clump of mistletoe?"

Of course the child agreed. That was something all eight-year-old boys must have in common, city or country, rich or poor. Simon weighed next to nothing, and Georgie was able to hoist him overhead onto a sturdy-looking branch. A few minutes later, Georgie noticed snowflakes landing on the sprigs of mistletoe scattered at his feet.

"We ought to go back to the house before it starts falling in earnest," he suggested.

Even from several feet below, Georgie could see Simon's disdainful expression. "It's snow, not artillery fire," the child said. "The ground isn't nearly cold enough for it to stick, at least for the next few hours."

"And we'll have frozen to death by then, so the snow will be of no import to us."

Simon landed neatly at the base of the tree. He would have been a worthy addition to any crew of housebreakers, if he hadn't been the heir to an earldom. "I like snow." He said it with the emphasis on the last word, as he had said "I like *cakes*" and "I like the *sea*" the day before. As if he were reminding himself of the things he liked, that there *were* things he liked, in the face of an otherwise unpleasant world.

No, Georgie was reading too much into the boy's statement. Simon liked snow because he was a child and children liked snow. "It's pretty, I suppose," he said, watching fat snow-flakes settle on the fir branch he carried. "Picturesque." And so it was, in an aggressively charming way.

If a gently born young lady were to sketch the scene, she would entitle it "Christmas in the Country" or something equally pleasant. The drawing would show a man and a boy making merry, and nobody who saw it would guess that Georgie was a crook, or Simon the misbegotten child of a count-ess and God knew who. Nobody would know that the child's putative father refused to leave his tower, that the house was a rotten shambles, and that the child was sad and unwell.

Georgie decided that he didn't need to think of those unsavory elements either. "It's beautiful," he said, tugging Simon's wool cap down low over his ears. "I'll race you back to the house."

As a rule, Lawrence didn't drink. He didn't like the taste of anything stronger than cider, and he had all too clear a recol-lection of his father's drunken rages to feel that intoxication was ever a good idea. But he had a notion that there was a bottle of brandy somewhere in this tower, and he meant to find it. This was a day that called for strictly medicinal doses of whatever spirits he could lay his hands on. He was either going to go downstairs and meet Simon, or he would stay here and incur Georgie's wrath. And he didn't think he was equal to meeting either of those fates entirely sober.

The brandy couldn't be in the study. Georgie had turned that room inside out, and if he had found a bottle of brandy he would have placed it on a shelf that bore a neatly lettered label reading "brandy," right in between the borax and the charcoal. In his bedchamber, he flung open the doors to his clothes press, but instead of brandy, he found neatly folded linens and unfamiliar clothing. He nearly took a startled step backwards.

This must be the clothing Georgie had purchased in Falmouth. Lawrence had worried that Georgie might have let his imagination run wild at the tailor, and that he would expect Lawrence to wear brightly colored waistcoats and fancifully arranged cravats. But what Lawrence saw before him was nothing if not sedate: a pair of coats in bottle green and brown, a few pairs of buff-colored breeches, two waistcoats, and an array of snowy white shirts and cravats.

It was all entirely unobjectionable. Lawrence couldn't help but smile when he imagined how bored Georgie must have found the task, choosing such drab attire among a haberdashery's worth of brighter and richer fabrics. He must have rejected bolt after bolt of silk and wool before settling on the least interesting of the lot.

But no. That's not what he had done. Lawrence looked more carefully at the contents of his clothes press. These waistcoats were similar in cut and color to the ones he already had. Georgie had tried to pick clothes that would feel familiar to Lawrence. That was just the sort of thing that he would think of, just as he had lined the walls of the study with that felt. He seemed to understand what Lawrence needed to get through each day, without Lawrence needing to specifically ask for it.

At some point, Georgie had become indispensable, not only to Lawrence's work but to his life—his heart, damn it. It wasn't only that Lawrence liked the way he looked and smelled and sounded. It wasn't only that he made Lawrence smile and want and feel in ways he hadn't ever thought possible. Those qualities were all well enough, but what stole Lawrence's heart was that Georgie grasped how his mind worked, when sometimes Lawrence didn't even know it himself.

He spread one of the waistcoats out on the bed, as if by studying it he might understand his attachment to the person who had chosen it. Frowning, he ran his finger along the line of ivory buttons. At some point, Lawrence had become used to loose strings, missing buttons, stains and holes and other signs of wear. This garment, fresh and unspoiled, seemed like it ought to belong to somebody else. Somebody who appreciated nice things. Somebody who cared about presenting a decent appearance to the world.

That was the point, after all. Today that somebody had to be Lawrence. He needed to care how he looked. Georgie had insisted that Simon would be troubled by seeing his father poorly attired. Lawrence had always thought it fitting that his outward dishevelment matched his inner disquietude. But today he needed the opposite to be true. He needed the outward appearance of neatness to create the illusion of inner stability.

He pulled out the green coat. Pinned to the lining was a note written in Georgie's perfectly slanted hand.

While not strictly correct, this attire will do for the country. As I don't foresee a trip to Almack's or a presentation at court in the near future, we can content ourselves thusly. In the bottom drawers you'll find boots, braces, and so forth. I placed a razor and a cake of shaving soap on the washstand. If you find yourself in need of a sustaining draught, I put a bottle of brandy in the top drawer of your writing table.

There was no signature. There was no affectionate closing. And there never would be—Georgie was too careful to risk his neck or Lawrence's in such a way. But the paper carried a trace of Georgie's absurd London perfume, and that was as good as any written declaration. Lawrence held the paper up to his nose and breathed in the scent.

Georgie and Simon arrived in the kitchens cold and disheveled and out of breath. Mrs. Ferris clucked and tsked as she carried over ginger biscuits and buttered muffins, which they ate at the long kitchen table. Janet sat down with them, nicking bits of muffin from Georgie's plate. This was likely grossly improper, for the heir to be eating in the kitchens with a pair of servants, but Georgie figured that if Lawrence couldn't be bothered to trouble himself with proprieties, then neither could Georgie. Besides, Simon seemed content by the wide kitchen hearth, amidst the clatter of pots and chatter of kitchen maids.

They drank their tea and slowly warmed up, listening to Janet tell Mrs. Ferris about shadowy goings-on at a cousin's house. From the bits of conversation that Georgie picked up, this cousin was decidedly up to no good.

"My mum says Davy had to spend half the night under a hawthorn bush," Janet said with a gurgle of laughter. "He came home half-blue."

Mrs. Ferris turned from the pot she was stirring, spoon still in hand. "Serves him right, capering about under a full moon." Then the two women glanced at Georgie and Simon before falling silent.

Smuggling, most likely. Before coming to Penkellis, Georgie's only knowledge of Cornwall had been that it was packed with smugglers. But he hadn't seen or heard anything, so he hadn't thought overmuch about it. As far as he knew, every new moon brought crates of tea and a fortune's worth of French brandy, but if it didn't affect Lawrence then it didn't matter to Georgie. Far be it from Georgie to begrudge a man his living.

Georgie supposed that if he had been born here, he might have been a smuggler too. Would he have been one of the men out in the fishing boats, bringing cargo ashore on moonless nights? Or would he have been one of those who ran the smuggled goods inland, from cove to barn to—

"Mrs. Ferris," he said suddenly, "is this Cousin Davy in fact David Prouse?" Oh, what a fool he had been. He had been so busy thinking of these people as superstitious peasants that he hadn't given them any credit for proper criminality.

"Yes," she said carefully. "Davy Prouse is my cousin, and Janet's too."

"He's the man the vicar overheard saying that Lord Radnor stole one of his sheep. Really, I must have maggots in my brain not to have put this together weeks ago. The cart driver I saw you arguing with—was that your cousin Davy as well?"

Of course there hadn't been any stolen sheep. The vicar had only overheard bits of conversation that weren't meant for his ears. Coded conversation, if Georgie had guessed right. Prouse was a smuggler, and he had lied about seeing Lawrence steal a sheep, and Georgie was inclined to think those facts were somehow connected.

"Simon," Georgie said, turning to the child, "John is warming his feet by the fire. Why don't you ask him to help you decorate the parlor with greenery? You can tell him I said he'll have the rest of the afternoon to himself afterwards. I'll be there in half an hour, and you can surprise me with how festive the room is." Simon pocketed some biscuits and a lump of sugar, then went on his way, Barnabus following along.

"Ladies." Georgie pitched his voice low enough that it wouldn't be overheard by any of the other servants. "If I were, right this minute, to pay a visit to the old stables, would I find anything of interest?"

Mrs. Ferris didn't turn around, but Georgie noticed that she stopped stirring the pot for an instant. Janet was the one who spoke. "'Course not. Only rats."

"I see," Georgie mused, "you would have taken care to have everything moved once you knew I was going to bring in servants from Falmouth." He remembered Lawrence's complaints about midnight noises coming from outside. Georgie hadn't taken him seriously, thinking the man just needed to grouse. But Georgie himself had heard horses and carts a few times; he hadn't thought much about it because Penkellis was such an eerie house that no strange noise or occurrence ever seemed out of place.

"Don't know what you're going on about," Mrs. Ferris said, her back still turned to Georgie.

Georgie pushed his chair away from the table and got to his feet. "I'll take myself off then. Fine day for a walk, all this lovely snow. Maybe I'll run into an excise officer and have a chat about why your cousin never pressed charges about his missing sheep." He made as if to reach for his coat.

"No, wait!" It was Janet, of course. Mrs. Ferris would have called his bluff, and rightly so. The last thing on earth that Georgie wanted was for Lawrence to come under scrutiny.

"Hold your tongue," Mrs. Ferris said to the other woman.

"There's nothing happening that would cause any trouble to his lordship," Janet said, laying a hand on Georgie's arm and looking up at him pleadingly. "We've taken such care to make sure that nobody comes near the stables."

Georgie could have slapped himself. So, that was why the servants had quit—Mrs. Ferris and Janet had done whatever was necessary to keep prying eyes away from Penkellis. They must have spread tales of Lawrence's evil doings. "I think there would be trouble indeed if it were known that the Earl of Radnor was turning a blind eye to smugglers using his property to store run goods," Georgie hissed. "Nobody would believe he didn't know."

"They would if they knew him," Janet protested. "It's not as if he has a hand in running the estate."

"If his eccentricities were to become common knowledge, you mean?" Georgie stepped into the larder and beckoned for the women to follow. Once the door was shut, Georgie went on. "That's hardly any better than having him known as a smuggler. The two of you have done your damnedest to have him branded a devil-worshiping madman throughout the neighborhood, presumably because you want to frighten people away from poking around Penkellis. You can't mean to have this nonsense said aloud in court."

"Who said anything about court?" Mrs. Ferris countered, hands on hips.

"That's what it would come to, if his name were to be tangled up in this business. Do you have any idea what would happen if word got out? Simon's relations would have the earl declared incompetent, and as the heir's guardians, they would have the running of this house and everyone in it. So if you want to keep your smuggler friends safe, you might want to think twice about making people wonder whether the earl has his wits about him."

"Now, now." The cook was looking up at him with concern. "Take a deep breath, Mr. Turner."

"Take a deep breath?" Georgie repeated, incredulous. "This is not a problem that will be solved with breathing, no matter how deep." His hands were clenched into fists at his sides, his nails biting into the flesh of his palms. "Can you even imagine how his lordship would take being summoned to testify in court?" A strange place, strange people, noisy and crowded and new. "What the devil have you done?" He wasn't shouting—he would never be so imprudent, even as furious as he was—but his voice was raised.

The realization struck him like a blow. He *was* furious. If he were the sort of man to punch walls or throw things, he'd have already put the larder into shambles. But Georgie never got angry. Annoyed, yes. Bored, most certainly. But anger didn't enter into it, let alone this full blown rage.

Now Janet and Mrs. Ferris were looking at him as if he were a spectacle. Janet's mouth was shaped into an O of perfect astonishment, and Mrs. Ferris's eyebrows were hitched so high they disappeared into her cap.

"What I'm trying to tell you," the cook said in patient tones, "is that none of that'll come to pass. The goods aren't on the property anymore. And they won't be, not so long as this place is crawling with outsiders."

"They won't be on his lordship's land, full stop. Tell whoever is behind this operation to avoid Penkellis in its entirety, or he will have to deal with me. And make no mistake, that will not be pleasant."

"We're in Cornwall," Mrs. Ferris was saying, as she regarded Georgie in utter bafflement. "His lordship would be surprised to learn his land *wasn't* being used by smugglers. Don't you worry your head."

"I'll worry as much as I damned well please. I neither know nor care about Cornish customs. All—and I do mean *all*—I care about is that his lordship not be troubled more than absolutely necessary."

He slid out of the larder and marched to the parlor, smoothing his lapels and straightening his cravat on his way.

He had spoken the truth. He would commit any number of outrages in order to keep Lawrence safe. All he had to do was imagine Lawrence in the dock, Lawrence in a madhouse, and he'd gladly unload a pistol into any Cornish smuggler who threatened the man he loved. Because there really was no denying it anymore, not even to himself: he loved Lawrence and was pretty damned sure Lawrence loved him in return. Not that it would do either of them any good at all.

CHAPTER SEVENTEEN

Lawrence was arrested on the threshold of the parlor, hoping another moment would give him the courage to enter the room. Georgie and a small boy—Lawrence's mind reeled at the knowledge that this was Simon, whom he had last seen as a babbling, chubby infant—were sprawled on the rug before the fire, playing a card game Lawrence didn't recognize. Barnabus was lounging between them, as if he were waiting to be dealt into the game.

"You've almost got it," Georgie was saying. "You're trying to pull the second card."

The child looked so much like his mother, pale and small, almost elfin.

Georgie shuffled the cards and held them out to Simon, who took what appeared to be the top card. He held it out, face up, to show Georgie, who let out a crack of laughter.

"A quick study. You were born to sharp cards."

Good heavens. Was Georgie teaching Simon, the future Earl of Radnor, to cheat at cards? If Lawrence had been under the impression that Georgie was an ordinary, respectable secretary, that delusion would have been quite crushed by this little tableau.

Georgie took the cards back from Simon and gave them a quick, competent shuffle. Or at the least appeared to do so; Lawrence assumed some sleight of hand was in play. He fanned them out, directed Simon's attention to one of them, and then restacked the deck.

Lawrence had known for a while that Georgie was not what he seemed. He was not a proper secretary, and therefore some manner of subterfuge had brought him to Penkellis. Lawrence ought to be disturbed, offended, afraid. He was none of those things. The strength of his affection for Turner overwhelmed any other stray notions, in the way a full moon blinded one to the surrounding stars. He knew they were there but couldn't make himself see them.

Lawrence took a tentative step forward, his new boots stiff and unfamiliar, his freshly starched cravat a strange presence under his chin.

Georgie noticed him first, shooting immediately to his feet. "Lawr—my lord," he said, giving a thoroughly correct little bow. "Allow me to present—"

"Simon," Lawrence said hoarsely. In two strides, he crossed to where Simon now stood beside Georgie. He hesitated for a moment, unsure what to do, and then impulsively took hold of Simon's hand. "Simon," he repeated, staring at the child's face, trying to find some trace of the infant he had held and comforted. "How was your journey?" he asked, because he had to say something.

"Most uneventful, sir," Simon said in a small voice.

Lawrence still held the child's hand. "You look so much like your mother." Something unpleasant flitted across Simon's face, and he looked like he wanted to tug his hand free. "I never thought to have a portrait made of her, but I wish I had, so I could show you the resemblance."

Simon swallowed. "My aunt has a portrait, but I haven't seen it."

"Whyever not?" Lawrence dropped the child's hand.

"They took it down after she ran off, sir. After"—he tilted up his chin, like a man about to take a punch—"after she disgraced herself." He said this with a matter-of-fact certainty that broke Lawrence's heart.

Lawrence drew in a long breath and felt his nostrils flare. He wanted to tell the child that his mother had committed no disgrace, that she had been faced with the choice between a pro forma marriage and utter scandal. Lawrence, while missing the child he had loved, could hardly blame Isabella for having left.

He couldn't very well say all of that to a child, though. "Your mother was a fine woman," he said. Simon's eyes went momentarily wide, and Lawrence heard Georgie's sharp intake of breath. "Perhaps you'll deal me in to whatever interesting card game you're playing here. I've always wanted to become a card sharp." He said this with a sidelong glance at Georgie, hoping to elicit a smile. But Georgie was staring at him blankly.

"Yes. Quite." Georgie nervously raked his fingers through his hair. "I apologize. I was only teaching Simon—Lord Sheffield—how to fuzz—damn it—how to recognize sleight of hand in the event he ever finds himself among unsavory people who do that sort of thing. He knows not to behave dishonorably."

Lawrence had never seen Georgie so uncomfortable. "I see," he said, striving for their customary ease. "An excellent plan, Georgie." As he watched, the other man's face turned red. What the devil? And then he realized: they were supposed to be distantly correct around Simon. They were Lord Radnor and Mr. Turner, earl and secretary. They were not on a first-name basis. They did not speak lightly about cheating at cards or marital infidelity.

To hell with that. He'd give Georgie his *Mr. Turner* if that's what he wanted, but he wasn't going to play act.

They got through a few hands of loo, which was the only game all three of them knew. Simon giggled whenever he won a trick, while Georgie sat ramrod straight, as if he were listening to a sermon rather than playing a silly game of cards. All Georgie's conversation was directed at Simon. He scarcely turned his head in Lawrence's direction. But when Lawrence was bent over his cards, he felt Georgie's eyes on him. Whenever Lawrence looked up, however, Georgie's gaze had slipped away.

The rhythm of card play distracted Lawrence from the alien strangeness of sitting in his newly transformed parlor with the child who was, in some sense, his. The room, which he had last seen at sixes and sevens while the laborers worked, was now lit by a multitude of candles that hinted at expanses of rich, soft fabric and polished wood. Lawrence found that if he kept his attention on his cards and his companions, he could avoid the sensation of being in a strange place.

They laid down their cards when one of Georgie's new footmen—Lawrence couldn't quite accept that these efficient strangers were his own servants—came in with a supper of cold meat. Georgie murmured something, and a few moments later the same servant appeared with a tray of bread and ham. Lawrence tried to catch Georgie's eye to give him a wordless expression of gratitude, but Georgie wouldn't turn his head to look at him.

Soon afterwards, Simon started to yawn and Georgie took the child up to bed.

"Come back when you're done," Lawrence murmured.

"Of course, my lord." Georgie bowed his head with infuriating deference.

The sight of the two of them going off together made Lawrence's heart jump. He had somehow, over the course of little more than a month, acquired something like a family.

But no. Simon would go back to school and the homes of his more civilized relations, and Georgie would eventually go back to London where he belonged. And Lawrence would be alone, once again. A month ago he would have looked forward to solitude, but now he felt that he was on the other side of a chasm he could not return across.

Lawrence finally allowed himself to take in his surroundings. In his memory, the room was blanketed beneath dust and cobwebs, half the windows cracked and the other half blackened with filth.

But this room looked like a picture in a book. Hell, it looked like a home.

Every sconce and candlestick held a lit candle. The enormous old hearth was filled with a roaring fire, casting a mellow glow on the room. Every available surface was draped with fir boughs and trimmed with ivy and holly. It was

Christmas Day, Lawrence realized. The scents of greenery
and wood fire, beeswax and furniture polish, filled the air.
Somehow, Georgie had found rugs and curtains that looked
like they had always been here. He made the room seem like
a place fit for happy, sane people, rather than feral cats and
wild squirrels.

As unfamiliar as the house now seemed, as strange as his
new clothes felt on his body, it all was somehow right, as if
Lawrence and Penkellis had been waiting around for Georgie
to set things right. Lawrence found himself forgetting that
there had ever been a time before Georgie came to Penkellis.

And he wondered what it would take to get him to stay.

He wondered whether asking Georgie to stay would be
the maddest thing he had ever done.

Georgie hardly knew where to look. Every time he let his
gaze stray to the man who sat beside him, he felt like he had
gotten a glimpse of a stranger. A very imposing stranger.
Clean-shaven, decently dressed and groomed, Lawrence was
every inch the earl. They were sitting on the parlor sofa, and
Georgie was at a loss for words for perhaps the first time in
his life.

"We gathered rather more greenery than was called for,"
Georgie babbled apologetically, noticing Lawrence taking in
the room. "It's a fortune's worth of beeswax candles, but I
thought we might as well do the thing right."

"I think you're a magician." Lawrence was swirling a glass
of brandy in one hand; his other arm was slung over the
back of the sofa, so near to Georgie's neck as to almost be

an embrace. Georgie could feel the heat radiating from the larger man's body.

"Not a magician." Georgie kept his back straight, his eyes fixed on the fire blazing in the hearth before them. He had the sense that if he relaxed a single muscle he'd slide not only into Lawrence's embrace but into a mess he'd never see his way out of. "Just very good at spending other people's money."

"Ha. I can stand the expense, as you know." Out of the corner of his eye, Georgie watched Lawrence bring his glass to his mouth and caught the glimmer of an unfamiliar ring, its stones the same misty blue as Lawrence's eyes. Could be blue topaz, but more likely pale sapphires or even blue diamonds. A fortune, in arm's reach. Didn't that just sum up these past weeks at Penkellis? A fortune in arm's reach, and Georgie too addlebrained to do anything about it.

"I liked your beard," Georgie blurted out. "But you look so very well without it." He reached out as if to touch Lawrence's newly smooth jawline, but then snatched his hand back.

Lawrence captured Georgie's wrist and kissed his palm, sending a rush of warmth up the length of Georgie's arm. "Is that why you're being so odd? I thought you were displeased with me."

Far from displeased. If only Lawrence knew how impressed, how proud Georgie was. "Distracted is more like it. I'm afraid that if I look at you for too long, I'll lose all semblance of decent conduct. The clothes fit, I see."

"Perfectly. How did you manage it?"

"I took some of your old clothes with me to Falmouth and gave them to the tailor to use for measurements."

"You thought of everything." Lawrence took a sip of brandy, another unfamiliar gesture that made Georgie take notice of his...lordliness, or whatever this quality was that made Georgie feel like the street urchin he had once been. "The child likes you."

"The feeling is mutual."

"I hope I'm..." Lawrence's voice trailed off.

Georgie squeezed Lawrence's hand. "You're doing wonderfully." He didn't say that Simon's life had been an exercise in lowered expectations, and that all Lawrence had to do was show up in order to secure a place in the child's inner circle of loved ones. "You were everything you needed to be. You were marvelous." And he had been—calm, engaging, patient. "What you said about his mother was exactly what Simon needed to hear."

Lawrence bumped his thigh against Georgie's. "Why don't you look pleased with yourself? You're the one who brought this about."

Georgie chanced another sidelong look. The earl's jaw seemed chiseled out of rock. Expensive rock. All that beautiful hair, unfashionably long though it was, had been combed and wrangled into a tidy queue. And that wasn't even mentioning the superfine wool coat, the perfectly polished leather boots, the immaculate linen. He looked precisely what he was: a wealthy country gentleman, a titled aristocrat, possessing every privilege to be had. "Frankly, because I only now realize that I strong-armed an earl into giving me free reign with upwards of a thousand pounds."

Lawrence was silent for a moment. "Ah. You mean now that I'm dressed the part you finally think you owe me some respect?"

Georgie shifted on the sofa. "Not exactly—"

"Bugger that. I wouldn't have thought you gave a damn for rank and privilege."

"I don't. That's the point." He searched for a way to explain without coming too near a truth that couldn't be unsaid. He wanted Lawrence to know what it meant for Georgie *not* to steal from him but didn't want to risk saying so much that Lawrence was repulsed by his character. "I ordinarily wouldn't think twice before taking every advantage of an earl." Even now, Georgie's worst angels were urging him to steal and thieve, to swindle and connive. Wasn't that what he had planned when he came here? To help himself to whatever Penkellis had for the taking? He had only altered his course when he decided that it was unsportsmanlike, unworthy of him to trick a man as unworldly as Lawrence. But looking at Lawrence now, groomed and polished, Georgie felt predatory stirrings and didn't know how to reconcile those urges with his fonder feelings. His thoughts were a tangle he couldn't unpick.

Lawrence's hand had strayed to the nape of Georgie's neck, where it drew idle circles. "Did you profit from these expenditures? As far as I can tell, you didn't buy yourself so much as a flower for your buttonhole."

"No." Not this time. But it would be so simple to slip that ring off Lawrence's finger later tonight. It would be the work of seconds, and he'd be on the stagecoach back to London before he even had any regrets.

"I wouldn't have minded if you had."

Georgie sighed. "You'd mind." Being stolen from was a blow to a man's pride, but he had never given a damn about that before.

"If someone I cared about was in need, I might wish to help."

"This isn't charity that we're talking about."

"What precisely *are* we talking about, Georgie?"

Georgie winced. "Let's not."

"Have it your way." The words might have sounded harsh if he hadn't had his fingers tangled in Georgie's hair. The intimacy of the touch, the gentleness of his voice, transformed the words into permission for Georgie to keep his secrets. "Come upstairs. I want you in my bed."

Georgie half wanted to leap to his feet and run up the stairs two at a time. But when he tipped his head against the back of the sofa and turned to face Lawrence, he saw the man in all his aristocratic splendor: the earl in full panoply. "I need you out of those clothes," he said, running his hand along Lawrence's thigh.

"That's rather the idea." Lawrence's voice was low and amused. "Unless you have something else in mind?"

Georgie licked his lips and saw an answering flare of desire in Lawrence's eyes. "No, no. I mean, of course it is. But…Lawrence, I don't want to be fucked by the Earl of Radnor."

A wrinkle appeared on Lawrence's forehead, and his hand went still. Georgie held his breath, but only the barest second passed before he felt the earl resume those slow circles on the back of his neck, heat like a brand. And then, finally, Lawrence asked, "Is that what you want me to do? Fuck you?"

The words sent a thrill of lust through Georgie's body. "Yes." It was a whisper. A plea. A confession.

"But not as the Earl of Radnor."

"As yourself." Georgie resisted the urge to smooth away the worried crease that appeared between Lawrence's brows.

"I'm not sure I know the difference."

"But I do." With Lawrence, Georgie had discovered a chance to be himself; with the resplendent Earl of Radnor, Georgie was simply a thief waiting for a chance. Or, worse, he was a thief who had lost the instinct, and without that he didn't know what he even was. "You go upstairs first." He kept his eyes fixed on Lawrence's to make sure his meaning was received. "Take off your ring and lock it up." Lawrence's eyebrows shot up, but he nodded. "Someplace safe. I'll be up in a quarter of an hour."

That was truth, of a sort, but without having to say the ugly words. Alone in the parlor, Georgie finished Lawrence's brandy and then reached for the decanter to pour himself another glass. He could already feel the warmth seeping through his body, smoothing the jagged edges of guilt and shame and need.

CHAPTER EIGHTEEN

Snowflakes fluttered past Lawrence's window, illuminated by the moon. The clock—now keeping reliable time, thanks to his secretary—had struck the quarter hour, then the half hour, but still there was no sign of Georgie.

Lawrence didn't know what had gotten into Georgie but gathered it had something to do with money. That, as far as Lawrence cared, was easily remedied. By the time he heard Georgie's light footsteps on the stairs, he was wearing his ratty old dressing gown and an ancient pair of trousers. He had, as requested, removed his signet ring. He'd have tossed it into the sea if that was what Georgie required. For that matter, he would throw the entire contents of Penkellis into the sea and it wouldn't make much difference to him. He had mines; he had money in the funds; he had land spread across this part of Britain. And for all his faults, he wasn't foolhardy enough to dispense with the services of good stewards and land agents. He had kept the Browne fortune safe for Simon and had wealth to spare.

He heard a rustling in the corridor, and he smiled when he realized that he knew what it was—Georgie's habitual smoothing of his lapels and straightening of his cravat. The next moment Georgie had pushed open the door, bolted it behind him, and promptly launched himself at Lawrence. The two of them landed helter-skelter on the sofa.

"You smell like brandy," Lawrence pointed out, as Georgie buried his face in Lawrence's neck. "Are you drunk?"

"Nothing so dire as that. Two glasses. Half-sprung at best." His eyes were as sharp as ever, but his mouth quirked up in an uncharacteristically silly grin. Perhaps it wasn't intoxication so much as his usually rigid self-control having slipped a bit. Lawrence sat up, taking Georgie with him. "There's something I wanted to show you."

Georgie made a sound of prurient interest.

"No, that's later," Lawrence said sternly. He reached over to the table beside him and brought out a soft leather pouch. Without explanation, he dumped its contents onto Georgie's lap.

For a moment the room was utterly silent except for the sound of ivy brushing against the window, and farther away an owl calling in the night.

"What nonsense is this?" Georgie finally asked, his voice strained.

"Some jewels I don't need, and which I thought you might find useful."

"Bollocks." He was holding his hands up and away from the jewels, as if they might be dangerously hot to the touch.

"This was my father's ring." Lawrence indicated a large emerald set in heavy gold. "I have no fond memories of it.

Quite the contrary, in fact. It's yours now. Sell it, if you like. Or wear it." Georgie's fine fingers were half the diameter of the late earl's meaty digits, but rings could be resized, and Lawrence might get an indecent thrill out of seeing his father's ring on his lover's finger. "It's yours to do with as you please."

"Like hell it is. This is ridiculous."

"Not as ridiculous as you telling me to lock my ring up so you don't accidentally rob me blind, or whatever flummery you were spouting downstairs."

"That's not—"

"Oh, and this vulgar number is my grandfather's watch fob." Using his index finger, he lifted a chain bearing several jeweled seals and pendants. "Grotesque. Your sensibilities are no doubt offended by its very existence. Take it and dispose of it how you will. I believe those are real diamonds, not paste."

"They're real," Georgie said promptly. Of course he would know paste from the real thing. "You're mad."

Lawrence raised an eyebrow.

"I don't mean that," Georgie quickly said. "You know I don't."

He did know. Georgie's confidence in Lawrence's sanity had changed Lawrence's own opinion of himself and was worth more than diamonds or gold. "In that case, here's a cravat pin. Diamond, of course. This," he said, holding out a necklace, "was a present from my brother to his wife. And matching ear bobs. It has no value to me, except to remind me of the lady my brother harassed to an early grave."

Georgie let out a low whistle. Hesitantly, he reached towards the jewels, sifting the strands of gold and rubies between his fingers. The gems glimmered and flashed in the candlelight even though the pieces hadn't been cleaned in years. Smaller rubies were arranged in an intricate flower pattern punctuated by larger rubies. It struck Lawrence that this must have been his late sister-in-law's choice, because Percy couldn't possibly have good enough taste to commission something so delicate.

"These belong to your family." Georgie let the necklace drop heavily onto Lawrence's lap. "They'll be Simon's. I can't."

"They aren't heirlooms. The family pieces are still in a bank vault. These are bits of frippery that mean nothing to anyone, least of all me. I had quite forgotten the necklace even existed."

"I can't," Georgie repeated.

Lawrence swept up the jewels into one big hand and crossed the room, flinging open the window. "In that case, you won't mind if I dispose of them."

"Don't you dare!" Georgie cried, jumping to his feet. "What if a crow flew away with that necklace?" Lawrence was about to protest that he didn't give a damn if that was precisely what happened, when Georgie took a step forward. "That necklace," he repeated. "My God. Who made it? It wasn't Rundell and Bridge, I don't think," he murmured with the air of an expert.

"So you'll take them." Lawrence didn't know the value of any of these jewels but figured the necklace alone would be enough to provide for Georgie in reasonable comfort for the rest of his days.

"I'm trying so hard not to take from you." An adorable crease had appeared on Georgie's forehead.

"It's a gift. You're meant to take it." When Georgie didn't answer, Lawrence moved his fistful of jewels closer to the open window.

"Stop! Damn you. This is—you're holding a pistol to my head."

"Would you like me to hide them someplace for you to pretend to steal? I could put it all back in the jewelry case—I assume you're capable of picking a lock?"

Georgie choked back a laugh. "If you had acted half so daft a month ago, I would never have tried to convince you that you were sane."

Lawrence took Georgie's hand and slid the jewels into his open palm, then closed each of Georgie's fingers around the gems, before wrapping his own hand around Georgie's fist.

"I'll concede that this might not be the moment I'd want brought up if my sanity were called into question." He settled a palm against Georgie's hip, satisfied by the way his hand nestled against the smaller man's body.

Georgie brushed a kiss against Lawrence's newly smooth jaw. "I suppose any decent person would protest about it being sordid and transactional. Payment for services, that sort of thing." And that was Georgie's way of telling him that he knew this not to be the case.

Lawrence pulled back just far enough to pull his watch from his pocket. "It's still technically Christmas. Consider it a Christmas present."

"Madness." With his empty hand, he was pushing open Lawrence's dressing gown.

"So I've been telling you." His dressing gown fell to the floor, and he was standing before Georgie, bare chested.

"I've wanted you from the beginning, you know. Since you thought I was a housebreaker." Something of the irony of that situation must have occurred to him—whatever he was must not be so different from a housebreaker, after all—because he smiled candidly up at Lawrence, crinkles forming around his eyes, such an unstudied expression of joy that Lawrence hardly could keep from laughing with happiness.

Georgie traced his fingers along Lawrence's chest, hoping the feel of taut skin and coarsely curling hair would distract him from the jewels he clenched in his other hand. But even when Lawrence kissed him in a confusion of lips and tongues and teeth, all Georgie could think about were rubies and diamonds, his mind calculating value and interest and contemplating such mundane matters as insurance.

None of that was surprising in itself; this wouldn't be the first time Georgie had focused on personal gain instead of…everything else. No, what surprised him was the wonderful, awful, sickening realization of what those jewels meant. No matter how he turned the numbers over in his mind, even if he were to sell them to an unscrupulous jeweler—hell, even if he were to use a fence—he would make enough money to stay far from the gutter for the rest of his life. He'd be safe. All he had to do was take Lawrence's offering, and he would never need to steal, swindle, or cheat again.

And if he weren't doing those things, if he didn't always have one eye open to every dishonest opportunity, what the holy hell was he supposed to do with himself? Another fifty years of…what? It was more than the question of how to fill the days and years. Georgie didn't even know who he would be if he weren't a swindler. He had been a clerk, an apothecary, a man about town, the younger son of minor peer. He had been one of Mattie Brewster's best men.

But he had never simply been Georgie Turner.

"Where did you go?" Lawrence asked, pulling back from the kiss, leaving Georgie blindly seeking, bewildered.

Half a dozen flippant answers sprung to mind. Half a dozen different ways to deflect and distract. Instead he tried for something nearer to the truth. "What will I do? Now that I'm to be a man of leisure, I mean." It wasn't possible to entirely do away with flippancy.

Lawrence looked down at him, misty blue eyes going wide with understanding. "Whatever you like, I hope."

If only he knew what that was. Georgie Turner swindled and connived to put as much distance as possible between himself and poverty, starvation, and humiliation. Absent that goal, what did he even want?

"You could stay here," Lawrence said carefully. "If you like." Georgie thought he heard a note of wistfulness, as if Lawrence didn't really believe that would come to pass.

"I want you to kiss me," Georgie said, because at least it was true. It was a start. And Lawrence did kiss him, soft and patient. Georgie pressed his back hard against the wall, and Lawrence took the hint, leaning forward against him so that Georgie had nowhere to go, nowhere to move, no choice but to kiss and be kissed.

Georgie squirmed, and Lawrence promptly eased away. That would never do. Georgie tugged him back.

"You like this," Lawrence said, unnecessarily, because surely at this proximity he could feel the evidence of Georgie's arousal.

"I like this," Georgie managed, squirming again, relishing the feeling of being gently trapped.

Lawrence worked a hand in between their bodies and started to untie Georgie's cravat. "Well then, if walls and...roughness are what you have in mind..." Georgie let out a sigh of pleasure. "I see that they are," Lawrence went on. "Then I'll see what I can do."

He tugged off Georgie's clothes without the least bit of finesse until they stood chest to chest, Georgie's head tipped back to properly enjoy the look of intent interest on Lawrence's face. Lawrence braced his forearms on the wall beside Georgie's head and brought his mouth down in a hard kiss. The harder Lawrence kissed, the harder Georgie kissed him back. The more aggressively Lawrence crowded Georgie, the more Georgie felt like he was melting against Lawrence's stone wall of a body.

And all the while, the jewels were heavy in his left hand, warm now with the heat from his palm.

Lawrence, holding him close, never breaking the kiss, steered him towards the bedchamber door. Georgie still clutched the jewels.

Lawrence pushed him onto the bed. Georgie still clutched the jewels.

Lawrence tugged off Georgie's shoes and trousers and then his own. Georgie clutched the jewels even tighter, until he felt gold filigree biting into his fingertips.

He watched Lawrence scan the room, his eyes finally alighting on something near the washstand. Georgie propped himself up on his elbows in time to see a tin box being placed on his bare chest. This was the tin the shaving soap had come in, the soap Georgie had bought in Falmouth with the notion that Lawrence would like it. The tin still bore the scent of sandalwood and cloves, which was how Lawrence's skin smelled tonight, masculine and expensive, rich and powerful—but still somehow Lawrence. It was into this box that Georgie placed the jewels that would buy him his freedom, his independence, but rob him of the only purpose he had ever had. They slid out of Georgie's hand and into the box, stone and metal colliding jarringly in the otherwise silent room. Lawrence placed the box on the bedside table where Georgie could see it.

And then Lawrence kissed Georgie hard, almost hard enough to be too much. Georgie ran his hands over Lawrence's arms, relishing the flex of his muscles as he braced himself over Georgie, loving every ounce of weight on top of him. Lawrence shoved Georgie's legs apart with a forcefulness that would have seemed dangerous if it hadn't been precisely what Georgie had asked for, if his eyes weren't carefully trying to read Georgie's face for signs of distress.

"Yes," Georgie breathed, to clear up any confusion in the matter. "Like that."

"You still want to be fucked?" Lawrence's voice was raspy and rude, and it went straight to Georgie's cock.

"Oh God, please." He had been thinking about it for weeks, with obscene frequency. Since arriving at Penkellis, every time he had let his thoughts wander, he imagined Lawrence inside him, on top of him, strong and sure and *his*. He dreamed of being fucked hard enough to not worry about the future or the past or anything else. He knew it wasn't possible, but he shut his eyes and pretended this moment, these touches and kisses and whispered words, were all that mattered.

"Am I sufficiently unlordly?"

Georgie made a sound that he had meant to be a laugh, but came out more like a sob. "Never." The man was a peer of the realm, a man of wealth and consequence, and Georgie had been a rank fool not to have properly considered him in that light. What a lackwit Georgie was to only see it after having spent a tidy sum on finery and fripperies.

But now, thanks to the contents of the soap tin, Georgie's predatory instincts were gone, and without them he felt like a compass without a needle. There was only desire, and something more. Something worse.

"I love you," he said, because now—naked, aroused, and with thousands of pounds worth of rubies on the table beside them—felt like as good a time as any to let the man know, if he hadn't figured it out already. He couldn't think of a single reason not to say it, which only went to show how addled his faculties were at the moment.

"And I love you," Lawrence said. He made it sound more like an action than a sentiment.

He caged Georgie in with his arms, he kissed his neck, he pressed Georgie into the mattress, as if all of those things were somehow acts of love. Georgie wriggled out of Lawrence's grasp, momentarily dispensing with the fiction that

PUBLIC HOLD SHELF:
Barcode: 37445302104793 Title: The Lawrence Browne affair

Barcode: 27396000168543
Request Date: 2/3/2023 2:33 PM

Notify by email:
JUSTINE7PAULSON@YAHOO.COM

PAULSON, JUSTINE

2/22/2023 6:01 PM

he was powerless beneath the larger man. He knelt over Lawrence's lap, straddling him. Then he took Lawrence's hand and guided it around to the cleft of his arse. He felt the rough pads of Lawrence's fingers skimming over his entrance.

"Like so?" Lawrence murmured.

"Yes." Georgie buried his face in Lawrence's neck, kissing and sucking that sensitive flesh as he tried to push back against Lawrence's hand. He heard Lawrence grunt in appreciation, felt Lawrence's hard prick touch his own.

Lawrence shoved him backwards onto the mattress with that combination of unchecked strength and watchful concern that had done away with all Georgie's defenses. The man knew what Georgie wanted and wasn't going to hold back, but he also wouldn't let Georgie be hurt. Georgie rolled onto his stomach, tilting his hips up as Lawrence crawled over him. "Yes," he repeated, his head buried in his folded arms. "There's oil in the bedside table." Yesterday, when he folded Lawrence's clothes and arranged them in the clothes press, he had also hidden away a bottle of oil he had swiped from the pantry. There were advantages to being the sort of conniving soul who thought three steps ahead, the kind of man who thought hiding an object was the same as stealing, only in reverse. He heard Lawrence remove the stopper, and just that sound was enough to send a thrill of anticipation coursing through him.

A moment passed, the only sound being Lawrence sliding his hand over his oiled prick. Georgie's own cock ached with need, his body cried out for more, now. Lawrence's hand rested on the small of his back before moving lower. Georgie felt the tip of a finger enter him and moaned at that first strange intrusion. And then nothing. Lawrence was still, barely breaching Georgie's entrance. Georgie pushed back, felt Lawrence shudder.

"I want to see you." Lawrence leaned low over Georgie, pulling his arms away from his face. "I need to see your face."

Georgie turned his head, resting his cheek on the smooth bed linen. Over his shoulder, he saw his lover's face, so unexpectedly young and sweet without the beard. He flicked a reassuring smile. "I need you inside me."

Lawrence added another finger, readying Georgie with painstaking care. Unable to take any more, Georgie reached back and wrapped his hand around Lawrence's shaft, guiding it to his entrance. "Please. I've been thinking about this for so long."

Lawrence's hands looked unsteady as he reached for more oil. Georgie gave a little moan of anticipation, willed himself not to push himself entirely onto the cock that was only barely touching him. Finally, Lawrence locked his hands on Georgie's hips and thrust all the way in with one steady, inexorable push.

Georgie made a mindless sound of pleasure mingled with intensely realized fullness. He felt like the head of Lawrence's cock was impossibly deep, further into him than made any sense at all. Lawrence, hands digging almost painfully into Georgie's hips, pulled back and then thrust back in.

"Fuck!" Georgie cried, his body on fire with sensation.

"Is that all right?"

It most definitely was. "God yes."

And he did it again, and again, settling into a rhythm. Georgie desperately arched back, sliding his hand underneath his body to take hold of his own needy prick. Georgie didn't know what he was saying, whether it was words or just nonsense syllables, but knew Lawrence wouldn't hold it against him.

He felt safe.

He *was* safe.

His climax was bearing down on him, and when he came, it was with Lawrence's arms around him, with the sounds of Lawrence's own pleasure ringing in his ears.

CHAPTER NINETEEN

Lawrence woke to the sound of wheels crunching on gravel and the icy chill of a cold breeze. It took him one sleep-addled moment to realize that this meant he hadn't properly closed the window last night after threatening to throw the jewels outside.

Lawrence tucked the quilts more firmly around Georgie, who was still fast asleep, burrowed beneath layers of quilts and Lawrence's own body. He eased out of bed and crossed into the study to shut the window. That would take care of the cold, but left the problem of the carriage wheels. Peering out the window, he saw a chaise and four swiftly approaching. He could discern the outline of a coat of arms on the carriage door.

He couldn't think of a single good reason why anyone, let alone a peer, would be arriving at Penkellis the day after Christmas with a winter storm brewing over the sea. Hell, he couldn't think of any reason why anyone would come to Penkellis on any day. His heart started to pound with anxiety over the unexpected arrival.

"Georgie," he said, nudging the man awake. "There's a visitor. A carriage is outside."

"Eh?" Georgie opened one sleepy eye. His hair, normally so tidy, was ruffled into wavy dishevelment. "Delivery?" he mumbled, his words swallowed by the pillow.

"There's a coat of arms on the carriage door."

Georgie sprang out of bed, flung open the clothes press, and threw a few garments onto the bed. "You. Dress." He retrieved his own clothes from the floor and readied himself; a few economical movements later he looked much the same as he always did—tidy clothes, smooth hair, an air of implacable coolness. If it weren't for the flicker of green on Georgie's finger, Lawrence might have imagined last night.

Lawrence's heart gave a thud that was equal parts satisfaction and disorientation. Last night, sated and happy, Georgie curled next to him, Lawrence had dumped the contents of the soap tin onto the mattress. He had found his father's ring and slid it onto Georgie's thumb, where it almost fit. Heavy, old-fashioned gold surrounding a large, strangely dull emerald, Lawrence's father had worn that ring every day.

Seeing that clunky emerald on Georgie's hand filled Lawrence with a dozen different kinds of pleasure, ranging from the basic joy of adorning his lover, to the dark thrill of doing something that would have enraged his unlamented father. Giving his father's ring to Georgie might have been the first time Lawrence truly felt like the Earl of Radnor. If he wanted to give his father's precious emerald to the man he loved, he could and would do precisely that.

Georgie caught the direction of his gaze and flashed a smile ten times brighter than the stone. Pointedly, he turned the ring so the jewel faced his palm. This was their secret.

He hadn't taken the ring off. He was going to keep it.

For a fleeting moment, Lawrence felt capable of anything. Strange carriages, housefuls of servants, none of it mattered.

Georgie looked away, breaking the spell. "You'd better get dressed."

"I…" Lawrence hesitated. The walls were closing in and the blood rushed in his ears, the sound of oceans and broken floodgates and raw, elemental panic. "I'm not sure I feel equal to…" To leaving his tower. To meeting new people. To dealing with anything unexpected.

To living a life.

Ashamed and angry with himself, he let out a long, miserable breath.

But then Georgie's hand was on Lawrence's arm. "Of course," he said gently. "I'll run downstairs and do what needs to be done. But get dressed just in case." They stood like that, Lawrence's hand wrapped around Georgie's smaller one, Georgie looking up at Lawrence with an unreadable, nearly bashful expression. Then Georgie skimmed a kiss along Lawrence's now-stubbly jaw and slipped out of the room.

For a moment, Lawrence had seen how things might have been if he had been a normal man, if his mind worked in the ordinary fashion. He could fall in love with his secretary, he could dare to hope that they might fashion some sort of life together. He could be a father to his neglected child. He could have a house that wasn't a crumbling ruin.

But he could not even go downstairs. No, he could not even *think* about going downstairs without the paralyzing certainty that his heart would pound through his ribcage and his mind devolve into primal chaos.

What Lawrence really wanted to do was bar the door, tinker with his battery, and pretend there was no carriage, no visitor, no world beyond to interfere with his peace. Every nerve in his body told him to hide. There was no way, despite Georgie's faith in him, that this could be anything other than madness, for what better word was there to describe a man who could not hear carriage wheels without panicking, who could not conceive of leaving his study without the sense of imminent doom?

Still, blood rushing in his ears, Lawrence set about the foreign rituals of shaving his face, tying his cravat, and putting on his ring. These felt like the rites of a strange religion, superstitions as laughable as the villagers sprinkling salt on their windowsills.

"I'm not certain I understand precisely who you put in the parlor," Georgie repeated to the flustered footman he had met in the hall. He had rushed downstairs, convinced that he was about to meet whichever of Lawrence's relations had threatened to dispute the earl's competence—one of Simon's uncles, presumably. But instead, the footman was saying something about the Standish carriage. "If Sir Edward Standish is not present, as you say, who arrived in his carriage?"

"Lady Standish, sir, and her brother."

In itself, that might not be remarkable—it wouldn't be so very odd for a man to pay a visit on his correspondent, even one living in such an out-of-the-way place as Penkellis—except that Georgie was convinced that Sir Edward Standish did not exist, and therefore his wife could not be in

Lawrence's parlor. He entered the room fully expecting to be met with a fellow confidence artist, or an assassin, or possibly armed robbers.

Really, anybody except a prim-looking woman in a high-necked traveling costume, sitting rigidly on the settee beside a man Georgie recognized immediately as Julian Medlock. Georgie schooled his expression to bland neutrality. The last time he had seen Mr. Medlock, Georgie had been helping to persuade one of Medlock's friends to invest in a thoroughly imaginary canal company. Georgie had been grave and clerkly with his sober attire and deferential manners, and of course he had used a different name. With any luck, Medlock wouldn't recognize him.

But just to be safe he stayed clear of the light that streamed through the newly cleaned windows.

"I'm George Turner, Lord Radnor's secretary. I'm afraid we weren't expecting the pleasure of your company, but—"

"I told you it was devilish bad *ton*, Eleanor," Medlock interrupted. "Can't you tell the place is at sixes and sevens?" Medlock's gaze landed on the wainscoting, where a hasty coat of paint barely concealed rot. These details had been obscured in last night's candlelight but now seemed painfully obvious. "The poor chap is likely still in his bed."

"Mercy, Julian. Radnor and I have exchanged letters by nearly every post for the better part of two years. A fine friend I'd be not to check on—I mean to say *call* on him when I'm in the neighborhood."

"Which would have been all well and good if you *had* been in the neighborhood, but you were not." He turned to Georgie. "We were visiting a relation in Barnstaple, which has to be a hundred miles away, although I'll be dashed if it didn't feel like five hundred. Two days on the road, and very muddy roads they were. Speaking of which, Mr. Turner," Medlock said, his voice now weary and beleaguered, "I trust that someone will tend to the horses. My sister did not lead me to expect any of the niceties." His gaze alit on a length of curtain that the maids hadn't had time to hem properly.

"His lordship keeps no horses, but the stables are clean and well-provisioned. One of the gardeners used to be an ostler, so your horses will be well cared for." Yesterday, Georgie had inspected the stables and other outbuildings himself, to make sure there were no casks of brandy or other smuggled goods.

Medlock looked dumbfounded by the existence of a man who kept no horses of his own.

"Very sensible," Lady Standish said briskly. "But there'll be no need for that. As soon as I see Lord Radnor, we'll be on our way."

Earlier, she had nearly said that she had come to check on him. She had also said that *she*—rather than her husband— was Lawrence's correspondent. Georgie regarded her appraisingly, and rang the bell for tea.

"Lord Radnor doesn't receive visitors," Georgie said. "And while he has the greatest respect for your husband—"

"About that," Lady Standish said, smoothing out the folds of her skirt.

"Truly, Eleanor, I would have sent you by yourself on the stagecoach"—Medlock's tone suggested that traveling by stagecoach was a fate equal to being burnt at the stake—"if I had known you meant to embroil me in this havey-cavey business. If this ever got back to London, I would positively sink into the earth."

"What my brother is alluding to is that my husband is away on diplomatic business. I've been handling his correspondence in his absence."

Medlock let out a strangled laugh. "His correspondence!"

Georgie narrowed his eyes. "The letters are signed by your husband. The signature and handwriting have been the same for several years now." Not for nothing had Georgie read through and sorted stacks upon stacks of letters. He had been looking for evidence of fraud, suggestions of a swindle, and instead, he had found—what, precisely? He narrowed his eyes and regarded the woman. A scientific mind, one with an understanding of business as well as explosive devices, lurked under that drably serviceable bonnet. He cleared his throat. "Lord Radnor has said that your husband had a head for business. That he handled his lordship's patents and licenses."

"That was me. Truly shocking behavior for a woman, I know."

The only thing that shocked Georgie was that she might not be cheating Lawrence.

"Don't be daft, Eleanor," Medlock said. "The man isn't shocked by your…unwomanliness, or whatever notion you've gotten into your head. You've just confessed to forgery, my girl."

"Not at all," Georgie said quickly. "I feel certain that Lord Radnor wouldn't object to Lady Standish using her husband's name." He still hadn't thrown Georgie out when he first realized his secretary wasn't what he seemed.

The tea arrived, carried in by a very correct Janet. Georgie sent her a grateful look. Even though the house might seem in disarray to a man like Medlock, who was used to country houses humming with activity, with butlers and footmen permanently stationed in the hall and grooms and stable hands at the ready to tend to visitors' horses at all hours, Penkellis was perfectly respectable, in a quiet sort of way. And now that two unexpected visitors—however duplicitous—had arrived, Georgie was even more relieved that Penkellis was fit for company.

"How did you—or Sir Edward, rather—enter into your arrangement with his lordship?" Georgie asked in between sips of tea.

"I was friends with poor Lady Radnor."

Simon's mother? Lawrence's mother? The Mad Earl's beleaguered wife?

Medlock plonked his cup into the saucer with a clatter. "The heavens positively overflow with poor Lady Radnors," he said, echoing Georgie's thoughts. "She means the most recent one. The current earl's sister-in-law."

"Poor lady," Lady Standish murmured. "She told me of her husband's brother, locked away in an attic. We were very young and thought it quite romantic."

Medlock looked like he might be sick.

"Of course he wasn't locked away at all. I gather he had locked himself *in* to avoid his relations, and who can blame him. In any event, she told me that he invented a system of pipes that brought hot water up from the kitchens so she could more easily wash her hair."

Georgie froze, remembering how Lawrence had hauled up bucket after bucket for his bath, and wondered what had happened to this hot-water contraption. In which of Penkellis's dust-shrouded bedchambers would Georgie find evidence of Lawrence's kindness for his brother's mistreated wife?

"And there were other inventions too," Lady Standish continued. "I was fascinated. I thought, here is a man who has been very kind to my friend, a man who has no fortune whatsoever of his own, a man who is a virtual prisoner in the house of his ill-tempered father and depraved brother. I thought that with a little effort I could help him turn his inventions to a small profit. I knew a little about business, because my father was in trade and he wasn't above letting me help. Don't look at me like that, Julian."

"Our father being in trade is the least appalling part of that narrative, dear sister."

Georgie raised an eyebrow. "You began this endeavor out of the kindness of your own heart, then." He knew perfectly well that Sir Edward Standish—which was to say, Lady Standish—took a fee for her labors. Kindness had little or nothing to do with it. Georgie felt once again on quite solid and familiar ground.

"Oh, goodness no." She actually laughed, a ladylike trill that had no place in this conversation. "I needed money too. Quite badly, in fact."

"Do strive for some conduct, Eleanor," Medlock said wearily. "Not all your private matters need to be aired this morning. Save some for supper."

She ignored her brother and continued addressing Georgie. "Well, it seemed a partnership would help both of us, but I wasn't such a fool as to think he'd do business with a woman. Besides—"

She broke off, her attention evidently arrested by a sight over Georgie's shoulder. Medlock was frozen, his teacup halfway to his mouth.

Georgie turned to see Lawrence standing in the doorway, his expression as dark as a thundercloud.

Rising to his feet with all the self-possession he could muster, Georgie greeted Lawrence and performed the necessary introductions. He wanted to know how long Lawrence had been standing there, but that was never a clever thing to ask. It was best to be the first one to speak unpleasant truths, to put just the right level of distracting shine on the ugly facts.

"Lady Standish and her brother, Mr. Medlock, have paid a call on us, my lord. Lady Standish is responsible for her husband's letters and business interests, so I don't doubt that the two of you will have many shared interests."

That wasn't so bad. Lawrence's expression even softened, his eyebrows less violently V-shaped.

"Welcome to Penkellis," Lawrence said, and he almost sounded like he meant it. He didn't come further into the room, but he didn't need to. He was dressed to go outdoors, in a topcoat Georgie had purchased last week. Simon was in the hall behind him, similarly attired; Barnabus had lumbered into the parlor and was drooling on the new carpet. Georgie gathered that Lawrence and Simon meant to take the dog for some exercise.

"I'm glad to see you in good health, Lord Radnor," Lady Standish said. "The contents of your last two letters left me a good deal concerned. So when I found myself somewhat near your home"—here, Georgie thought he heard Julian Medlock snort with derision—"I knew I had to pay a call."

"My last two letters?" Radnor repeated, a furrow appearing between his eyebrows.

"In which you detailed the functioning of the trough battery and the scheme for burying the device underground. None of it made the least bit of sense."

Oh, damn. Those were the letters Georgie had written, hoping to mislead Standish sufficiently to prevent him profiting off Lawrence's invention while Georgie figured out how to steal it himself. He coughed apologetically. "I believe I wrote those letters. Perhaps I misunderstood the mechanism for the battery. How stupid of me."

Lawrence's eyebrows had reverted to ominous slashes across his brow. And rightly so, since he knew that Georgie was perfectly capable of explaining the telegraph and the battery.

Lady Standish did not seem to notice. "Ah, that explains it. It was an unfamiliar hand."

Lawrence narrowed his eyes, and now he looked very threatening indeed. He knew Georgie was up to something. Georgie instinctively moved closer, drawn by some half-formed and misguided intent to reassure his lover. But as he stepped out of the shadows, a beam of light struck him full in the face.

"Oh!" It was Medlock, damn him. Georgie stepped out of the shaft of light but it was too late. "I knew you looked familiar." He bit his lip and held his finger in midair for a long moment, during which Georgie thought he might expire from suspense. "Gerald Turnbull!" he finally announced with an air of satisfaction, as if he had calculated a particularly difficult sum without pencil and paper.

"He's already said his name is George Turner, my dear," Lady Standish said. "He can't be your Gerald Turnbull. Although those names *are* terribly similar. Perhaps you were introduced to Mr. Turner and misheard it as Turnbull."

"That must be it." Medlock did not sound convinced. "You had something to do with those canals Reggie was so keen on." He stopped abruptly, no doubt remembering that his friend had lost a frightful amount of money in the scheme. Medlock was too much the gentleman to discuss money, or crime, in mixed company, but he turned a sharply appraising eye on Georgie.

He knew.

Medlock was not the only one regarding Georgie carefully. Lady Standish looked like she was about to start asking questions about canals. No doubt she knew more about that topic than Georgie ever would.

But it was the look on Lawrence's face that stopped Georgie cold. He looked like a man who finally understood something he wished he hadn't ever known.

I as good as told you, Georgie wanted to cry. *You knew I wasn't honest.* He had begged Lawrence to lock up his valuables, for God's sake.

"I'm taking the dog for some air before the snow gets too deep," Lawrence said. "It's nearly noon," he added, with a sweeping glance around the room that somehow seemed to condemn them all for their layabout ways. "Nobody leave." Those last words he said with a pointed look at Georgie, as if he were afraid that Georgie might flee the premises. That assumption wasn't far off the mark. In the ordinary course of things, Georgie would have disappeared as soon as his

swindle was exposed. He would have grabbed his satchel and
run.

He still wanted to. But he wouldn't. He would give Lawrence an explanation. It would be humiliating, probably for
both of them.

And then Lawrence would be done with him.

CHAPTER TWENTY

The sky grew menacingly gray as the snow fell with greater urgency.

"We'll have to put them in those two rooms at the end of the corridor," Janet said, coming up behind Georgie in the hall. "I'll send up some clean linens."

Lady Standish and Mr. Medlock would spend the night, possibly two nights if this snow lasted. Yesterday's light snow had dwindled into mud, but today's storm might make travel impossible, not only for the visitors but for Georgie if Lawrence asked him to leave.

Like a jolt from careless handling of Lawrence's battery, Georgie realized that he'd have to leave no matter what. Medlock was a notorious gossip, and now that he was in possession of a particularly delectable bit of news there would be no shutting him up. The Earl of Radnor, who supposedly had madness in his blood, had a confidence artist under his roof. It would be a matter of days before news got back to Mattie Brewster about where to find his prodigal swindler. And then he'd come looking for him here, at Penkellis. Georgie wouldn't expose Lawrence to that risk. It was bad enough that Lawrence's name would be linked with his own.

But where to go? Certainly not London. For all Georgie knew, he'd step off the stagecoach and find himself tossed directly in the Thames by one of Mattie's men. Perhaps the Continent, then. Another time that prospect might have sounded appealing, but now Paris and Milan were only places that didn't have Lawrence. He rested his head against the cold windowpane and sighed.

"Come, now," Janet said, laying a hand on Georgie's forearm. "Nothing to get fussed about. Those rooms are right as rain. The chimneys don't smoke, at least not too badly, and we've gotten rid of nearly all the mice."

She had mistaken the cause of his grim mood. "Quite right," he said absently. "Please have Mrs. Ferris send up a tray of sandwiches for the guests."

He went upstairs to pack his things. Everything he owned fit into a valise and a satchel with room to spare. There would be no last-minute pilfering of candlesticks or teaspoons. There would be no soap tin filled with jewels either. Lawrence had given those gifts when he had underestimated Georgie's secrets. Taking them would be as good as theft, and Georgie couldn't bring himself to steal from the man he loved.

The look of suspicion and betrayal on Lawrence's face when Medlock had recognized him had told Georgie all he needed to know. Up until that moment, Lawrence had probably thought Georgie a housebreaker, a common thief, not someone who lived and dined with his victims and stole their money along with their peace of mind.

When Lawrence had found out that Georgie had interfered with Lawrence's correspondence, he must have guessed that Georgie wasn't after the family silver. He was after Lawrence's inventions.

It hardly signified that Georgie wasn't, at least not anymore. Lawrence wouldn't believe him. Why should he? Georgie himself could hardly believe that he had passed up this opportunity. And for what? Love? What rot.

But it wasn't rot at all. Georgie knew that what he felt for Lawrence, and what he was prepared to give up for him, was the closest he had ever come to being honest, to being good.

There was a tapping on the door, and Georgie's stomach dropped. He wasn't ready to talk to Lawrence, because talking to him meant parting from him.

"Come in," he called.

It was Janet who entered. "Brought you gin." She handed him a bottle. "You look like you need it."

He took a swig directly from the bottle. There was no sense in observing the niceties where gin was concerned.

"Do you want to talk about it?" She took the bottle back and drank.

"No." He wiped his mouth with the back of his hand. "I'm a fool."

"You and every other bloke I've met."

"Law—Lord Radnor isn't."

"Oh, it's like that, is it?" She looked over her shoulder to confirm that the door was shut.

Georgie shook his head. "It isn't like a damned thing I've ever known about."

"You'll be wanting another drink, then." She held out the bottle, and he took it. "Are you leaving?" She looked at the valise that sat open on his bed.

"I'll be sacked as soon as his lordship gets back."

"And why would he be so daft as to sack you, after you made this place livable? He may have kicked up a fuss about you bringing the lad here, but he didn't seem too put out about it this morning when the two of them set off on their walk, did he? Thick as thieves, they were."

Georgie pinched the bridge of his nose to hold back tears. He would not cry; he would not face Lawrence with red eyes. It was stupid to be so proud and happy that Lawrence had found a way to be a father to Simon.

"It wasn't all me. You and Mrs. Ferris worked tirelessly." It was true. Despite Mrs. Ferris's initial hesitancy, she was ruling over the kitchens with a natural authority. Georgie hoped Lawrence wouldn't dismiss all the servants after Simon went back to school. Simon deserved a decent home to return to. Lawrence deserved it too.

But that was all out of Georgie's control. He'd be far gone by the time Simon went back to school. He'd never hear again from anyone at Penkellis. These weeks would dwindle to a vague dream, a time when he had worked to build and create, not simply to scheme and take; a time when he let himself care and be cared for.

Georgie didn't realize he was crying until Janet used the corner of her apron to wipe his cheeks. "Now, that'll never do," she chided. "Take a deep breath, and go say whatever needs to be said. His lordship isn't going to sack you, and you'll see that you worked yourself into a state for nothing."

With an effort, Georgie attempted a smile. "Thank you." She was trying to be kind, and for no reason at all. Georgie couldn't take much more of it.

Lawrence stomped the snow from his boots and sent Simon and the dog off to warm up in the kitchens.

He found Georgie in the study, looking out the window, his back to the door. When he turned to face Lawrence, something dark and dismal flickered briefly across his face, but just as soon disappeared. He was once again his usual cool, collected self.

Lawrence spoke first. "Tell me your real name."

"Georgie Turner." His posture was stiff and his expression betrayed nothing. "I didn't use a false name when I came here."

Lawrence nodded. He felt vaguely, senselessly relieved that he hadn't been addressing the man he loved by a false name for so many weeks.

Georgie cleared his throat. "I'll leave, but—"

"Like hell you will." If Lawrence had his way, he'd never let the man out of his sight. He latched onto the first relevant piece of information he could think of. "It's snowing." Fragile flakes still clung to the dark wool of Lawrence's coat.

"I didn't plan to hurt you," Georgie said.

"Who said you did? For God's sake, sit down." Lawrence peeled off his topcoat and tossed it over the back of a chair before sitting. "I've known for some time that you're no ordinary secretary. And you've known that I know. It didn't matter yesterday, it doesn't matter today, and it's not going to matter at any point in the future." Lawrence had never been so certain of anything, but as he looked at Georgie's shuttered expression, he knew he would have to work to convince the man. "Start from the beginning and tell me what was going on with Lady Standish's brother."

"I sold one of Medlock's friend's shares in a company that doesn't exist," Georgie said, sitting at the end of the sofa farthest from Lawrence's chair. "I would have done something similar to you."

Lawrence raised a skeptical eyebrow. "You planned to sell me shares in a fictitious company?" He would have thought he made a poor target for that sort of scheme—he had plenty of money and cared little about making more.

Instead of looking at Lawrence, Georgie busied himself in brushing imaginary lint from his sleeve. "I would have taken your plans for the telegraph and used them to, ah, endear myself to a business associate with whom I've had a falling out."

"I see." Stealing a man's work seemed rather worse than preying on a man's greed. Lawrence ought to be shocked, no doubt. But he found he didn't care what Georgie had done to earn his bread before. There was a good deal of bitterness in Georgie's voice when he spoke of this friend, and Lawrence wanted to know why, but that would have to wait until later. "But you didn't."

"Not yet."

"I don't think you would have." He moved to the sofa and cupped Georgie's face in his hand, tilting it up towards him. "I don't think you went to bed with me last night planning to steal from me." He remembered how very sad Georgie had sounded when asking Lawrence to lock up his ring.

Georgie turned his head away. "That's true. Irrelevant, but true."

Lawrence took in a long breath. "When did you change your mind? Was it before…before we…" Before they fell in love, he meant. But those words seemed ill suited to a conversation about swindles and theft.

"Weeks ago," Georgie said tightly, still looking at his hands, Lawrence's ring glinting in the scant sunlight. "You might not hate me now, but you will. If I had taken your plans, and you had ever sought redress, your sanity would have been called into question. I would have seen to it that you had no proof of your invention."

"This doesn't change the way I feel about you. I knew you were some kind of thief, but I thought you were after the silver. Every morning I woke up and wondered whether you'd still be here."

"And whether your silver and paintings would be here," Georgie said dryly, not meeting Lawrence's eyes.

"I didn't give a damn about the silver or the paintings. I thought I've made that clear. Why do you think I made such a point of giving you the jewels last night? Those are worth more than all the paintings and silver put together." *You're worth more*, he wanted to say. "Now, let's get rid of Lady Standish and her miserable brother and enjoy the rest of the day. I told Simon we'd play snapdragon."

Georgie closed his eyes and let out a sigh. "I can't. I told you. Medlock recognized me from when I swindled his cousin."

"Bugger Medlock. What do I care what he thinks?"

"He'll start talking when he gets back to London. It's excellent gossip, so I can hardly blame him. The Earl of Radnor is being swindled. And he knows absolutely everybody, so it'll be no time before all of London knows."

"And that matters to me precisely why?" Lawrence had gone nearly thirty years in complete indifference to public opinion and wasn't about to change his ways now.

"Because..." Georgie opened his mouth and shut it again, as if unsure of what to say. "Halliday is concerned that Simon's relations will try to wrest control of the estate away from you."

"Pardon?"

A faint grimace flickered across Georgie's face. "One of Simon's relations got in touch with Halliday, wanting to know whether there was any case to be made that you might be mad. Halliday wrote a letter to a friend of my brother's, who offered to send me to look into matters." He laughed, dry and mirthless. "Of course, if word gets out that you're harboring a confidence artist under your roof, that will only help Simon's uncles get you declared incompetent. Which is why I need to leave. I need to hide somewhere else. Now."

Lawrence's mind scrambled to make sense of this. Of course one of Simon's relatives—probably the same uncle who had taken down Isabella's portrait—would try to have Lawrence declared insane. It was only a wonder that it hadn't happened yet. He settled on the one aspect of Georgie's narrative that didn't directly involve him. "Hide?"

He watched as Georgie took a breath and seemed to come to a decision. "I came here not only to spy on you but to hide from the former associate I mentioned. I betrayed him, so he needs to make an example of me."

"He wants to harm you?"

Georgie's gaze cut away to the floor.

"To kill you?"

"I owe him." He said this so baldly, speaking of his own anticipated murder with such matter-of-fact ease, that Lawrence was momentarily stunned. "I planned to swindle a very sweet, slightly daft old lady. But I couldn't go through with it."

"This sounds like honorable behavior."

Georgie waved a bored hand, a tired dismissal of the idea of honor.

"Nobody is coming to Penkellis to murder you. London street criminals don't creep into old castles to dispose of their enemies."

Georgie looked at him with raised eyebrows. "He has to. Mattie Brewster can't be known to tolerate double-crossers."

"Go abroad."

"I have no money."

"You have the jewels. I'll give you ready money, if that's what you're talking about."

Georgie shook his head. "My brother and sister live in London. And you're here. There's no life for me on the Continent. But if I stay here, I'll put you all in danger, and I won't do that."

And you're here. That made it sound like Georgie *would* stay, if not for this Brewster bastard. "I'll come too," he said rashly. "We'll tour the Continent. Your criminal friend can't possibly hunt you across Europe."

Lawrence had been to London as a young man and to Exeter twice to visit his tutor. Those trips had been…deeply unpleasant. Christ, the idea of going so far as the village church sounded ghastly. Even in the safety of his study, he could imagine narrow streets, strange buildings closing in on him, unfamiliar people like so many rocks in his boot.

But he would do it for Georgie. Just like he had gone downstairs last night to see Simon. And that had turned out fine, hadn't it? Better than fine.

"Let's not make promises we can't keep." Georgie laid a hand on Lawrence's arm. "Neither of us is in a position to make any promises at all."

Lawrence wanted to protest. There were a dozen promises already forming on the tip of his tongue. He wanted to promise to love and protect Georgie as best as he could, as long as he would let him. He wanted to promise to follow Georgie to the ends of the earth or anywhere else he needed to go.

But Georgie was right. He wasn't in any position to make those promises. He could barely walk downstairs to greet his own son, and his entire body flinched at the prospect of having to venture even farther.

For all he had come to depend on Georgie, he knew that Georgie could not depend on him in return.

So instead of uttering useless promises, he nodded his head in bitter assent.

Chapter Twenty-One

Georgie slipped through the corridors that had become as familiar to him as the narrow alleys and back passageways of London. He kept his footsteps silent, even though there was no reason for secrecy. Some habits were hard to break.

He tapped on Simon's door. The child was supposed to be resting after lunch, but Georgie doubted that would last long. Sure enough, he heard the sound of giggles and scuffling coming from within, and when he pushed open the door, he found Simon and Barnabus engaged in a heated debate over the fate of a long black sock.

When the dog noticed Georgie, bearer of treats and giver of excellent head scratches, standing in the doorway, he immediately let go of the sock, causing Simon to tumble backwards in a riot of laughter.

"Down," Georgie ordered the dog, who obeyed as best he could while wagging his tail at top speed. Georgie realized with a start that he would miss this furry mongrel. When he finished with a job, he never let himself shed a tear over the places and people he would never see again, but he already knew that his usual defenses were of no use to him at Penkellis.

He'd miss ramshackle Penkellis, with its senseless tangle of corridors and decayed greatness. He'd never see it in the spring, when the overgrown garden must teem with masses of wildflowers. He'd miss getting to know Simon better, and he wished he had time to figure out why the child had seemed so unwell the first few days after he arrived. He'd never hear Janet and Mrs. Ferris's explanation of what stolen cauls had to do with smuggling rings. He'd never know what Lawrence's next project would be.

Maybe the problem was that it didn't feel like the end of a job. Not only was he walking away empty-handed for the first time, but he felt like he was about to leave the best part of himself behind. At Penkellis, he had gotten a taste of what life would be like with a purpose, with a sense of belonging, the very things he had scorned in his flight from the gutter. He had never understood what use fine feelings were to a man who was half-starved.

But now he thought he did.

That was why he couldn't take the jewels. It would have been so easy to slip them into his coat pocket and get on the next ship for Calais, or even go back to London and use the rubies to buy off Brewster. But then every time Lawrence thought of the necklace, the ring, the gaudy watch fob, he'd wonder if Georgie had really gotten what he came for after all. And Georgie didn't want Lawrence to remember him as a glorified thief who had made off with the family jewels.

He cleared his throat. "I thought you might want to visit the stables to see Mr. Medlock's carriage and horses," he told Simon. "You'll need your warmest clothes."

Georgie didn't need to bring Simon to the stables, nor did he need to make sure that there was enough hay and straw for the horses and that the servant who had been press-ganged into service as a stable hand was competent in his new position. But he wanted to. These small tasks had made him feel like he belonged here, and even though he had known all along that this was an illusion, he wanted one last time to feel needed, to pretend that this was his home.

They set out for the stables, Barnabus trotting alongside. The snow fell heavily enough that when Georgie looked over his shoulder, their footprints were already covered by fresh snow. Lady Standish and Lord Medlock would be stuck at Penkellis until tomorrow at the earliest. As soon as the snow melted enough to pose no danger to carriage wheels, they'd be on their way to London.

Georgie would be gone before then. He needed to reach Mattie Brewster before any gossip did. Otherwise there was the risk that Brewster's men would come to Penkellis, and Georgie couldn't let that happen. It was time for Georgie to pay for all the wrong he had done, and the price would be leaving Penkellis.

"Listen!" cried Simon, tugging at Georgie's sleeve.

At the sound of snow-muffled hoofbeats, Georgie went rigid, imagining it was Mattie Brewster coming for him. But Brewster couldn't have found him yet, and even if he had, he'd hardly come on horseback, least of all on the huge black stallion that was bearing down on them.

But still Georgie's heart pounded in his chest as the rider brought the horse up short in front of Georgie and Simon.

"Blast it all, why don't you watch where you're going?" the rider shouted from his mount. "I nearly trampled both of you. Can't see a damned thing in this storm." Muttering what sounded like foreign profanities under his breath, he swung off his horse and came to land in front of Georgie and Simon.

He was tall and wore a magnificent, many-caped greatcoat. His hat had been the height of fashion before being ruined by the snow.

"I suppose one of you will tell me where to find the stables?" Even through the falling snow, the man's sneer was visible. "Assuming there are stables, and I'm not meant to leave my horse tied to a tree in the middle of a blizzard."

Simon gave a small gasp and squeezed Georgie's hand. "Uncle Courtenay!" he squealed. "You've come!"

"Courtenay is *where?*" Lawrence bellowed, causing the housemaid to take a step back. He had never seen her before in his life, this neatly dressed servant who had the temerity to knock on his study door and announce that the kingdom's greatest reprobate was here at Penkellis.

"In the blue room, my lord. Mr. Turner ordered that he be put there until better accommodations could be sorted out."

"Better accommodations—like hell he is." The last Lawrence had heard, Isabella's wastrel brother was in Constantinople, where he had fled his creditors. Even the Antipodes would have been a good deal too close, as far as Lawrence cared. "He's not staying another minute under this roof."

Courtenay had always been a blackguard, an infamous scoundrel, for as long as Lawrence could remember. Christ, he had been friends with Percy, which would have been bad enough—birds of a feather, and so forth. But where Percy had contented himself with duels, drunkenness, and domestic cruelty, Courtenay dabbled in political radicalism, overt sedition, and orgies of depravity.

Lawrence brushed past the servant and made for the blue room, his heavy steps causing the candle flames to dance in their sconces. The blue room, his arse. Georgie had given up his own room? Infuriating. To be sure, Georgie had no need of his own room—he had spent the last two nights in Lawrence's bed, and Lawrence had no intention of letting his lover sleep anywhere else. But for Georgie to give up his claim to a bedchamber, and for the comfort of such a one as Courtenay, offended sensibilities Lawrence hadn't even known he had. Courtenay could go to the local inn or bed down in a cow shed, for all he cared.

He absolutely ought not to be anywhere near Lady Standish or her prig of a brother, certainly not even in the same county as Simon.

The blue room, however, was empty, its door standing ajar, with no trace of either Georgie's or Courtenay's belongings within. Lawrence strode downstairs, taking them two at a time. He was dimly aware of footmen and housemaids scattering as he approached, but he paid them no mind. Never had he cared less how many strangers were present in his house, how much noise they made, and whether they interfered with his work. His only concern was finding Courtenay and throwing him into the nearest snowdrift.

"I was expecting a shambles, dear Laurie." The voice was cold, urbane, and tinged with a vaguely foreign accent.

Lawrence spun on his heel to find Courtenay himself leaning against a pillar in the great hall.

"Don't call me that," Lawrence spat, as if forms of address could possibly matter in these circumstances. But Courtenay had always taken a patronizing, elder-brotherly air, and Lawrence would be damned if he'd allow it under his own roof.

"Of course, you're Radnor now." As Courtenay spoke, he emerged from the shadows. "I dare say you hardly remember me," he drawled.

"Go to hell, Courtenay." The bastard had to know perfectly well how notorious he was.

"So you *do* remember me." A cruel smile twisted Courtenay's lips. "How flattering."

"Get out of my house," Lawrence ground out.

"No shelter for a weary traveler? That's not quite in keeping with the spirit of the season, I fear. And to think, I came all this way to make sure my nephew was in good hands."

Lawrence snorted. "Since when do you give a damn about Simon? Or anything but your own pleasure?"

"I could ask you the same thing, now, couldn't I? For how many years have you been living like a hermit in a ruin of a house? When my idiot sister wrote that Simon was to come here for his holiday because her own brats were breaking out in measles, I half expected to find him alone among the rocks and the sheep or whatever it is you have in Cornwall."

Lawrence narrowed his eyes. How did Courtenay know anything about his house or his habits? He raised an eyebrow. "You can see for yourself that the house is perfectly habitable."

He had never been so grateful for Georgie's machinations. "And I have guests in the parlor this very moment, so if you'll excuse me." He gave a slight, insignificant bow. "Oh," he said over his shoulder, "you'll find that the Fiddling Fox in the village offers acceptable lodgings."

"Have you grown too respectable for your old friends, Lawrence?"

There was something about the man's tone that made Lawrence halt and turn around. "We never were friends," he ground out.

"A pity, that. But I'm the only friend Simon has, let's not forget."

"How dare you—"

"Enough." The facetious drawl was quite gone from Courtenay's voice now, replaced by something that in a less despicable man might be called earnestness. "I know he's never been here before. I know he's never had so much as a letter from you." They both knew Lawrence couldn't deny it. "And now you've taken a fancy to acknowledging him. That's all well and good. But when I found out that my daft sister had sent Simon to *you*, I traveled night and day to get here."

Lawrence reeled at this information. "You traveled— why?"

"Because until an hour ago I was under the impression that Penkellis was no better than a lunatic asylum, and you no better than a bedlamite. I have to say I'm delighted to be wrong so I can get out of here as soon as the weather permits. I wasn't looking forward to having to throw my nephew over my saddle and take him back to France. My mode of living doesn't quite accommodate children, as you know."

Before Lawrence could contemplate why Courtenay knew anything about the goings on at Penkellis, the parlor door opened and Julian Medlock stepped out.

"Radnor, I hate to be a pest, but the tea is quite cold. Good God, is that—" He put his quizzing glass up to his eye. "Heavens above, it's Lord Courtenay." He took a step back as if there were a live tiger in the hall. "Eleanor, stay where you are. Don't come out."

Lady Standish promptly appeared by her brother's side. "I should think Lord Courtenay has better things to do than interfere with middle-aged matrons, Julian."

Courtenay didn't even look in their direction. "Simon and your secretary are in the kitchens, drying off your dog. I mention that in case you were wondering whether I'd murdered and disemboweled them, all for want of better amusement."

"You can't mean for that fellow to stay here," Medlock protested, still peering through his quizzing glass. "He's a menace."

"We're all snowed in," Lawrence growled, not making any effort to make his tone amicable. "I didn't ask any of you lot to come here, so you'll all have to make do. If you're worried that Courtenay will lure you into orgies or opium eating, then lock your doors." He stared at Medlock until the man retreated into the parlor.

"And as for you," he said, turning to Courtenay, "did you write to my vicar?"

"You may not remember this about me, Laurie, but I'm not much in the habit of corresponding with vicars. Not in my line, you know."

"Damn you. Did you write to Halliday inquiring about my mental competence, or didn't you?"

Courtenay regarded him appraisingly. "I couldn't very well let Simon live with a lunatic, now could I? And I was a good deal too far away to see for myself, so the vicar seemed the best bet."

"What exactly did you tell him?" A suspicion was forming in Lawrence's mind.

"I told him that he'd assure me of your mental competence or I'd see to it that you were quietly thrown in an institution and your property made over to your heir."

That would explain it. Halliday, prone to worry on the best of days, would have gotten it into his head that Lawrence was in grave danger. "Why do you care?"

"Simon is my nephew. I wasn't going to let him run loose in the company of a mad recluse." He spoke like it was a matter of course, as if ten years earlier he hadn't thrown his younger sister into far worse society than Lawrence ever could have been.

"Would that you had so much concern for your relations' safety when Isabella was alive." It had been Courtenay who had introduced Isabella to the man who got her with child.

Courtenay's nostrils flared, but other than that he betrayed no sign of anger. "You think that doesn't weigh on me? She was my sister, my friend. And Simon is all I have left of her." He looked sincere, but appearances could be deceiving where Courtenay was concerned. "And listen here, Laurie. I'll gladly murder anyone who harms him, you included."

Lawrence met the man's challenging glare with one of his own. "Good."

For a moment, Courtenay held Lawrence's gaze, then gave him a single nod. Lawrence nodded in return, as if they had struck a truce.

Lawrence went down to the kitchens to tell Georgie about their unfortunate new arrival, but when he pushed open the baize doors there was no sign of the secretary. Servants bustled about, Simon sat on a stool by the fire, eating a scone, and Barnabus sat by the garden door, but Georgie wasn't there.

"Where's Mr. Turner?" he asked the room at large.

"He went to see to the linens," Mrs. Ferris said, not meeting his gaze.

A sick feeling began to grow in Lawrence's stomach. "When did he leave?"

Mrs. Ferris looked at him and shook her head. Lawrence saw what he should have noticed right away: Barnabus was stationed by the door, instead of begging for Simon's crumbs.

Lawrence strode across the room and flung open the garden door, letting in a blast of cold air and a flurry of snow. But he saw no footprints, no trace of Georgie.

"Where is Mr. Turner?" he repeated. "Where did he go?"

Dazed, he retreated to the safety of his study, only to find that even there he felt the walls closing tightly around him, his heart pounding furiously in his chest.

CHAPTER TWENTY-TWO

It wasn't until they had been snowed in for two days that Lawrence realized he was, effectively, hosting a house party. A terrible, boring house party with guests who heartily disliked one another and with the painful absence of the one person Lawrence wished were present, but a house party nonetheless. The servants contrived to keep everyone fed, Lady Standish carried the conversation at mealtimes, Simon cavorted with the dog, and Lawrence played the part of the thoroughly drunk host.

"Your library is appalling," Courtenay announced, throwing open the door to Lawrence's study. "It's shocking. There were mushrooms growing on Seneca, which is neither more nor less than the fellow deserves, but all your brother's naughty lithographs are ruined. Disgraceful."

"I daresay you have some expertise in disgrace," Julian Medlock murmured archly, glancing up from the letter he was writing. Lawrence had forgotten that the dandy had decided to make himself at home in the study while his sister fiddled with the telegraph. Why the fellow was draining inkwell after inkwell in writing letters when the post hadn't been collected in two days, Lawrence couldn't attempt to guess.

"Get out," Lawrence grumbled, holding his glass of brandy close to his chest. "The lot of you."

"Would that I could," Courtenay said, a single eyebrow raised, his gaze never straying from Lawrence, "but my valise and my coin purse went missing at around the same time as your secretary."

Lawrence looked up sharply at Courtenay. Georgie hadn't taken the jewels, not even the emerald ring, and the idea of his wandering penniless through the storm had troubled Lawrence as much as the sheer fact of the man's absence. He had repeatedly told himself that Georgie was resourceful, that he was conniving, that he certainly wasn't fool enough to die of exposure.

"Yes, I thought that would get your attention," Courtenay said. A lock of hair fell onto his forehead, and Lawrence remembered the old rumor that he slept in curling papers. "I do love a good—"

"Will you look at this, Radnor?" Lady Standish interrupted, rising to her feet behind the sofa and shaking out her skirts. "Your battery is not the problem. It's just that there are too many wires. Each additional wire multiplies the likelihood of something going awry."

"I know," Lawrence assented wearily. They had been through this at least a dozen times this morning. "But what use would fewer wires be?" There were twenty-six letters in the alphabet, twenty-five if they were to eliminate C, per Lady Standish's pragmatic suggestion. What the devil could anybody do with fewer wires than that?

"The point isn't to be able to communicate in perfect English prose," she said. "That's what the post is for."

"A fat lot of good the post does when you're snowed in," Medlock chimed in.

"Listen," Lady Standish insisted. "What you have right now is a way to communicate urgent, prearranged messages from one point to another. Say, from the coast to London."

That was more or less what Georgie had thought. Lawrence felt another miserable pang at his secretary's absence. "A way to signal a strange ship's approach," he said, echoing Georgie's suggestion.

"Or favorable conditions for a crossing. That sort of thing."

Lawrence nodded and knelt on the floor beside the telegraph. They spent the rest of the afternoon reconfiguring the device. It was pleasant working with Lady Standish; after such a prolonged correspondence, they were almost like old friends. Once he had gotten over the initial shock of discovering that she was a woman—and a youngish woman too, when he had been expecting a man considerably older than himself—he found himself recognizing in her conversation turns of phrase that she had been wont to use in her letters. Lawrence at first had to pretend that he was dictating a letter to Standish, but after a few hours and too many short circuits to count, he felt nearly comfortable with her.

Lawrence had never had this many people in his study at once. It had been years since he had even been in a room with so many people. It was unpleasant, and even the thought of his sanctuary being invaded made his heart squeeze uncomfortably in his chest. Medlock was silent, except for the incessant scratching of his pen on paper. Courtenay sprawled in the chair by the fire, thumbing through whatever books weren't too damaged to be read, and then later quietly playing cards with Simon when the child tentatively poked his head into the room. He would have strongly preferred them all to go far away.

Except Lady Standish, because together they had accomplished more in a single day than they had in months of correspondence.

Except Simon, too, because seeing him filled Lawrence's heart with a degree of joy he hadn't thought himself capable of.

Except that old roué Courtenay, because Simon clearly adored the bastard.

And hell, he'd even keep Medlock, if for no other reason than because his presence seemed to be a prerequisite for his sister's company.

So while he still much preferred being alone, this was…not horrible. He felt the walls closing in on him, the heat rising to the surface of his skin, but it never got unbearable. He had always assumed that if one of his episodes progressed too far, he would be plunged thoroughly into madness, and then be as lost to reason as his brother or father. But that hadn't happened. Not now, not when Georgie had turned the house upside down, not when Simon had arrived.

Not madness, then. And it never would be. He finally believed what Georgie had been trying to tell him, and Georgie wasn't even here to look smug about it. There were days and weeks and years opening before him, and every one of them would be without the person who had helped him see that he had a future.

"Radnor?" Lady Standish looked like she had been trying to get Lawrence's attention for some time now. "Do you need to rest?" She pitched her voice low, so as not to be overheard by the gentlemen or Simon. He recalled that she had traveled some distance to check up on him. She knew he was a hermit; she knew his family's madness. And she was treating him as a friend.

No, she *was* a friend. Somewhere in between their disputes about the relative merits of brine and acid as electrolyte and their arguments about copper wire, they had become friends.

"I wanted this machine to send letters, not prearranged messages. I wanted a way for people to correspond instantly, without the hassle of letters crossing in the post or the annoyance of forgetting to send letters." He still regretted all those unposted letters Georgie had found that first day—so many wasted words, so many conversations that had never taken place. "I wanted a way for people"—he busied himself in uncoiling a length of wire—"people like me, perhaps, to not be quite so alone."

Lady Standish put her hand over his. "There's time for that. You have decades to work out the details. Right now, though, I think we ought to go to the Admiralty. What was the name of that fellow who had asked you for the plans?"

It took Lawrence less than a minute to lay his hands on the letter from the Admiralty. This study, from the neatly labeled bottles and vials, to the meticulously organized papers, was Georgie's doing. He had left his mark on every inch of this room, to say nothing of the rest of Penkellis.

He had reshaped the house, he had reshaped Lawrence's life, and now he was gone.

Against his better judgment, Georgie peered over the side of the fishing boat. The ocean was choppy and frothed with white in the storm, and when Georgie looked inland he could see the cliffs covered in snow.

The fishermen—Mrs. Ferris's smuggler cousins—assured Georgie that they would reach Plymouth tomorrow. Or perhaps it was tomorrow night. Their speech—whether it was a foreign tongue, a rustic burr, or a thieves' cant, Georgie neither knew nor cared—was almost unintelligible. He was in the uncomfortable position of having to trust that these strangers weren't going to dump him overboard to spare themselves the inconvenience of having to sail out of their way. But Mrs. Ferris had spoken to them very sternly, in the same tongue they now used among one another. Whatever she had asked for, none of the sailors had the temerity to deny her to her face.

At least Lord Courtenay's coat was warm, with all its superfluous capes of heavy, soft wool. Georgie hadn't scrupled to steal it, along with the man's valise and coin purse. He would have stolen Courtenay's hat as well, if it hadn't been ruined by the snow. Lawrence didn't care much for Courtenay, and that was enough of a reason for Georgie to rob the fellow blind even if he hadn't arrived at precisely the moment when Georgie needed to make a quick escape.

Pulling the coat tightly around him, he realized that helping himself to Courtenay's belongings and persuading Mrs. Ferris to aid his escape had been the easy part. Now he had to figure out where to go.

In the stolen coin purse was enough money to get him to Paris, maybe further. But he hadn't asked the fishermen to carry him across the channel. No, he had asked them to bring him to Plymouth, where he would travel by the mail to London.

And once in London, well, he would choose the method of his demise, most likely. Either the gallows or a knife in the back.

At the moment he was leaning towards the knife in the back. If he delivered himself to Mattie Brewster of his own accord, the man might not look too closely into where Georgie had been—and who Georgie had been with—these past months. That would keep Lawrence safe and out of reach. Lawrence would be able to live peacefully at Penkellis, undisturbed. Georgie would either be killed as a traitor or put back to work for Mattie. Both fates appealed to Georgie about equally, but at least all the people he loved would be safe.

"Drink." A fisherman shoved a flask under Georgie's nose. Georgie took a long drag of what tasted like apple brandy.

"Thank you," he said, returning the flask.

The fisherman grunted and left Georgie alone.

Then there was the other option. Riskier, but Georgie had never been one to shy away from danger. Georgie only had one card that was any good whatsoever, and if he played it right, he could...well, not precisely win, because there was no winning in this game, but he could make sure that Brewster lost.

Halliday arrived at Penkellis as soon as the snow had melted enough to allow foot travel from the village.

"You could have warned me," Lawrence said, greeting the vicar in the hall. He had been looking forward to confronting Halliday ever since he learned that the vicar had thought Lawrence's sanity needed inquiring into. Never mind the fact that Lawrence himself had been quite convinced of his own lunacy. One expected one's vicar to have more sense.

Halliday's habitually concerned expression grew several degrees more anxious and he ran a finger between his neck and his collar. "Oh?" He was plainly striving for innocent curiosity but failing miserably.

Lawrence drew himself up to his full height, effectively towering over Halliday. "You knew Courtenay was out to get me declared mad, and instead of simply telling me, you went and hired a spy. You put a man into my own house."

The vicar's brow furrowed. "Now, that isn't entirely fair. What would you have done if I had said that Simon's maternal relations were investigating your competence? You would have thrown me out on my ear, and then you'd be in Bedlam before you even knew what happened."

"Besides," said a voice from the doorway. Courtenay, of course. The man was forever materializing from the shadows like a nasty insect. "You couldn't blame the fellow if he were a bit concerned about your..." He gestured at his own head. "What with your pedigree."

"That's terribly rich coming from someone who called my late brother a friend," Lawrence retorted. "Pedigree, my arse."

"I take it the matter is moot?" Halliday asked. "You're satisfied of Radnor's mental state? Mr. Turner saw nothing amiss."

"Yes, yes," Courtenay answered. "You can't imagine how relieved I am. I had visions of needing to rescue a small boy from the clutches of a monster, and instead, I find this." His gaze traveled around the hall, taking in the furnishings Georgie had hastily put in place. "Shabby and tired, but respectable. In all events, it's clear enough that you've none of your brother's predilections, Laurie. I see no courtesans, either dead or living, on the premises. No evidence of any recent orgies, more's the pity. No pregnant servants, no creditors banging on the doors. Utterly, boringly respectable." He paused, blowing some hair off his forehead. "God, I can't wait to get out of here."

"You're welcome to leave." Lawrence gestured helpfully at the door. "More than welcome, in fact."

"The mail coach arrived in Penryn this morning," Halliday said. "So the roads must be clear."

"I'd run off to pack my bags, but of course my bags have vanished, right along with the fellow you hired to keep an eye on Radnor," Courtenay told the vicar.

Courtenay was the only one who had dared allude to Georgie's absence. Lady Standish instinctively knew it was a delicate matter, and Simon seemed grimly accustomed to the idea that people he was fond of might disappear.

"I'll give you whatever you need to get back to the rock you crawled out from," Lawrence growled. Twenty pounds, thirty pounds, whatever it took to get Courtenay out of his hair would be money well spent.

But instead he found himself taking tea with the vicar, because that was evidently what one did with afternoon callers. A maid arrived with a tray of tea and biscuits, and Lawrence let himself be swept into the parlor. Lady Standish and Simon arrived, as if summoned by the presence of tea, both chattering about their progress in laying wires from the study to the kitchens. Lawrence couldn't figure out the purpose in that endeavor, except that it kept both of them busy.

Courtenay was absolutely right that it was boring, but he was also right that it was perfectly respectable. Ordinary. Sane. Unremarkable. Lawrence had never even aspired to such outright normalcy. If anyone had told him in October that before the end of the year he'd be taking tea with Simon, the vicar, Standish's sister and brother-in-law, and one of Percy's nearest and dearest, he'd have thought it more likely that he would open up the window of his study and discover he could fly.

He knew he had Georgie to thank for easing Lawrence's way back among the living. And Lawrence had done nothing for him in return. Georgie hadn't even taken the jewels, the one thing that Lawrence *could* give him. He had simply disappeared into thin air, and Lawrence knew that he would never see the man again.

No, Georgie hadn't disappeared into thin air. People didn't simply evaporate, for heaven's sake. Georgie had gone somewhere, and based on what he had said, there were few safe places he could have gone.

But there was a niggling doubt that he hadn't gone someplace safe at all. It was past time for Lawrence to stop feeling sorry for himself and start figuring out how to help Georgie. He put down his teacup and paced the length of the parlor, searching his brain for some clue as to Georgie's destination. The roads had been blocked, and no horses were missing from the stables, which mean that Georgie had left Penkellis on foot. Which was a stupid thing to have done in the middle of a blizzard.

But Georgie was clever. He was brilliant. Either he was holed up in a cottage within an easy walking distance, or he had found some other means of leaving.

Either way, he would couldn't have acted on his own, and there was only one person at Penkellis who was in a position to help. Lawrence strode out of the room and was in the kitchens before he could second-guess himself.

"Where did he go?" Lawrence asked, ignoring the flutter of curtsies from the kitchen maids.

Mrs. Ferris put down her rolling pin and looked at him levelly. "Tell me why it's your business again?"

"I need to know whether he crossed the channel." Whether he was safe. "And if you want to have this conversation in plain hearing of a dozen strangers, it's up to you."

She followed him into the larder. "I don't know where he went," she whispered. "But he didn't say anything about France, and he knows full well I could have gotten him there."

So Georgie knew about the smuggling. The Ferrises had run goods inland for generations, and Lawrence accepted it as a fact of Cornwall life, much like weather.

"What exactly did he ask you?"

She hesitated a moment, wiping her hands on her apron. "He asked if I could get him close to London. And I told him I could send a boat as far as Plymouth if the wind was right, and that he could travel by land the rest of the way."

If Georgie had gone back to London, with all the risks that city held for him, there had to be a reason, and Lawrence didn't doubt that Georgie had a plan. And he had a grim sense of foreboding that he was going to do something dangerous. Something noble.

And damn it all to hell if Lawrence wasn't going to do the exact same thing.

CHAPTER TWENTY-THREE

As soon as the smugglers set him ashore, Georgie stripped off Courtenay's sodden greatcoat and pawned it along with the contents of the stolen saddlebag: a silver hairbrush, an ivory and tortoiseshell shaving kit, and a proliferation of shirt studs. He didn't even bother to change into dry clothes before boarding the stagecoach for London. Likely he looked and smelled like a stowaway, but he couldn't bring himself to care.

When, two days later, Georgie climbed down from the stagecoach in Charing Cross, he was greeted by the odor of coal fire and a blanket of fog that bleached the city to the color of dust. Tired and disoriented from the long, uncomfortable journey from Cornwall, he somehow hadn't expected it to be winter in London. He had missed all the good parts of autumn while he was at Penkellis, alphabetizing papers and falling in love.

Georgie had always been careful not to let people at any shop or tavern get too used to the sight of him. Impermanence was almost as good as invisibility. He slipped in, he slipped out, and he didn't retrace his footsteps for a good long while, lest anyone start to wonder why Gerard Turnbull looked so much like that rascal Geoffrey Tavistock and what either of them had to do with Georgie Turner.

Today he would ignore his inclination towards secrecy and subterfuge, to say nothing of his instinct for self-preservation, and do his best to attract notice. He walked slowly eastward from Charing Cross, deliberately lingering near the busier thoroughfares and walking twice around some blocks. He arrived, cold and aching, at his destination: a coffee house on Wych Street that was frequented by people from all walks of life. If he sat there long enough, bareheaded and in plain view, somebody would recognize him. And then all he would have to do was wait.

At a table near the door, he sipped his coffee, jarringly hot and bitter after so many weeks without it. Alert for a narrowed glance, a low whisper, a too-quick flash of movement, he had to remind himself that he wasn't hiding, that he welcomed every stray gaze and curious look. The constant hum of chatter, the almost musical clinking of cup and saucer and spoon, seemed uncomfortably loud after the quiet of Penkellis. The swarm of people in and out of the coffee house and along the street outside was foreign and unsettling. He felt like he was seeing the world through Lawrence's eyes; everything was loud and busy and fast, pregnant with danger.

All the more reason to leave Lawrence in peace. By going to London, Georgie would keep Brewster from going to Penkellis. It was an old trick, doing something flashy and obvious to put a mark's attention precisely where the confidence man wanted it. Georgie had known that principle before he knew his letters.

There were more direct ways to attract Brewster's notice. Georgie could have walked right up to the front door of Brewster's house, a nondescript building in Whitechapel. Or he could have gone to the old warehouse Brewster's gang used as a place of business. But those methods made it too convenient for one of Brewster's men to kill Georgie behind closed doors, dispose of his body, and call it a day's work. Georgie might be reckless, but he wasn't suicidal.

He finished his coffee and ordered another.

All told, it took four hours before he felt a tap on his shoulder, an ominous pressure between his shoulder blades.

He forced out a slow breath, striving for a semblance of calm. He shot a look out of the corner of his eye and saw enough of his assailant to know it wasn't Mattie but one of his men.

"I thought for sure he'd want to talk to me," Georgie murmured, too low to be overheard by the other patrons. "I won't have much to say if you do anything drastic with that knife, friend."

"He doesn't want to talk." Georgie recognized the voice as belonging to Tom Vance, a man who unloaded cargo from ships and made sure some of it disappeared. They had worked together only once, when Georgie helped dispose of a stolen crate of silks. "He offered twenty pounds for your body. *Dead* body, Turner." Tom stood behind Georgie's chair, bending companionably to Georgie's ear, the knife concealed between their bodies. Georgie darted a look around the coffee house. Tom had come alone. "Twenty pounds," Tom repeated, as if daring Georgie to argue with him for valuing a spot of murder as well worth the sum.

"Seems a waste," Georgie said blandly, without turning his head. "I earned him hundreds of pounds last year alone." If he could only persuade Tom to bring Mattie here or somewhere else too public for bloodshed, then Georgie could do what he did best. He could lie and connive and somehow bring Mattie around. Somehow.

Failing that, he was going to run like hell. Every bone in his body told him to run now, now, before that knife made the decision for him.

"That was before you nearly got the lot of us transported. Damn it, Georgie. We thought you had scarpered. You ought to have, damn it." There was regret in Tom's voice, but the blade on Georgie's back didn't drop. "He can't let you caper about the city after that trick you pulled. Otherwise it makes it too easy for any of us to turn our backs on one another the next time we get picked up. And you know it." He was right. Georgie knew it. He always had. "Why the hell did you come back?"

Georgie took a sip of coffee, forcing his hands to remain steady despite the audible scratch of steel against the wool of his coat. "Take me to him, Tom. I'll talk to him, make him see it my way. And then he'll be grateful to you for—"

"Not this time, Georgie."

There was a silence that stretched out too long. Georgie understood that Tom was trying to figure out what to do next. Stab Georgie in the middle of the coffee house and let the chips fall where they did? Drag Georgie outside and stab him in the nearest alley? Bring him somewhere more convenient for murder? Georgie didn't wait to find out.

With a single movement, he pushed his table over, moving with it as it fell. That put a healthy distance between his back and the knife and caused enough confusion for Georgie to slip out the door without a backwards glance.

Spending three days in a carriage was a hellish prospect, but Lawrence needed to get to London. Even thinking about it, he felt his chest constrict and a wave of heat spread across his skin. He had to remind himself that this miserable state was temporary, not the prelude to a permanent state of madness. It didn't feel the least bit temporary, though. It felt like doom itself, and Lawrence desperately wanted to retreat to his study.

Instead, he cleared his throat and attempted a casual tone. "Simon, how would you like to go to London?"

The boy looked up eagerly from the game of cards he was playing with Courtenay near the hearth. "With you?"

"Yes, I have a small matter of business I need to conduct in person, but after that we can visit Astley's Amphitheatre." Filled with people, noise, and animals, visiting Astley's was an objectively terrible idea, and it wasn't even the most unpleasant task he'd face in London. "I've never been."

"May I visit Astley's?" Courtenay asked, affecting an air of hopeful innocence.

Simon clapped his hands together, an expression of undiluted merriment on his face. Lawrence was simultaneously jealous of the child's affection and reluctantly glad the two seemed to get on so well. "Oh yes, Father," Simon said. "Please can Uncle Courtenay come too?"

Lawrence went rigid. Simon had never before called him *Father*. He *wasn't* Simon's father, and from what he gathered, the child knew it. Which, paradoxically, gave the term that much more meaning. He felt a warm rush of pride and happiness that nearly displaced his anxious fear.

Lawrence grunted his assent. Of course he would agree to anything Simon asked.

Courtenay smirked, the insolent bastard. "I have some business in London as well," he said. "Some loose ends that need to be tied up before I return to the Continent."

So it was settled. Lady Standish and Lord Courtenay worked out the details between themselves, and early the next morning Lawrence found himself packed into the Standish carriage along with Simon and Lady Standish. Courtenay was to ride alongside while Medlock would return home by post chaise.

Lawrence moved as if in a fog, allowing himself to be bundled in a blanket like an invalid, a hot brick placed beneath his feet.

As the carriage began to roll, Lawrence squeezed his eyes shut. It had been years since he had been in a carriage, since he had been anywhere farther than Penkellis's borders. But this was what he needed to do to make sure Georgie was safe, so he'd do it.

He felt a light touch on his arm and looked down to see Lady Standish's gloved hand resting on the sleeve of his coat. "Is there anything I ought to know?" she murmured. "Any way to make this less unpleasant? I gather that there must be a pressing reason for you to make this trip, and if I can help in any way, you must know that I'll be only too glad to help." Lady Standish was no fool and didn't need to be told that Lawrence's venturing any further than the garden gate was a major event.

Lawrence nodded. "Thank you." He tried to imagine what Georgie would do, what measures he would invent to make

Lawrence feel more at home, less in the wilderness of confusion and nerves. "If you could see to it that I have bread and ham when we stop for supper, perhaps?" It sounded childish, pathetic.

"Of course," Lady Standish said briskly, as if nothing were amiss. This, Lawrence reminded himself, was friendship.

As the carriage drove past the Penkellis gates, Lawrence absently dropped his hand to his side, unconsciously reaching for Barnabus, who, of course, wasn't there. No Barnabus, no Georgie, no familiar places or things.

He tried to put his rising anxiety to the side. He couldn't conquer it, so perhaps he could ignore it. Or, at least, exist alongside it for as long as he needed to get to London and ensure that Georgie was safe. As soon as he knew that Georgie hadn't foolishly delivered himself part and parcel to the man who wanted to kill him, then Lawrence would go back to Penkellis and hole up in his study for the rest of his life.

"Look!" Simon called, his voice alive with excitement. "Tell the coachman to stop!"

"Oh, dear," Lady Standish clucked. "We'll have to bring him back to the house. Otherwise, the poor creature will jog alongside us until he becomes quite exhausted."

Lawrence opened his eyes and peered out the window. There, running beside the carriage, was Barnabus. He rapped on the roof. "Stop!" Once the carriage had come to a stand, he unlatched the door and patted his knee. Barnabus promptly jumped into the already cramped carriage and settled himself on the floor on top of Lawrence's feet.

"Well," Lady Standish said. "That's loyalty, I suppose."

"More like he's never seen me step outside the house without him," Lawrence countered. He felt the edge of his anxiety blunt a little bit, as he focused on the dog's heavy weight on his feet, the rhythm of the sleeping animal's breathing.

He shut his eyes and slept.

Prisons all smelled the same, like piss and illness, with a hint of blood and gin. It was the same odor as the gutters Georgie had come from, so in a way it felt only right that he ought to be here now, iron bars separating him from all the things he didn't deserve—freedom, warmth, sunlight. Born in the rookery, dead on the gallows—it had a certain symmetry that to Georgie's exhausted mind looked like justice. He was getting exactly what he deserved.

He slumped against a damp, sticky wall. No sense being precious about his clothes anymore, was there? He couldn't shut his eyes for more than a minute, because he knew enough not to sleep too deeply in the kind of company you found in a jail cell, but the next thing he knew, there was a man standing before him, nudging Georgie's leg with his heavy, booted foot.

"You. Turner," the man said, continuing to prod even though Georgie's eyes were open. "Up. The governor wants to talk to you."

Georgie got to his feet and brushed the dust off his trousers, even though they were beyond salvation after so much time on that little boat and even more on the stagecoach.

"On with it," the man insisted, impatient. "Haven't got all day."

They went down a corridor and into a small cube of a room that held nothing more than a deal table and a couple of chairs. The single dirty window was covered in bars, affording no possibility of escape. Not that Georgie wanted to escape. He had, after all, come here on purpose.

The door slammed behind him, and he was momentarily alone, the heavy oak blocking out the sounds of the prison beyond. He sat in one of the chairs, every joint in his body aching with fatigue. He shut his eyes, only opening them when the door slammed shut behind him.

"What do we have here?" The man who entered the room was of middle age, slightly balding, wearing the sort of somber, nondescript clothing that Georgie would don to play the part of a clerk. He consulted a paper that he held in his hand. "Smythe says you tried to turn yourself in, saying you know something about the Brewster gang and confessing to—well, that's quite a list, isn't it?"

"You aren't a magistrate," Georgie said, his voice sounding thick and remote.

"Lord, no." The clerk seemed amused by the notion. "Can't bother the judges with every lunat—ah, helpful fellow who comes in off the streets. Tell me what you know, and I'll make sure that it gets passed on to the right people."

After all this, they weren't going to listen to him? And what if the right people included Mattie Brewster, who must have an informant in Newgate? Georgie would have laughed if he weren't too tired to force out the sound. "I'm George Turner. I worked for Mattie Brewster for almost ten years. I know the password to speak to him. I can give you details about the Herriot case and the Landsdowne forgeries. I played a principal role in both. I'm confessing to larceny, forgery—"

"Steady now, Mr. Turner," the man said, smiling patiently.

"George Turner. I've been in Newgate before, for God's sake. I was ten years old the first time I was arrested." He had stolen a lady's reticule. After shedding a few tears and telling the magistrate a pretty story, he had gotten off with a slap on the wrist and a shilling from the lady herself. He tried to tamp down his desperation and summon up some remnant of that crafty Georgie Turner who had outwitted and outlied thieves and thief takers alike.

The trouble was, now that he actually wanted to tell the truth, to finally confess his sins and do something decent for a change, he didn't know how to be persuasive.

"The Brewster gang's meeting place is the top story of a warehouse on Ironmonger Lane. Knock twice, and when they open the door, say you're there to see the old codger about a pot of prawns." Georgie had come up with that himself, and for a few days it had been highly diverting to hear everyone who entered Mattie's inner sanctum—lords and ladies, ruffians and penny whores—utter such a stupid, commonplace phrase. After a while the joke had staled, but Mattie hadn't bothered to change the password.

"A pot of prawns, yes indeed, my lad. I'll get right to it. How about you stay here while I do just that."

Georgie bit back a groan. If this didn't pan out, he didn't have another plan. Attempting to talk to Brewster hadn't worked, so Georgie had resorted to ruining him. He had thought that by giving evidence against Brewster, he'd protect the people he loved. If Brewster were in prison, he couldn't go to Penkellis and harm Lawrence, nor could he harass Jack and Sarah.

The only catch was that Georgie, too, would be in prison. Or worse.

When the clerk left, the door bolted firmly behind him, Georgie slumped in his chair and tried to rest. He couldn't have said how long passed before the door opened again.

"You're an idiot."

Georgie jerked to attention. In the doorway stood his brother, wearing a grim expression.

"Jack, what are you—"

"I could ask you the same. You realize that once they realize you weren't lying, they're going to try to pin every unsolved racket onto you. Damn it, Georgie." He slapped his hat onto the table and slumped into the chair across from Georgie.

Of course Jack had found him. He had people all over London whispering in his ear.

Jack scrubbed a hand through his hair. "Sarah will be worried sick, you know."

Georgie had known Jack long enough to understand that this was code for *I'm worried*. "I didn't know what else to do."

"You could have stayed in Cornwall, or gone to Paris, or gone anywhere else on earth, for God's sake, Georgie."

"I didn't want Brewster to hunt me down in Cornwall."

"Ah, so you came here to make it easy on him? To give him a sporting chance?"

"No," Georgie said slowly, weighing whether to confide in his brother. Oh, hell, he didn't have much to lose at this point. "I was worried that he'd harm Radnor."

Jack's eyes flew open, and an expression of bewildered shock flickered across his face for the briefest instant, before his features resumed an even grimmer expression than before. "Ah, fuck me. Wasn't expecting that."

If Georgie were even a little less tired, he would have laughed at his brother's confusion. As it was, he huffed out a sound that was more like a feeble wheeze. "Nor was I."

"So you're here to get yourself hanged so Mattie doesn't go near your fellow."

"Getting hanged wasn't in my original plans," Georgie said dryly.

Jack drummed his fingers on his thigh. "I'll go to Mattie and warn him. That way if Bow Street decides to check up on your story, they won't find anything. They'll think you're a lunatic or that you're mad for attention. We'll get you out of prison and then figure out Brewster afterwards."

"But what about Lawrence?"

"Bugger your Lawrence. He's an earl. He can fend for himself. Besides, Mattie's going to be pretty clear on the fact that you aren't in Cornwall. He won't have any reason to go there."

"What about you and Sarah?" Georgie felt a wash of hot shame sweep over him as he admitted to his brother that he had put him and their sister in danger.

"I can take care of myself. As soon as Sarah got back in town, I stationed one of my men outside her shop, and so far Brewster hasn't shown up."

That was hardly reassuring, and they both knew it. Especially now that Brewster knew Georgie had returned. So much for this plan, Georgie thought. Now he was going to molder in prison while Brewster did as he pleased. And if he did get set free, he had only one recourse: he'd have to go directly to Brewster.

CHAPTER TWENTY-FOUR

L awrence glanced again at the scrap of paper he had carried in his pocket all the way from Penkellis. It was creased and soft from having been clenched in his fist.

"Are you quite sure you don't want me to come with you?" Lady Standish asked again when Lawrence made no move to exit the carriage.

"You and Simon go see the lions at the Tower," Lawrence insisted. "Keep an eye on Courtenay." As bizarre as it was to see Courtenay play the part of a doting uncle, Lawrence had yet to see anything less than proper in the man's conduct. Still, having Lady Standish there might curb any stray impulse on Courtenay's part to revert to bad habits and wander into the nearest brothel.

They had arrived in London in the middle of the night. Lady Standish had insisted that they all stay at her home, and Lawrence had been too weary to protest. He scooped Simon up in his arms to carry him upstairs, and the next thing he remembered was waking in an unfamiliar room. Moments later, a pair of servants had arrived with a bath and pitchers of steaming water.

The result was that when Lawrence finally emerged from the carriage and climbed the steps to this narrow, unassuming house, he was freshly washed and shaved, his hair neatly combed into a queue. Somebody had even bathed Barnabus, which was just as well, since Lawrence wasn't going anywhere without the dog. All this strangeness was bad enough, even with the dog's companionship.

He assumed an expression that he hoped approximated good cheer and waved to Simon, who was happily sitting on the box beside the coachman as the carriage drove away. Before lifting the brass knocker, he bent to scratch Barnabus's furry neck. A moment passed and still nobody came to the door. He felt exposed, vulnerable, standing on this strange doorstep on an unfamiliar street in a city he didn't want to be in. Lawrence had gotten this address from Halliday; in this house lived the man Halliday had written about investigating Lawrence's mental state. He lifted the knocker again and let it fall, and the unpleasant clank of metal against metal jolted unpleasantly through his body. London was a noisy, chaotic place, and every sound chipped away at the veneer of calm he had tried to assume.

After another interminable moment, Lawrence heard footsteps, and then the door was opened. It was not a servant who stood in the doorway, but a gentleman. He was close to Lawrence's own height and leaned heavily on a walking stick, which was perhaps why it had taken him so long to answer the door.

"How can I help you?" the gentleman asked, with a wary glance at Barnabus.

"I'm Radnor," Lawrence said simply, watching as the gentleman's eyes went wide. He looked like he wanted to take a step back, but then his manners won out over prudence. "I'm looking for Oliver Rivington."

"Of course. I'm Rivington." He gestured for Lawrence to come inside. "And you're Halliday's earl. Not a recluse after all, I see. Georgie must have been—" He stopped.

"Right," Lawrence said. "About Georgie. Where is he?"

"Georgie?" The man's astonishment could not have been feigned. "He's supposed to be with you." His lips went tight with concern, then he gestured for Lawrence to enter. "Come in, come in. There's nothing to do but wait for Jack."

Rivington led the way to a small sitting room that smelled of lemon oil and brandy. "I went to school with Halliday," the gentleman said. "And he wrote me a kind letter when I was recuperating from my injury." He gestured at his leg. "When he mentioned in passing that his patron's, ah, mental state had been called into question and that he was in danger of being plunged into some kind of legal proceedings, I offered to help."

Barnabus must have sensed Lawrence's disquiet, because he pressed his body close to his master's leg and kept his ears pricked up. At that moment, the front door opened and slammed shut.

"My fuckwit of a brother is in prison," called a voice from the vestibule. There was the sound of a coat being shrugged off, keys dropped on a table. "Some or another noble-minded shite."

The new arrival appeared in the doorway to the sitting room. "Lord Radnor," Mr. Rivington said pointedly, "allow me to present Jack Turner, Georgie's brother."

Lawrence drew in a sharp breath. Georgie's brother. Which meant Georgie was in prison.

"So you're Georgie's fancy man." The man was a larger, rougher version of Georgie. Where Georgie looked carved by hand in ivory, this man was roughhewn from stone. And evidently he lived here, in this respectable little house, along with the handsome gentleman with the bad leg.

"Don't torture him," Rivington chided. "He's as worried as you are."

Barnabus let out a low growl. "I came to see that he was safe," Lawrence said.

"Well, he isn't," Jack spat. "I'm trying to see that he isn't hanged, but once a man is in Newgate, there isn't much I can do."

But there might be something that Lawrence could do.

Lawrence declined Rivington's offer to drive him, instead asking for instructions on how to reach his destination by foot. He needed to burn off some of the anxious energy that was stopping him from thinking clearly. In the absence of wood to chop or water to swim in, that left walking.

So with little more than a vague sense of where he was heading, he and Barnabus kept up a brisk pace as they strode along the pavements. He didn't know whether it was the sight of Barnabus or his own thunderous expression that caused people to keep their distance, but Lawrence was given a wide berth, even when he skirted the edge of a rookery.

This squalid warren of dilapidated buildings and dirty streets could have been the slum where Georgie was born. Barefoot children loitered in doorways, wearing little more than rags. Women leaned out of windows, and skinny dogs roamed the streets. The smell of filth and gin hung in the air despite the chill. When a pair of boys Simon's age briefly ventured too close, Barnabus let out a low growl. Lawrence suspected that these urchins were a team of pickpockets. Might as well spare them the trouble. He dug a couple of pennies out of his pocket and tossed two coins to each of the boys.

When he emerged into a solidly respectable neighborhood, he looked over his shoulder at the rookery, glad to be out of it. He could only imagine how desperately Georgie must have yearned to do the same, to get as far away from that place as possible. However little Lawrence liked the idea of Georgie defrauding innocent people, he had never really doubted that Georgie had every reason to take his fate into his own hands. Still, seeing the alternative with his own eyes made Lawrence understand just how much a man would do to escape a place like this.

He arrived at his destination, took a reassuring look at Barnabus, and crossed the wide courtyard of the Admiralty.

A uniformed sailor stationed by the door moved to block his entry. "Can I help you, sir?"

"I'm Radnor." Lawrence didn't break stride, and the sailor stepped aside to make way for the brutish lord and his enormous dog. "I'm here to see Admiral Haversham." Haversham was one of the fellows who assisted the Lord High Admiral. More importantly, he had written to Lawrence about the telegraph.

"If you'll take a seat, sir, I can see if his lordship—"

"Most unnecessary," he said as he walked up the stairs, Barnabus trotting beside. "I'll find him myself."

As he had hoped, the prospect of a peer of the realm— one of the historically deranged Earls of Radnor, no less— barging into the chambers of the Lord Commissioners of the Admiralty, accompanied by an eight-stone mongrel who snarled at anyone who approached his master, was enough to send the young man skittering ahead to lead the way into the proper set of rooms.

Lawrence had never been in a building like this: wide marble corridors hung with portraits of men long since dead, people who must all know one another bustling purposefully about, a vaguely efficient and martial air. Perhaps boys who went to school or men who joined the army or navy could get used to the sensation of being a bee in such a grand hive. But Lawrence felt sorely out of place; he belonged among the crumbled stones and rotten wood of Penkellis, not here. If it weren't for Georgie, he'd turn on his heel and leave, never stopping until he reached home.

Instead, he tried to swallow his fear. He reminded himself that this would soon be over, no matter how terrible it was. Besides, he knew that he looked every inch the earl. He was wearing the clothes Georgie had bought, and he was freshly shaved. Nobody needed to know how uneasy he was, nobody but he could hear the blood rushing in his ears or feel the heart pounding in his chest.

He walked through a final set of doors and found a gray-haired man reading a letter at an enormous desk.

"Haversham?"

"Yes, what's the meaning of this?"

"I have your telegraph." Lawrence pulled a sheaf of papers out of his coat pocket and slapped them onto the glossy mahogany surface of the desk.

"Telegraph?" Haversham flipped through the papers. "Are you Lord Radnor?" he asked, looking over the rim of his spectacles. "I was under the impression that you, ah, didn't come to town much."

Lawrence arched an eyebrow and gestured at his person, as if to say, *guess again*. He swept the telegraph plans out of the older man's hands. "You can have these after you've granted me a favor."

"Excuse me? No, no. Not possible. The Admiralty has decided that we don't need this kind of device. The war is over. We're at peace. No need to send urgent messages."

"Then I'm free to sell the plans to anyone else?" Lawrence grabbed the papers off the man's desk. "A private person or another government, perhaps?"

Haversham turned an angry shade of puce. "Certainly not."

"Good. Then we can discuss price."

The older man made a noise that Lawrence interpreted as grudging assent.

"All I require is that you pull some strings to have my secretary, George Turner, released from Newgate."

"This is most irregular," Haversham sniffed.

"We both know I could hire a solicitor or throw my weight around in some other way in order to have my secretary set free." But those courses of action required time and a level of participation on Lawrence's part that he'd rather avoid. "I suggest we spare ourselves the inconvenience."

"Tomorrow I can discuss the matter with my—"

"No. Today."

"Lord Radnor," Haversham said, "these things take time. Messages need to be sent to the appropriate parties."

"If only there was some device that allowed for messages to be sent instantaneously," Lawrence said pointedly, waving the papers in his hand. "Besides, you'll do well to remember whose son I am, whose brother I am. There's no telling what I might do if I'm crossed." As if on cue, Barnabus bared his teeth. "You have until tomorrow morning," he said, and Haversham blanched. Lawrence nearly felt bad for the man. But there was power in being considered beyond reason, and Lawrence fully intended to exploit every advantage he had.

"Somebody has mighty special friends."

"What?" Georgie was half-asleep, slumped against the slimy stones of the cell wall.

The guard snorted. "You're to be released."

"What?" Georgie repeated, staggering to his feet. "Why?"

"I don't know. They don't tell me things," the guard groused. "All I know is that there was a runner from the Admiralty and the next thing I know I'm being told to let you go."

The Admiralty. That couldn't mean… There hadn't been time for Lawrence to find out about Georgie's imprisonment and request help from his acquaintance at the Admiralty.

Well, never mind what it meant. Georgie shrugged into the coat the guard thrust at him and walked out the open cell door before anyone could think better of setting him free.

The foggy gray London sky was blindingly bright after the darkness of Newgate. Georgie started walking in the direction of Jack's house, for lack of any better plan. At least he'd get a meal and a bath along with whatever scolding Jack saw fit to dole out.

Worse than the scolding would be the pity for Georgie having lost his heart in a foolish way. Perhaps even a little bit of respect for Georgie's attempt to do something that wasn't entirely self-serving.

Georgie didn't want any of that. He didn't deserve it, and he didn't think he could sit there and endure anything like kindness when he knew how little he merited it. After a lifetime spent stealing and scheming, he belonged at Newgate more than he belonged in a comfortable chair by his brother's fire. He didn't regret the past, but all those years spent harming—yes, harming, even though he tried his best not to think of it that way—innocent people had left their mark. He wasn't a decent person anymore, and there was no use trying to live like one.

He was exhausted. It had been days upon days since he had slept properly. After so many hours on the cold floor of the prison, his bones ached with every step. Judging by the scruff on his jaw, it had been nearly a week since he had shaved, so he must look as rough as he felt. The very model of a ruffian, like something out of a Hogarth sketch depicting a cautionary tale of hard living.

That suspicion was confirmed when he crossed into a respectable neighborhood. A nurse tugged her young charges to the opposite side of the street. A lady and gentleman out for a stroll steadfastly refused to look at him. Georgie tugged the brim of his hat low on his forehead, obscuring his face.

He sat heavily on a bench in Grosvenor Square, facing the house he had frequented for his last job. The Packingham house. He didn't know why he needed to come here, whether it was to rub some salt in his wounds and remind himself of how he had nearly robbed that poor lady, or whether he wanted to cling with both hands to the first good deed he had ever done, which was to spare Mrs. Packingham.

The wind whipped through the square, and Georgie half-heartedly pulled his coat tighter around his chest. His gloves had gone missing—which was to say they had been stolen—at Newgate, along with his coin purse. Georgie could hardly begrudge any fellow thief his takings. All the same, he was bitterly cold.

The door to the house opened, and he saw Ned Packingham load the old lady into her carriage. She appeared unaltered, which stood to reason; her fortune was intact, her nephew still danced attendance on her in hopes of inheriting her estate, and all was well—or at least as well as it had been before Georgie had arrived. He wondered if the nephew untangled her embroidery silks as carefully as Georgie had, or if he lazily snipped off any stubborn knot, leaving her with frustratingly short strands.

Tears prickled in his eyes. This was why he never let himself think about his marks after he was done with them.

Tired and miserable as he was, he knew that he was thinking of Mrs. Packingham to avoid thinking of Lawrence. He had very carefully not let himself wonder how Lawrence and

Simon must be getting on without him, or about how Lawrence might be distressed by the arrival of Simon's uncle. He was trying not to think about Lawrence at all.

One of Georgie's earliest memories was of his sister's cat. He couldn't have been much more than a baby, if Sarah was still living at home. The cat had kittens, and Sarah and Georgie's father had insisted that they needed to be killed. He had brought up a bucket and drowned them, one at a time. Georgie, confused by his sister's tears and unsure why the soft kittens required a bath, had toddled over. "You hold them under until the bubbles stop," his father had said, as if he were teaching Georgie how to toast a crumpet rather than how to drown a newborn cat. Georgie watched as the bubbles stopped, one kitten, then the next, then the next, all the while Sarah cried in the background.

That was what he was trying to do to his love for Lawrence, but no matter how hard he fought to push his feelings deeper, they kept bubbling up.

All he had to do was shut his eyes, and he could almost smell Lawrence's scent, feel the pleasant coarseness of his beard against Georgie's face, imagine the way he stroked that mongrel of a dog with his huge hands.

Georgie imagined Lawrence putting an arm around him, comforting and warm.

And then, out of nowhere, there *was* an arm around him. But it wasn't Lawrence. It was Mattie Brewster.

CHAPTER TWENTY-FIVE

Under other circumstances, Lawrence might have been amused to discover how many doors were opened to him by virtue of his rank, his wealth, and his presumed dangerousness. But today he was too busy pretending not to be panicking to within an inch of his life.

He playacted the role of imperious aristocrat. When in doubt he simply channeled Percy—arrogant, entitled, reckless—and people promptly gave him whatever he desired. He wanted his secretary released from jail? It was done. He wanted to know precisely what his secretary had tried to confess to the magistrate? A runner was dispatched to find out, while Lawrence drank brandy in a cozy parlor next to Haversham's office. He wanted a hackney to take him and his enormous dog to a warehouse in Cheapside? Not five minutes later he was headed along the Strand, Barnabus sitting beside him on the carriage bench.

Lawrence had never been inside a warehouse before. As far as he knew, he had never even been *outside* one either. This particular specimen was a dirty brick building, boxy and unimpressive, with tiny windows barely breaking up the monotonous facade. As he climbed the short set of stairs to the door, he saw a faded, peeling sign indicating that the building was the property of some or another shipping company. But this was the address Georgie had given as Brewster's headquarters.

Lawrence, figuring that a wretchedly unpleasant and harrowing couple of days could hardly get much worse, had decided to dispense with Brewster. Any man fearsome enough to make even the unshakable Georgie Turner flee on the spot needed to be done away with. Lawrence, after the misery of the past week, was in a foul enough temper to put a bullet through the head of a man far less deserving of death than Mattie Brewster. He patted the coat pocket where he had placed Percy's dueling pistol.

Not that it would necessarily come to bullets or death. If Brewster could be dealt with in some other way, that would be acceptable, as long as the man never again had anything to do with Georgie.

I owe him, Georgie had said. Bollocks on owing. Bollocks on debt. Georgie was his own man, free to live his own life, and anyone who argued otherwise would have to answer to Lawrence. Georgie had made that point to Lawrence again and again—that Lawrence didn't need to repeat his father's or brother's sins or even atone for them. He was his own man, and he could live his own life. Lawrence was going to make that happen for Georgie.

He knocked on the door and, when asked, uttered the inane password. The door was opened by a man in rolled-up shirtsleeves and dirty trousers who looked warily at

Barnabus. Lawrence was momentarily astonished by the man's dishevelment, before recalling that this was precisely how he had dressed only a few weeks earlier. Self-consciously, he smoothed his gloved fingers down the lapels of his spotless coat, a tangible reminder of Georgie's care.

The man gestured wordlessly for Lawrence to precede him up two steep, rickety flights of stairs. At the top was a sort of landing with nothing but a flimsy-looking door. Could Brewster be protected by nothing more than a few sets of stairs and a cheap door? But then again, Lawrence was learning that power wasn't measured in fine buildings and armored doors but rather in what one could make other people do.

The door swung open, revealing a dim room lit only by the late afternoon light that streamed through a few small windows. A handful of men stood around the perimeter, their watchful eyes turned to Lawrence's entrance. In a chair, with his back to the window, sat a man whose features Lawrence couldn't distinguish in the dark, but from his placement and the way the other men oriented themselves with regard to him, he had to be Brewster.

"Mattie Brewster?" Lawrence asked, addressing the man in the chair. "You're not to lay a finger on Georgie Turner."

The seated man laughed, a disconcertingly affable sound. "And who are you to be telling me what to do with my fingers?"

Lawrence had been prepared for a rough accent, a voice that sounded of vice and crime. But this man sounded like a genial cockney costermonger.

"I'm Radnor." He wasn't certain if the criminal classes were up to date on the peerage, so he added, "Lawrence Browne, Earl of Radnor."

But Brewster responded promptly. "I lent money to your brother when he was at Oxford. He was a nasty bastard."

"And I'm worse. Which is why you aren't going to touch Turner."

"Oh, but it's a bit late for that, you see." He gestured to a shadowy corner that held a bundle of rags. The bundle of rags moved, and Lawrence saw that it was a person. A dirty, unshaven, badly—

It was Georgie.

Fear gripped Lawrence like a tight band around his chest, but he didn't let any emotion show on his face. He was pretending to be a half-mad, ruthless, dangerous man, not a lovestruck schoolboy. He sauntered over to one of the windows and calmly put his fist through it. From somewhere behind him came the sharp intake of breath. Good. He was making precisely the impression he sought. "Let him go. Bow Street knows where I am." Which was true—Lawrence hadn't made any secret of his intentions. "You have"—he shook the glass from his glove and pulled out his watch—"a bit less than a quarter of an hour to make yourselves scarce before the thief takers show up. Give me Turner, and you'll have just enough time to get out of here."

At the mention of Bow Street, a few of the men around the edges of the room shifted.

"And if I don't?"

"Then I take out my pistol, and presumably one of your men shoots me dead. You're tried as an accessory to the murder of a peer. Not an enviable position." He didn't even look at Georgie but heard a faint sound of protest come from that corner. So very faint that Lawrence felt certain Georgie was hurt, but it would ruin his act if he showed the least bit of human concern. "While we're on the topic, if any single hair on Mr. Turner's head is hurt at any point in the remainder of his life, I'll see to it that you pay. I have nearly unlimited resources and absolutely no scruples whatsoever. At the moment," he said casually, "I'd gladly cut off your balls and feed them to your henchmen. I'll almost regret it if I don't get a chance to. Give me Turner, though, and perhaps I'll get distracted."

When Brewster didn't move immediately, Lawrence flashed him his fiercest, maddest grin and coolly punched another window. This was the value of pricey Italian leather gloves, no doubt. One could break an infinity of windows with no harm to oneself.

Barnabus, his dander up and his teeth bared, was standing beside Georgie, snarling as if he were ready to devour anyone who came near. Lawrence would remember to buy him some buns as a reward.

Brewster, his eyes briefly narrowing with speedy calculation, turned calmly to the man nearest to him. "Let's go," he said, as if he were suggesting a walk in the park. He didn't spare a look for Lawrence or Georgie, or even for any of his men, who followed him single file out of the room as if nothing unusual had happened.

As soon as the door clicked shut, Lawrence fell to his knees by Georgie. "Are you all right?" He pushed the hair off Georgie's face. There was a bruise forming over one of his eyes, and he looked achingly pale and tired, but he gave Lawrence a shaky smile.

"They only hit me a couple of times."

Lawrence earnestly regretted not having cut off Brewster's balls while he had had the chance.

"I thought I was seeing things," Georgie murmured. "Are you really here? In London?" He reached out a hand and touched Lawrence's jaw with cold, bare fingers. "With Barnabus? Where's Simon?"

"Hush. He's with Lady Standish and bloody Courtenay visiting the Tower. I suspected that you were going to do something"—he nearly said foolish, but then realized he was talking to a man who had risked life and limb for him—"heroic, so I thought I'd help."

"You make a very good hero yourself."

Lawrence snorted. "They only listened to me because they were afraid I'd be as deranged as my brother."

Georgie's eyes were shut, his head tipped back against the wall. If Lawrence kept blathering on, Georgie would likely nod off.

"Come on," Lawrence said. "I have a hackney waiting. You need food and a bed."

"You have a hackney waiting," Georgie repeated, and laughed as if that were the most hilarious thing he'd ever heard. "A hackney waiting while you scare the life out of Mattie Brewster."

"You're delirious." Lawrence got an arm under Georgie's knees. "Hold on to my neck."

"Very dashing," Georgie mumbled into Lawrence's cravat as he was carried down two flights of stairs. "Feats of strength."

Lawrence deposited Georgie into the hackney and gave the driver an address.

"You're not getting in?" Georgie asked, his eyes half-closed.

"No." He was barely holding himself together and had enough nervous energy running through his body to fuel a walk to Sussex and back. He didn't think he could take being cooped up in a carriage. "Take care, Georgie," he said, shutting the door.

Georgie woke in an unfamiliar bed, but it was too dark to figure out precisely *whose* unfamiliar bed. That wasn't so unusual—his life, thus far, had been a series of beds, very few of them slept in for more than a month at a time. But he had no recollection of falling asleep in this bed or anywhere else. He ran his hands over a quilted coverlet and smooth linen sheets, felt the plumpness of a featherbed. Not an inn, then. He took a deep breath, and his nostrils filled with the scent of lavender and the sort of laundry soap that had to be special ordered.

His eyes adjusted to the dark, and he made out the faint pattern of stripes on the walls. He remembered having been with Oliver when he bought the paper. That put him in Jack and Oliver's spare room, then.

He was unaccountably disappointed to realize this. He knew he couldn't be wherever Lawrence was staying. That *take care, Georgie* had been as definitive a good-bye as he'd ever heard. Lawrence was likely glad to wash his hands of a man who had been in business with the sort of scum he'd seen in the warehouse today, Georgie included.

It had never been meant to endure, this thing with Lawrence. Nothing Georgie ever had was meant to endure.

Transient friendships, impermanent addresses, mutable identities, interchangeable lovers. How foolish he had been to lose sight of that.

He must have fallen back asleep, because when he next opened his eyes, there was bright light seeping in from around the edges of the curtains. Too tired to move, he shut his eyes again.

When he heard the squeak of door hinges, he cracked open his eyes.

"Not dead, then." It was his sister.

"What are you doing here?" His voice was a dry croak.

"You ought to be glad I am. Jack and his gentleman were going to let you sleep forever and take turns spoon-feeding you your broth, or some such addlepated nonsense. I told them men have no place in a sick room, not that you're sick." Sarah flung open the window curtain, letting in a blinding stream of light. "And you're daft if you think I'm going to hide away every time one of my brothers does something stupid. I grew up on the same streets as you and Jack, and I don't need either of you treating me like a damsel in distress. What rot." She leaned over the bed, tilting his head towards the bright light of the window. Her lip curled in dismay. "You look horrible. I'll bring up Jack's shaving kit. I've also got you a new waistcoat."

Georgie nearly smiled. "That's your proposed course of treatment? Shaving and haberdashery?"

Sarah regarded him with a gimlet eye, and Georgie was struck by how much he had missed her. She dressed in her usual subdued, although modishly tailored, dove gray. Her hair was smoothed into a sleek, dark coil. At a few years under forty, she exuded the sort of nonchalant gentility that made nobody question her origins. There were times when Georgie thought she was an even greater fraud than Jack and himself. "If you mean to act the part, you have to look the part," she said.

Which was more or less what Georgie had told Lawrence time and again. "What part?"

"To start with, the part of a man who doesn't lay abed for three days."

Three days! He had been here *three days?* His shock must have registered on his face, because Sarah responded, "You needed it. But now it's time to get up."

He sat, feeling weak as a kitten. "Did, ah, anyone call on me?" Pathetic, pathetic.

But Sarah didn't go in much for pity. "No," she said simply. "Jack said that your Lord Radnor was staying at Lady Standish's townhouse but that he isn't there with her anymore."

That explained how Lawrence had gotten to London; getting a hermit, a small child, and an enormous mongrel to London would be child's play for a woman who built batteries and applied for patents in her spare time. She could likely masquerade as Wellington and command armies, if that struck her fancy.

And now they had returned to Penkellis, leaving Georgie in London, where he belonged.

Sarah stepped out when the bath arrived. Georgie soaked until the water cooled, then shaved and dressed in the new clothes Sarah had laid out. She had been right, of course, in the annoying way that older sisters often were. He did feel better now that he was clean and tidy. When he glanced in the looking glass, he saw his usual reflection: a neat and gentlemanly sort of person, perhaps slightly pale and with traces of purplish circles still under his eyes, but nothing jarringly different from what he always saw in the mirror.

Had he expected to somehow look less like a swindler? More like a man stupidly, uselessly in love?

Sarah knocked and entered the room, bearing a tray of muffins.

"What am I going to do?" He wasn't sure if he was asking his sister, his reflection, or neither.

"First, you're going to eat something."

He slowly chewed a few bites of muffin, gathering that they were not going to have a conversation until he complied. "I've, ah, burnt a few bridges."

"I'd say you have." She pulled a length of ribbon and embroidery floss from her pocket. "Jack'll give you work, though."

True. But Georgie had never wanted to be beholden to Jack, nor to anyone else. "It's utterly humiliating," he said.

"What is?" She didn't look up from her stitching, which made it easier for Georgie to be honest.

"I've spent years scheming and lying, and now I haven't anything to show for it. No work, no skills, no friends." He was totally alone. "Only a trail of people I've hurt."

Sarah was quiet a moment. "I ran into Lily Perkins the other day. She looks about a hundred. Hardly any teeth. Her boy was born the year after you, remember?"

Of course Georgie remembered Jimmy Perkins but didn't know why Sarah was bringing him up. "He took the king's shilling, I think?" Was Sarah suggesting that Georgie ought to have joined the army?

"He died last year in Waterloo. His friend, the boy with the red hair—"

"Jonas Smith."

"Right. He was arrested for petty larceny. Transported. Nobody expects him to survive the journey. He has a wife and two daughters—God only knows what will become of them."

"Why are you telling me this?" Was he supposed to feel guilty for not having tried to earn an honest living, or ashamed that he wasn't reaping the consequences for his misdeeds?

"You didn't have too many options. There wasn't anyone to set you up as an apprentice, or teach you a trade. God knows you're no saint, but throwing your lot in with Mattie Brewster wasn't the worst thing you could have done."

"I could have tried to become a clerk. I'm very good at sorting papers and keeping records, it turns out." It was pitiful that this was the only honest talent he could name.

Sarah laid her work in her lap and looked steadily at him. "Why do you think you were good at what you did?"

He heard the past tense there and didn't argue. "Good at swindling? Because of my natural distaste for honesty, I suppose," he quipped.

"No, that's not it," she said seriously. "You like helping people. You like making them happy."

"And then stealing their money."

"No, you aren't listening to me. I know you stole money, and if you want to figure out a way to live honestly, I'll be glad of it. But why were you good at it? Walk over to St. Giles and ask any lad if he'd tell a few lies in order to put food in his mouth. Half of them would merrily stab you if it meant they'd have a guarantee to see next summer. You aren't any more or less dishonest than the next person with an empty belly." She bent her head over her work. "I always felt bad that you had to leave after a job."

Georgie goggled at her. "What?"

"You became fond of your marks. At least a little. And then you had to take their money and disappear. That's not easy on a man like you."

Georgie reeled. "I dare say it wasn't easy on them either."

"Enough!" she snapped. "You can feel guilty to your heart's content after I go back downstairs." She rose to her feet, tucking her embroidery back into her pocket. "But so help me, Georgie, figure out a way to live your life so you're not always saying good-bye." She swept silently out of the room.

Sarah was right, of course. It had always taken him so much effort to convince himself that he didn't care for his marks, that his interest and liking for them were only part of the act. In the end he fooled himself better than he ever tricked one of his marks. He had stolen their money, but without even realizing it he had swindled himself out of a life, out of friends and purpose and meaning.

But what had happened with Lawrence was of another magnitude entirely. Georgie had known almost from the beginning that he wouldn't have the heart to harm Lawrence. He had gone out of his way to do the opposite—to help him, to help Simon. Lawrence had repaid him in kind. He had somehow traveled across the country to rescue him.

And then he had left.

Georgie stood and walked to the window on weak, shaky legs. Three days in bed had taken their toll. The window looked over a quiet side street lined with a few spindly trees. He could stay here, he supposed, in this small room with pretty wallpaper and a cozy feather bed. He could do a bit of somewhat honest work for Jack and try to build a sort of life for himself.

Still fully dressed, he lay on the bed again, drifting in and out of sleep. He was tired to the marrow of his bones. Only when the shadows on the wall had shortened and then lengthened again did he rise, and even then he still felt sapped of strength.

When he opened the bedroom door, he heard voices and the clink of china and glass that meant a meal was in progress. Suddenly, his stomach seemed to remember the past week of irregular meals. As little as he wanted company, he couldn't ignore the rumbling of his belly.

Pausing on the threshold of the tiny downstairs parlor his brother and Oliver used as a dining room, he saw that Sarah had stayed for dinner. They had neared the end of the meal, by the looks of things, and were now lingering at the table over the last few bites and some easy conversation. Jack and Oliver kept the bare minimum of servants—fewer servants meant fewer chances of their relationship being exposed for what it was—and the maid hadn't come to clear the table, so the cloth was littered with napkins and crumbs and the detritus of a meal well enjoyed.

Jack's arm was casually slung over the back of Oliver's chair, as if that were where it belonged. As Georgie watched, Oliver tipped his head back against Jack's arm and turned a bit to smile lazily at his companion. To Georgie's amazement, Jack smiled back. Georgie could count on one hand the number of times he had ever seen his brother smile. But here he was, giving Oliver as soppy a grin as Georgie had ever witnessed in his life.

It was Sarah who first spotted Georgie. "Finished your beauty sleep?"

All three of them ignored Georgie's protests, shoving him down into a chair and heaping food onto his plate. He had a few bites of pigeon pie, and then before he knew it, he had eaten every last scrap of food on the table. He must also have consumed a fair bit of wine, because his head was pleasantly muzzy.

His family—it occurred to him that Oliver was family too—was carefully refraining from asking him any questions. Occasionally, Jack opened his mouth, only to receive a pointed glare from Sarah and a jab in the side from Oliver's elbow. They were treating him with kid gloves, as if he were fragile and in danger of breaking.

He *was* fragile, truth be told. Whatever had happened with Lawrence had left his heart pulpy and exposed, like flesh after a bad burn. He wanted to bury it back away, pretend he had never found it in the first place.

Draining the last few drops of wine in his glass, he glanced at his brother, who was flicking a crumb off Oliver's lapel. How, despite their shared origin, was Jack's heart a functioning organ, while his own was a putrid and vulnerable wound?

"I'm going back to Cornwall," Georgie said impulsively, answering the question they weren't asking, the same question he had been torturing himself with all day.

"You're in no state to travel," said Sarah. At the same time, Jack coughed, choking on his wine.

"Have you, ah, been invited?" Oliver asked tactfully.

"Not precisely," Georgie admitted. "Not at all, in fact." He thought of Lawrence's parting words. "Far from it." But it was worth trying.

"You don't need to go anywhere," Jack protested. "You can stay here as long as you like."

"Or don't leave at all," Oliver added. "We always meant that room for you."

Georgie hadn't known that and now felt tears welling up in his eyes. "Thank you."

"But how will you…" Jack's voice trailed off. "What will you do there?"

What would he do there? He'd sort Lawrence's correspondence and make sure the smugglers didn't set foot on Penkellis soil. He'd write a stern letter to the headmaster at Harrow, demanding that he make sure Simon got enough to eat. He'd invite Lady Standish for a few weeks in the spring, he'd talk to the vicar about holding a fete for the village, and he'd train Barnabus to do something other than sleep.

He'd kiss Lawrence every chance he got.

"What Jack is getting at is whether you have any particular thievery in mind," Sarah said. "He's wondering whether to start bribing magistrates in Cornwall."

Georgie winced. "Nothing like that."

"A job, then?" Jack asked hopefully.

"Not that either." Although he'd like to continue as Lawrence's secretary.

Three pairs of eyes were fixed on him. Georgie supposed that after a lifetime spent in relentless pursuit of wealth and security, the idea of running off to Cornwall without even the prospect of common wages demanded some kind of explanation.

"I want to be with him, if he'll let me. As far as money…" That was the crux of the issue. There was no guarantee that things would work out with Lawrence, and then he'd be older and poorer and with no better prospects than he had now. "I'll have to hope for the best."

A silence descended on the room. Sarah and Jack exchanged a look of concern. Georgie thought he saw his sister's mouth form the words *send for a doctor*.

In the continued silence, they were able to hear a tap at the front door and the subsequent patter of the housemaid's boots across the vestibule. Jack and Oliver pulled apart, reverting to their usual role of cordial business partners.

"Who could that be at this hour?" Sarah murmured.

A moment later, Lawrence was standing on the threshold of the dining room.

CHAPTER TWENTY-SIX

Georgie had never hallucinated, but there was a first time for everything. If his mind were to dream up any possible vision, surely it would be that of Lawrence, with Simon and Barnabus by his side, no less. Georgie glanced around the room and saw that everyone's gaze was riveted to the doorway where Lawrence stood, so perhaps this was actually happening.

Finally, Oliver spoke, a stream of polite meaninglessness that bridged the gap between the impossible and the real and gave Georgie a moment to acclimate himself to a world in which all the people he cared about were here, safe, crammed into one small dining parlor. Oliver and Sarah murmured and gestured until everyone was seated in the improbable space—Simon perched on Lawrence's knee, Barnabus's head on Georgie's lap, and Jack leaning against the wall with his arms folded as if he might just oversee some bloodshed before the evening was through.

Simon, Oliver, and Sarah were the only ones capable of conversation, which meant that the company was treated to an enthusiastic disquisition on the topic of Astley's

Amphitheatre. The child looked exceedingly well, his cheeks rosy and his eyes bright. Whatever had happened in the past week, it seemed that carriage travel agreed with him.

The same could not be said for Lawrence, who was pale and drawn and looked very much like he had lost half a stone. The hand that wasn't wrapped around Simon's middle was clenched, clawlike, into the arm of his chair. He looked…well, Georgie supposed that he looked like a man who would much rather be anywhere else.

And yet. Here he was. He hadn't gone back to Penkellis. He had come here, and now Georgie felt something like hope.

Georgie finally caught his eye, and Lawrence's mouth twitched up in the ghost of a smile. Georgie smiled back and knew his own effort was equally pallid.

Somebody—Sarah?—turned the conversation so that Oliver was leading Simon to the mews to inspect the horses, and Sarah was bodily tugging Jack out of the room. When the door finally shut, closing Lawrence and Georgie into the dining room alone, Lawrence sank back into his chair and sighed.

"Are you all right?" Georgie asked.

"Not really," Lawrence said. "But I suppose if a trip over muddy roads to London, a visit to the Admiralty, and an encounter with a den of thieves hasn't combined to throw me into a state of irretrievable madness, then I'm quite safe from that fate. How about you?" He gestured at the fading bruise under Georgie's eye.

Georgie nodded. "What a pair we are," he murmured. "A few days in London and we're quite shells of our former selves."

"Are we?" Lawrence asked, his voice low and grainy. "A pair, that is? I thought we were. But then you left…" He shook his head.

"You know I had to go."

"I do. But I had thought we were…I thought you would be there, by my side. And then you weren't."

"For what it's worth, I would have much preferred staying at Penkellis, despite the mice and the drafts."

Lawrence huffed out a laugh. "Penkellis rates higher than an abduction. Good to know."

"Yes, and"—Georgie hesitated, his heart feeling like it was exposed in all its embarrassing gore on the outside of his clothes—"I was just telling my brother and sister that I mean to go back to Penkellis, whether you'll have me or not." This was what it felt like to plummet off a cliff without knowing whether one would land on jagged rocks or simply in shark-infested waters. He was terrified in all directions. Even if Lawrence didn't deny him—especially if Lawrence didn't deny him—his life as he knew it was over.

Lawrence took hold of Georgie's hand. "Are you certain you want to come to Penkellis, though? To be cooped up in a rotten tower? You deserve more."

Georgie wasn't going to stand for one more second of this nonsense. He hauled his weary body into Lawrence's lap. "If we're going to talk about deserts," he said, looking down into Lawrence's tired eyes, "I can assure you that I've done nothing to deserve a life with a good, brilliant man. Nothing."

"Rubbish." But he settled his hands proprietarily on Georgie's hips. "I'm not certain it would be a life, Georgie."

Georgie shook his head. "It's a life. It's always been a life. Even if you never left Penkellis again—but I think you will, Lawrence—it would still be a life. And I'd be so happy and proud to be with you, if you'll let me."

"Let you, my arse. Beg you, more like." He let go of Georgie long enough to rummage around in his pocket. "You left this behind." He held out the heavy emerald ring.

Georgie felt his heart—feeble, sordid thing that it was—soar.

They got back to Penkellis in the first week of January, when the snow had melted but the landscape was still bleak and forbidding with no end of winter in sight. Simon was with them, and Lawrence felt a surge of raw delight whenever he saw his friend and his child together.

The day after rescuing Georgie from that whoreson criminal, Lawrence, fueled by the residue of the courage he summoned for the previous day's adventures, had paid a visit to the headmaster of Harrow.

"I'm not going back this term," Simon had told Georgie in tones that rang with awe. "Papa was fearsome. He said barely anything, just glowered like a bear and people did as he asked." That had been Lawrence's strategy the entire fortnight he spent away from Penkellis: speak as little as possible, glower and glare as much as possible. The headmaster had grudgingly agreed that eight years was perhaps premature for a boy to go to school, and that Simon's seat could be kept open, should they choose to reevaluate the matter next year, or the year after.

After Harrow, they had paid a visit to Simon's maternal aunt and demanded Isabella's portrait, which Simon was to hang in his room at Penkellis, where he would now be living permanently. Simon also had in his possession a sketch Courtenay had done of the villa where they had lived in Tuscany. Lawrence didn't have the heart to tell the boy his uncle was a scapegrace of the rankest nature, so decided to swallow his criticisms for the time being.

Penkellis was now visible on the horizon, a jumble of jagged lines and mismatched pieces. It was odd to see it at a distance after scarcely leaving its shadow for so long. He had no affection for the place, only the sort of desperate longing that a fox might have for its hole.

That night, they collapsed on the sofa almost as soon as Simon had gone off to bed. Lawrence had asked one of the new servants—he had been half-astonished to find them still at Penkellis, sweeping and polishing and otherwise keeping the rot at bay—to move Georgie's things into the old dressing room. After all, Georgie was supposed to be Lawrence's secretary; if they both kept odd hours and found it convenient for the secretary's bedroom to be moved closer to the earl's study, there was nothing so very strange in that.

"Lady Standish suggested building a new house," Lawrence said tentatively, stroking Georgie's hand and admiring the way the light played off the emerald he once again wore. "Something closer to the London road, with proper plumbing and chimneys that emit more heat than smoke." Someplace that wouldn't reek with bad memories and mouse droppings alike.

Up until that point, Georgie had been lounging languidly against the arm of the sofa, his feet kicked up on Lawrence's lap as he regarded Lawrence from beneath half-closed lids. But now his eyes sprang open. "Are you certain you would like that? You're rather…attached to this place." He gestured to the study at large.

"True, but that's because it's mine. It's…I don't know, *safe*. Which sounds ridiculous, I know—"

"It doesn't," Georgie said firmly, squeezing Lawrence's hand. "At all."

Lawrence squeezed back. "Well, a new house could truly be my own. We could put more of that stuff on the walls to dampen the noise."

"Hot water," Georgie added wistfully. "Windows that shut properly."

"A library that isn't being consumed by fungus."

"Floors that don't threaten to give way under your feet." He knelt up and arranged himself so he was straddling Lawrence's lap. "Building a house would put a good many men to work."

"It'll also spread goodwill, which ought to get you and Halliday off my back for a while."

"About that." He bent to kiss Lawrence's jaw, which was once again stubbly with what would likely be a proper beard by spring. "I think Mrs. Ferris has the goodwill situation in hand."

"Oh?" Lawrence found it hard to concentrate with Georgie kissing the soft underside of his jaw.

"I think she's been using talk about cauls"—kiss—"and hexes"—kiss—"to keep people away from Penkellis."

Lawrence shook his head. "Can't be that. The villagers already know about the smuggling ring. This is Cornwall.

Nobody needs to be told twice not to look too closely at the contents of empty barns."

"No, not that." Georgie started to unwind Lawrence's cravat and kiss the skin beneath. "She knew you wanted to be left in peace, so she did everything in her power to keep people away."

Lawrence let that sink in. "As a kindness?" Georgie murmured an assenting sound into Lawrence's collarbone. So, he had had a friend in the house all those years he had fancied himself alone. And Sally had less reason than most to befriend a Browne. "She will have a very good stove in the next house."

"I believe a monetary reward would not go amiss."

"I tried that years ago. Offered her a tidy sum to set herself and her son up." He hadn't been able to help her when Percy was alive, so setting things right for her was the first thing he had done after his brother's death. "She accepted the help to buy Jamie's commission, but nothing for herself."

Georgie's body momentarily went rigid with alertness. "Oh, damn me. This is the boy in the navy. The *navy*." He put his fist to his forehead. "That's why she took that caul. She gave it to her boy when he first went to sea."

"What on earth are you talking about?"

"*She* stole your neighbor's caul—it's supposed to be a talisman against drowning. Listen, write a letter to your friend in the Admiralty recommending her son for promotion. Really, whatever it takes to get her to retire from a life of crime."

Lawrence nodded. He could do that. "Speaking of which, I met with my solicitor while I was in London."

"Christ. You really went all in with unpleasant tasks."

"I settled a sum on you."

The kisses stopped. "No."

"Yes. It's done, so you can burn the money or donate it to orphans. I don't care."

Georgie pulled back. "That's not why I'm here."

"I know, and even if I didn't, there's a soap tin of jewels on my nightstand that testifies to your lack of mercenary motives. My point is, I need you to have something of your own. Just in case." *That way you're free to leave*, he didn't say.

But Georgie must have understood, because he took hold of Lawrence's loosened cravat and wound it around his hand, tugging Lawrence close with false menace. "Listen here, my lord," he said with a touch of his old insolence. "I'm not going anywhere, and you're out of luck if you think you can get rid of me. You can build a dozen new houses, and I'll simply follow you about from house to house, like a bad case of bedbugs. Where you are, I am, so get used to it."

Lawrence didn't think he ever could get used to it. He couldn't imagine a future where he would take for granted the gift the universe had given him in Georgie Turner. So he settled for the next best thing, which was to close his eyes, smiling, as Georgie proceeded to undress him.

Need more Cat Sebastian?

LORD COURTENAY'S ROMANCE IS NEXT!

Coming Summer 2017

ABOUT THE AUTHOR

CAT SEBASTIAN lives in a swampy part of the South with her husband, three kids, and two dogs. Before her kids were born, she practiced law and taught high school and college writing. When she isn't reading or writing, she's doing crossword puzzles, bird watching, and wondering where she put her coffee cup.

Discover great authors, exclusive offers, and more at hc.com.

Give in to your Impulses . . .
Continue reading for excerpts from
our newest Avon Impulse books.
Available now wherever e-books are sold.

TALKING DIRTY
A FORTUNE, COLORADO NOVEL
by Jennifer Seasons

DARING TO FALL
A HIDDEN FALLS NOVEL
by T. J. Kline

An Excerpt from

TALKING DIRTY
A Fortune, Colorado Novel

By Jennifer Seasons

Jake Stone has always been an outsider, even in his hometown. So when Apple Woodman comes poking her pert little nose around his business, trying to sniff out juicy bits for a book she's writing on the town's history, he decides he's had enough. He'll give her the answers, at a price: one piece of clothing for every question. If the town's good girl librarian wants the dirt on this bad boy then she's going to have to bare all to get it.

Jake joined her at the bar, turning her attention, and she took a deep, steadying breath. It was now or never. She placed her elbows onto the bar, and leaned toward him.

He scowled.

Of course he did. He was always scowling around her. Earlier had merely been his five-minute reprieve. "Put those away before you hurt someone."

Now he was sounding downright grumpy too. *Huh, funny thing.* "Why would I do that?" She asked and gave her girls a little squeeze with her elbows and inwardly sighed at the lengths she was willing to go to for the things that mattered most to her. He muttered under his breath and scowled some more. *Good.* "I don't see anyone here complaining." She added just to taunt him.

Not that anyone could, really. Her back was to the tables. Jake was the only one who was getting the full display, exactly as she'd intended.

"I'm complaining." He practically growled, yanked a white bar towel from its holder and began polishing the bar top.

He sounded surly, but Apple knew that secret about Jake, and she was not at all ashamed to take advantage of it now.

He'd forced her to it. "Why? Because you've been trying to scam a peek at my boobs since I started growing them in sixth grade?" She tipped her head to the side and blinked all big and innocent behind her oversized reading glasses. "Are you feeling sad about that?"

He scoffed at that—*after* he glanced at her chest again. She totally had him. "Of what? All the cases of blue balls your rack gave me when I was fifteen?"

"What if I offered to make up for all those missed opportunities? All those Spin the Bottles and Sixty Seconds in Heaven that didn't pan out?"

Jake stopped wiping the bar and pegged her with a look, his dark eyes filled with barely controlled skepticism. "And how would you do that, juicy fruit?" He asked, referencing her childhood nickname—the one *he'd* given her the year she'd come into her body.

If letting Jake finally see her topless was going to get him to actually open up and tell her what she needed to know about that first settlement in Fortune, then by all means she'd take her shirt off. It was worth it to her. Plus, it would quell that one nagging question she'd *never* had about them, which was awesome. Because she'd *never* wondered. "What if?" Not once. Why would she?

More to the point, she was willing to do it because she was desperate. Enough so that she'd bare what she had for Jake. Because the truth was, beyond needing to prove to herself that she could achieve her dreams, he wasn't all that wrong about her "spending habits". Not that she was a mess with finances or anything. But she didn't make that much as the librarian and it had been a hefty advance (to which she'd paid off the last big hunk of her school loans with. Responsible. Appropriate). And now she was out of cash, out of savings— debt free, but still broke.

This was her opportunity. Her shot. Right here and now. No matter how devalued she felt over how it was playing out.

Being a published author had always been her dream. And she was *this close*. She'd be an idiot not to flash him her goods if it meant finally wrapping things up. Only this time he wasn't offering to pay her his hard-earned summer lawn-mowing job money—and she was no longer such an innocent little good girl. It was just Jake. They'd known each other since she was three. Besides, if there was a question mark dangling over them—which there *wasn't*. Not in her head at anyway—then this was a quick and painless way to turn that question mark into a period.

No question mark, no doubts—no dissatisfaction over what might have or might not have been.

Apple took a deep breath. "I'm offering a trade. If you finally tell me what happened to the original founders of Fortune, I'll show you my breasts. You've always wanted to see them." Or so his drunken teenaged self had said, if that source could be trusted.

Jake laughed at that. "What makes you think I'm still interested?"

"Because you're a guy." Apple gave him a level look, unfazed.

He merely shrugged, his broad, defined shoulders moving under his faded green T-shirt. Then he slid her a quick glance "Maybe I am. But you're going to have to do better than that if you want me talking."

Apple leveled him with an incredulous look. "This is a big deal. Big offer from me here, Jake. What else could you possibly want?" And then she thought of everything she'd tried already and felt exasperated all over again, so she added on a frustrated rush, "What's it going to take to get you to finally spill your family's story?"

The look he shot her had Apple slowly straightening from the bar, her pulse skittering. She'd never seen that particular gleam in his eye before. It was dark and intense and unreadable. Dangerous even.

She swallowed hard.

Then he placed his elbows on the bar and leaned toward her. He didn't stop until they were almost nose-to-nose and she could see amber flecks in his chocolate eyes.

"Here's the deal, all right? If you really want me to talk about my myself, my family—hell, about *all* my frigging secrets because I know you and you're too damned nosy and won't stop with just my ancestors . . ." He stopped suddenly and took a deep breath, his last words hanging suspended between them. But his gaze held hers steadily as one uncomfortable heartbeat, then two, passed before he continued speaking. This time he was more animated, seemingly building up steam about something.

"Shit, you won't stop until you've taken up permanent residence inside my head and know things about me I don't even care to understand. Why? Because you're Apple Woodman and you can't help yourself. It's what you've always done. And you think caving and fulfilling some outdated PG-13-rated teenage fantasy is going to be all it'll take to get me singing about stuff I've never told *anybody*?"

He straightened and crossed his arms, his face set in stern lines as he shook his head once—just once—with impact. "Nope. No good. There's only one thing you can do." He raised a hand, his long, thick index finger pointed straight in the air.

Apple eyed him warily now as she slowly inched back from the bar, feminine fear racing across her skin. Maybe this wasn't her brightest idea, after all.

"Oh yeah, what could that be?"

Jake leaned over the bar toward her again and crooked his finger at her, urging her closer. His gaze held hers as he smiled, slow and devastating, and said the words that sent her reeling, "If you want me to talk, juicy fruit, I get to see *all* of you naked."

An Excerpt from

DARING TO FALL
A Hidden Falls Novel
By T. J. Kline

Emma Jordan has returned home after her father's
death to run the animal sanctuary that had been
his legacy. But strange things start happening,
and it seems that someone is out to shut her
down, someone who doesn't mind putting lives
in jeopardy to see it through. When Hidden
Falls' sexiest fireman starts to ask questions,
Emma needs to make sure his charm doesn't
distract her from keeping her dreams alive.

Emma tried to still the way her stomach flipped and somersaulted but when he climbed down from his raised truck, she couldn't help but admire the fine figure he cut walking toward her. He had enough height that his massive muscles looked proportional instead of hulking. Yesterday he'd looked a little too pretty boy for her usual tastes but today, with his jaw unshaven and his hair slightly mussed, he was walking, breathing male perfection in maroon cotton and denim. He'd have been absolutely perfect, if she wasn't so worried he was here for an alternative reason.

"Two days in a row?" Emma crossed her arms in front of her. "To what do I owe the pleasure?"

"I'm here professionally this time, I'm afraid." He stopped in front of his truck.

Her pulse pounded in her veins, making her feel lightheaded. She couldn't let this happen, but she had no idea how to stop it. Her only choice was to try to play it cool and stall for more time. A small voice of reason reminded her that he wasn't Fish and Game, Animal Control or the police department. She latched on to that one thread of hope.

"And what sort of business could the local fire department possibly have with me?"

Ben pulled a folded newspaper from his back pocket and held it up. She couldn't make out anything but one word: Bobcat.

She'd already read the article this morning, had already tried to convince herself that there was no reason for the paper's unwarranted attack to sting. She'd already begun planning ways to rebut the accusations made against her. But it was going to take time, and money, and she had neither.

It didn't take a genius to figure out that this wasn't going to be a benevolent visit. "Did you bring a warrant? Because you're not coming any further into the facility without one."

"Yesterday I was generous."

"Yet, here you are again." She didn't look away, wouldn't give him the satisfaction of seeing her fear, but she could feel the muscles in her back and legs quaking nervously, praying he didn't see it.

"Do I need to call my brother down at the police station and get one?" He mimicked her stance, crossing his arms over his massive chest. But when he did it, it made his biceps bulge and the sleeve of his shirt ride up his arm enough to reveal what appeared to be a wolf's head as part of the sleeve tattoo circling his right arm.

Heaven help me, she prayed as her heart bounced to her stomach and back up again before speeding up to triple time.

"Tell me, did this town harass my father this much? It might account for his stroke."

"I can't say it did." His tipped his head to one side. "You know, maybe shutting yourself and the sanctuary off from the rest of the town hasn't been the best idea. Perhaps if you let people see what you're doing here, they'd be backing you instead of believing this." He waved the paper slightly.

"You're saying that if I open my doors, they'll welcome me with open arms."

"Maybe."

"Bullshit."

She moved down the stairs to stand in front of him, trying to give him the impression that she wasn't intimidated by him. However, his sheer size was even more impressive this close and her idea backfired as her gaze slid up to meet his. "For your information, I wasn't the one to close the doors to the public. That was my father's doing. And I plan on reopening them as soon as I can, but it's going to take some time."

His dark gaze slid over her slowly, as if he was trying to read her thoughts, feeling more like a caress than an appraisal. It intrigued her, actually making her heart skip a beat. Her reaction to him annoyed her. She wanted to be unaffected by him, to not feel this slow heat sliding through her veins, to not have the urge to grab his shirt and jerk him forward for what she was sure would be a kiss to make her forget any before. A slow grin tugged at the corner of his mouth, a dimple creasing his left cheek.

Damn cocky man knows exactly what effect he has on women.

Emma wasn't about to be just another of the harem she was sure fawned over him. She didn't care how good looking he was or how his muscles might ripple when he walked. Okay, she *appreciated* it, but that wasn't the same thing as caring. She would keep her wits about her when this particular handsome man smiled at her, if only because she was sure most didn't, and she was smart enough to hide any attraction she might have to him beneath her annoyance at him wielding his authority over her this way.

She narrowed her eyes, studying him. She wanted to tell him to leave, to order him off the property and insist he not come back without a warrant. She had no idea what he really wanted and she already had enough trouble with the town and its rumors. However, she got the feeling that, if causing her more trouble had been his intent, Ben would have called in the police already. She tipped her head back, trying to get a better look at him and felt her make-shift bun loosen, coming unwound. Just like her resistance.

"Fine. I'm not sure why you're here, but I have nothing to hide." She jerked at the end of her hair, letting her auburn tresses fall around her shoulders, shielding her like a curtain and headed for the golf cart. "Well? What are you waiting for? Hop in. I don't have all day to waste."

Ben slid in beside her, his arm brushing against hers, the heat from his skin practically burning her. He exuded raw sexuality, making the close confines of the golf cart seem even smaller, and she edged farther from him on the small seat. Twisting the key, her gaze fell on the folded newspaper Ben set in his lap and she was able to read the full headline.

Damn! When was this town ever going to cut her some slack?